*The media frenzy can hide the truth
or bury it in a high-profile murder case.*

From MEDIA JUSTICE

"Okay. Tell us the bad news," said Johnnie, crossing her shapely legs.

"You've looked at the charges. You know who the defendant is. His reputation. You sure as hell know who the defense is. You've seen the evidence. And you know what the media is saying about us."

Bill James answered. "They're saying the white guys are beating up on another brother."

"Yes," acknowledged Frank. "And the media, bless their exploitable little hearts, are already pitching their tents."

Bill added, "It would be a lot easier if Art could do this one." He had run the option past Frank, but he wanted it on the table so the team could toss it around.

Frank was resolute. "If I pull him off the Cappelletti case, we'd lose it for sure."

Johnnie was shocked. "You think we might lose? We have more evidence against that child murderer than we have against Williams."

L.A. District Attorney Frank Fallen answered, "This is a great time to be a murderer in Los Angeles."

MEDIA JUSTICE

G. B. POOL

SPYGAME PRESS

LA CRESCENTA, CALIFORNIA

MEDIA JUSTICE

Published by SPYGAME Press
First Edition/ October 2004
Trade Paperback / February 2005

For more information, contact:

SPYGAME PRESS
Gayle Bartos-Pool, Publisher
P.O. Box 12141
La Crescenta, CA 91224-0841

Visit our website:
www.spygame.org

Hardcover ISBN: 0-9749446-0-2
Paperback ISBN: 0-9749446-1-0

Hardcover Library of Congress Control Number: 2004091729.
Paperback Library of Congress Control Number: 2004108534.
Pool, G. B. First Edition. First in the Series of Ginger Caulfield Mysteries.
Media justice: a Hollywood murder and the media frenzy that follows/
G. B. Pool

PRINTED IN THE UNITED STATES OF AMERICA

In memory of my mother,

Doris Bartos

ASK YOURSELF,

WHAT DO YOU VALUE MOST?

CHAPTER 1

This wasn't the first time Ginger Caulfield had seen the video on television. She'd viewed it a dozen times at police headquarters, but now it looked more like a made-for-TV movie when it ran on the nightly news. That's probably what the studio's executive producer had in mind, but he wasn't exactly Alfred Hitchcock. One of the local news anchors was doing the voice-over, explaining what was happening on the screen, as though it needed clarification.

In the original version there was no commentary, just the cold, stark reality of the deed. But Ginger could have given a better description of what led to the discovery of the video. After all, she'd been dumped into the middle of this mess, and she knew the characters involved and knew what really happened and why. Hell, she was even considered a suspect . . . Wait a minute. That's getting ahead of the story. After all, Mrs. Ginger Caulfield was just a Pasadena housewife with a "questionable background," as the defense attorney had tried to spin it. But this is how it started . . .

July 11, 1995

A balmy breeze carried the scent of gardenia and honeysuckle up the beach. Soft music played out across the inky water, while the waning moon cloaked the sand in thick black velvet. Even in the shadows there was a sense of the lush life in the air. As long as the Malibu hills weren't burning or washing away, the Pacific Coast Highway was a sumptuous drive.

The house sat high above the surf with its rear windows flung open so that you could pick up the faint sound of the tide as it was dragged back into the deep. Though, on the night in question, the ocean was just so much background music.

A trickle of luxury cars entered the exclusive neighborhood just off the highway, but at that hour most of the residents were either enjoying a quiet evening at home or warming loge seats at the Ahmanson. The only thing passersby could see was the high-tech track lighting illuminating the interior of that prime California real estate.

Clear white light flooded the highly polished hardwood floors and pooled on stark, ultramodern furniture made from bleached and blond woods. A crystal chandelier hung suspended from the whitewashed ceiling over a glass-topped dining room table. From a distance the whole structure appeared ethereal. It looked as if a gust of wind could lift it off the cliff and carry it out to sea.

Two amorphous figures seemed to float behind the sheer curtains billowing in the breeze. Marcella, a striking, light-skinned black woman, wearing a diaphanous gown in the palest shade of peach, glided across the floor like a vapor.

With her was Adrian, her constant companion for the past year. He was wearing a soft green silk kimono with giant mums splashed across it in shades of the faintest pink and yellow. Adrian, too, was a very light-skinned black, but rumor had it his skin was bleached. Even his hair was a curious shade of golden blond.

The pair skipped barefoot to the open kitchen. The space was all white cabinets and frosted glass. The only ornamentation was a cluster of forest green canisters sitting on the white tiled counter. Everything else was hidden behind roll-down partitions or glass-fronted doors.

Marcella opened the refrigerator and pulled out a tray laden with fruit and cheese for an evening snack. Adrian expertly opened and then poured white wine into two chilled tulip-shaped glasses with pale green leaves winding up their stems.

Returning to the living area, Marcella draped herself across the huge white couch that encircled half the airy room. She threw her head back and laughed while Adrian struggled with the brimming goblets and the bottle of wine, spilling and mugging as he crossed the floor.

He assessed the damage, stopped, and then slurped from both glasses, daring her to comment. Setting the half-empty wine glasses on the coffee table, he refilled them. Then he used the wine dripping off his fingers like perfume and daubed some behind his ears. She laughed again, while he grabbed for a piece of cheese.

Marcella continued her vamping on the couch. She had picked up a handful of green grapes and was holding them over her head like a Greek goddess, pulling off one at a time and eating them slowly, sucking her fingers with gleeful noise.

"I can do better than that," said Adrian, grabbing another bunch of grapes and dropping down on the couch. He placed the bunch between his toes and dangled them in her direction. She flipped her body under his feet and tried biting at the grapes above her head.

Marcella squealed, "Hold still, hold still! Wait a minute. Do you ever wash your feet?"

They giggled together like a couple of schoolgirls. Adrian dropped the grapes between his toes and howled even louder.

He leaned off the couch to retrieve the grapes he had dropped. He started feeding them to Marcella, pushing them into her mouth as she shrieked with laughter, choking on the sweet juice.

She finally managed to say, "What, no crackers?"

The duo convulsed with delight, rolling on the white couch like two playful pups.

VIEW FROM SURVEILLANCE CAMERA:

A grainy, colorless figure moved through blurry shadows to the side of the house. It stopped beside a magnificent profusion of bird-of-paradise, but in the dark the brilliant plumage of those radiant flowers was rendered lifeless. The figure stared upward at the large windows partially obscured by sheer organza curtains.

The watcher tensed at the sound of the antics going on inside. Then the lone figure slowly made his way around to the stairs leading to a secluded area of the redwood deck that encircled three sides of the spacious living room. Along that narrow side of the house were floor-to-ceiling windows that wrapped around to the back.

The solitary figure stood outside the windows, watching the cavorting going on inside. From that vantage point, the two on the couch were mere apparitions floating on white light. The figure clenched his gloved fist, then suddenly, in one swift move, he raised his hand and smashed it through the window.

At first Marcella and Adrian must have thought it was an earthquake. They sat up on the couch and prepared to hold on for a wild ride. That was when the sound of shoes crunching over broken glass caught their attention, and they saw the figure coming through the shattered window toward them.

Marcella reeled back on the couch, surprised. Then, for an instant, she got a perturbed look on her face. Adrian turned his head slightly. His hands were partly raised as if fending off an insult, when the first shot rang out.

The dark figure kept pumping and firing the shotgun, over and over again. When he finally stopped, he hesitated a moment before taking a few tentative steps forward until he was standing next to the couch. His body obscured the surveillance camera's view of the scene in front of him. He didn't move for several seconds. He was looking down, star-

ing, expecting movement. Slowly, he backed away until he got to the shattered window. He turned his shoulders slightly to avoid several jagged pieces of glass still hanging from the wooden frame. Behind him were the two illuminated bodies sagging on the white couch, which now had dark splotches spreading over it. The solitary figure took one last look, and then turned slowly toward the opening . . .
CUT.

That is where the grainy videotape would have abruptly stopped in the made-for-TV movie. Too bad it hadn't been found earlier to spare everyone the endless hours of talk and opinion and guessing and misreporting and . . . well, you know. But the circus must go on.

This is the rest of the story.

The pale hardwood floor glistened as the morning sun streamed through the open windows, while the curtains moved softly in the breeze. There was no dust, no lint, only a thick pool of drying blood next to the crimson-stained couch. Near the largest puddle was a smaller smudge. This one was a series of whorls and lines, resembling a huge fingerprint . . . in red.

Outside, the sound of gulls swooping up and down the beach was competing with a faint, high-pitched whine. Within a minute the screeching turned into the wail of sirens rushing up the coast road toward the house perched on a rock above the sea. The pale blue morning was slashed by red lights gyrating wildly across the front lawn.

In less than an hour the oleander bushes that encircled the yard were strung with yards of yellow crime-scene tape, until the lawn looked as if it had been rolled with toilet paper in a graduation prank. The beach on either side of the house was cordoned off, and there were more blue uniforms swarming over the grounds than in a Mel Gibson movie.

Inside the house, the pace was a little more subdued. The few people allowed indoors were virtually silent as they methodically went through their paces. A tall, good-looking man stared out the front window at the Barnum & Bailey atmosphere being generated on the lawn and backing all the way to the highway. He half-wished they'd get mowed down by a speeding truck, but then he'd have to write that one up, too. He shook off the feeling and went back to work.

"Get me some pictures of this area and—hey! Watch your step! That's a good footprint right there," he said, pointing to various areas around the window.

Detective Lawrence Patrick had been with LAPD for more than fifteen years. He frequently told his wife it seemed a hell of a lot longer. He called some of his cases "time bombs," because he never knew when one would blow up in his face. His wife laughed and quietly wished he'd quit and join his brother in the printing business. Lawrence wasn't driving a squad car anymore, but the twelve-hour days, the countless cups of high-octane coffee, the endless stream of human debris, and the pounding headaches were wearing him down.

Larry was a trim man in his late thirties. He worked out, laid off the jelly doughnuts, and kept his nose clean. And in this town that meant something. His brown hair was showing early signs of gray, but he still had clear eyes. He told his wife, when the eyes glaze over you're either bored, on drugs, or dead. Some days he wondered which he was—and he didn't do drugs.

The police photographer sidestepped the footprint on the polished floor and took several close-up shots from different angles. He paused to look at Detective Patrick.

Pointing to the female, deceased, he asked, "You know who that is, don't you?"

Larry didn't bat an eye. "Yeah. Trouble. Big trouble."

The photographer stood up and glanced around the

room. "What do you think *he'll* say?"

Detective Patrick shook his head. His people were working quietly around him, dusting for prints and picking up what few pieces of lint they could find.

"By the book, people. This one's gonna be a bitch."

CHAPTER 2

By 10 a.m. the circus atmosphere was complete. Every local TV channel with a news copter, camera team, or a reporter-in-the-field was going wall-to-wall with the "story of the decade." This was the umpteenth story this decade alone. You couldn't turn on the television without seeing a twenty-something reporter expounding on life and death like they had a clue. Half the audience had fillings older than most of these kids and their fillings had a better grasp of what was important than did these journalistic ninety-day wonders.

The scene was always the same. Television news crews appeared like mushrooms in a soggy field. Lights and video-cams sprouted on shoulders like so many Quasimodos. News vans were parked on every available piece of real estate for a quarter of a mile in either direction. Overhead were the obligatory news copters casting shadows on the people skittering around below. All you could think of were vultures circling.

Electrical cables were strewn over the ground like a huge nest of snakes. In the midst of the tangle was a pair of size 5 Nikes. In them: Myrna Blankenship. She was giving orders to the people around her while listening to directions from the program director through her IFB. There was no smile on her face. Myrna usually did the fluff pieces on Channel 11, but she was coming up in the world. Now she got the dead-body assignments, as long as they were found during the 6-to-10 a.m. time slot. She heard the "Go!" signal from the studio and became activated.

"This is Myrna Blankenship, Channel 11 *View on L.A.*, reporting from the picturesque seaside city of Malibu and the once peaceful road outside the exclusive oceanfront home of Marcella Williams . . ."

Twenty feet away another news maven was standing amid yet another coil of reptiles, holding forth. This was the perky Tina Lake from Channel 10 *News & Entertainment.* She was saying . . .

" . . . the former wife of television superstar Desmond Williams. Desmond Williams starred in the 1970s series *Buddies,* with Van Preston . . ." A little voice through her earphone corrected her. "Press-*cott,*" she enunciated. "And in the popular 1980s adventure series *Follow the Sun,* set in beautiful Hawaii. Desmond Williams has been . . ."

Standing near the bird-of-paradise on the front lawn was Channel 12 *L.A. Comprehensive News* reporter Steve Gonzales. Steve had worked his way up from the weather desk to covering news stories in less than five years. Fortunately for him, the guy he replaced had dropped dead from a heart attack while jogging. The studio decided to go for a younger face and body. Steve was saying . . .

" . . . a household name for the past two decades, branching into made-for-TV movies and motion pictures since the cancellation of his last series. Desmond Williams has brought many famous characters to the screen, such as: Big Man Jack from the movie *Kill or Be Killed,* Dr. Charles Good from the movie *Madman*, and of course, Police Detective John Law in the action-adventure thriller *John's Law* that . . ."

Positioned in the middle of a vacationing neighbor's yard was Gary Johnson, one of the few black reporters in the business. He worked for yet another local TV channel. This was Channel 8 *L.A. Hot News,* and Johnson was considered one of the hottest reporters around. A graduate from an obscure journalism college, the kid was setting the news business on fire with his exposés on conditions in mental health facilities and discrimination in hiring practices with small businesses located in predominately white and Asian neighborhoods.

The Channel 8 camera panned the murder house, trying to play down the mummers' parade building along the highway, and then went to a close-up on Johnson as he picked up the story.

" . . . was set in the San Pedro area where they are currently filming the sequel. But those spectacular car chases came to a screeching halt at the home of his former wife, Marcella Williams. A close friend and neighbor who was jogging on the deserted beach found the bodies of Ms. Williams, thirty-six, and Adrian Wells, thirty-nine, in the early morning hours. This reluctant hero noticed that a large, wraparound window of the pricey beachfront house was broken."

The camera pulled back, revealing another person standing next to Johnson. Still in jogging clothes, the man was visibly nervous before the cameras; perspiration soaked his tired gray sweat suit. His eyes had that wild look of somebody not used to the glare of the lights. But this *was* California.

"And your name, please?" asked the reporter.

"Uh . . . Jerry Crowell."

"Mr. Crowell, what exactly did you see this morning?"

Jer was nervous. He had no idea what to do with his hands. He kept wringing them like a nervous groom. "Well . . . I work out a lot. I . . . I jog . . . on the beach . . . every morning. I've been doing it for years. You just get to know a place. I always go down the beach toward Malibu Cove for several miles, then turn around and head home. By the time I'm on my way back, the sun's coming up and I can see it reflect in the windows when I jog past. Today, it wasn't there."

"And what was that, Mr. Crowell?"

"The sun . . . it wasn't there. The Williams' house . . . I . . . I didn't know her all that well, but everybody knows she used to be married to Desmond Williams. Anyway, her house has all these windows that face the ocean. Every morning I see the sun reflect off them. This morning the sun wasn't there."

"So you climbed the cliff steps from the beach, went up the back stairs to the house, and saw the broken glass before entering the murder scene. What made you go inside, Mr. Crowell?" asked the penetrating reporter.

"Well, I . . . I didn't go inside exactly. I could tell something was really wrong. I mean all the glass and stuff. That's when I looked in and . . . and saw . . ." Jerry took a big swallow as he recalled the sight from earlier that morning.

Less than an hour later Channel 10 was revving up for another media moment. Once again it was focused on Tina Lake as she began her interview with Jerry Crowell. Ol' Jer had lost some of his initial shock to the murders, and the cameras were no longer as intimidating. Tina picked up on this, so she graciously provided a grim face to go along with the gruesome story. The only problem was that she was listening more to the person talking to her through the IFB in her ear than to poor Jerry. Her head was nodding, but not to what he was saying. He got part of his story out before Tina tuned back into the dissertation.

"Take your time, Mr. Crowell. What was that terrible thing you saw through Marcella Williams' rear window?"

"It was awful. Marcella . . . and her friend . . . I didn't recognize him at first, but the police said it was him."

"And who was the other victim?" she prodded.

"Adrian Wells."

Jer didn't know Adrian Wells from Orson Welles, but the buzz among the news types was that the late Mr. Wells (Adrian, not Orson) was somebody the media and Hollywood adored.

Tina turned to the camera to impart her vast wisdom. "Yes, Adrian Wells was the owner/operator of the 'Ampora,' a fashionable West Hollywood 'waterhole.' Mr. Wells's . . ."

Ms. Lake was speed-reading from a 3x5 card in her hand,

but the word "amphora," wasn't in her lexicon, and the nuances of the popular "watering hole" from the Golden Era of Hollywood had escaped her.

Within fifteen minutes Channel 12 was ready for its chance at Jerry Crowell. Reporter Steve Gonzales was standing on the curved driveway in front of the crime scene, mike in hand.

" . . . blood-soaked body was discovered early this morning along with the body of Marcella Williams, former wife of television and motion picture star Desmond Williams. A good friend and neighbor, Jerry Crowell, who lives nearby, discovered the bodies. Tell us in your own words, Mr. Crowell, what happened this morning?"

Jer had just about used up his fifteen minutes of fame, but he was getting a lot of mileage out of it. He was growing accustomed to the limelight and even had one of the makeup people touch him up before the camera started rolling for his interview with Steve Gonzales. He also found time to change into a designer sweat suit, sans sweat, and train his hands to stay in his pockets.

"I've lived here for eleven years and nothing like this ever happened before. I was jogging on the beach early this morning when I noticed something was wrong at Marcella's house. Her big side window had been blown out. I thought there might be trouble, so I ran up the steps to the house and looked through a window. Marcella and her friend, Adrian Wells, were lying on this huge white couch. Blood was everywhere. I went to the place next door, but they weren't home. I climbed back down to the beach and was heading to my house when I saw a guy coming toward me with a cellular phone, and . . ."

CHAPTER 3

Unless she wanted to watch an old movie, Ginger Caulfield couldn't get away from the "murder of the century." She channel surfed until she landed on the Channel 11 *View on L.A.* news program. Their studio set was modern, slick, high-tech. The news anchors sat behind a console right off the *Starship Enterprise.* The only thing missing was the comm button on their chest. Instead, the news people wore the Channel 11 logo—a stylized camera eye with the number eleven in silver in its center.

The noon anchor was John Roberts, a man in his early fifties with perfect hair and perfect teeth. Not a hair on his head had changed since he started reporting fifteen years earlier. Ginger and her husband, Fred, swore Roberts must keep it in a drawer at his desk. The guy was perfection. His suit never wrinkled and neither did his forehead. He had either heard it all before or the slime and gore on the TV monitor didn't seem real, so to him it was just another day at the office. He picked up the story from there.

" . . . the neighbor telephoned the police, who confirmed that the bodies were those of Adrian Wells, the prominent restaurateur, owner of the posh Hollywood nightspot the Amphora, along with Marcella Williams, the former wife of famous television and motion picture star Desmond Williams, whose best known movie, *John's Law,* grossed more than a hundred million dollars at the box office."

The scene abruptly switched. At first Ginger thought the channel was breaking for a commercial, but sadly, she was wrong. The news director was running a montage of publicity stills of Desmond Williams and then the trailer from the star's popular action/adventure movie, *John's Law,* with Williams as the super-smart, streetwise black police detective, John Law, strutting, punching, and loving his way around the city. The voice-over was describing the action flick in heart-racing detail:

> "If you think it's rough in your neigh-
> borhood, you ain't seen nothin' yet.
> The streets in L.A. are mean. Life is
> cheap...and hard. It takes something
> tough to clean them up. It takes the
> law—*John's Law,* the new action picture
> starring the toughest of them all,
> Desmond Williams. He *is* John Law. He
> fights hard and loves hard. That's why
> they call him the L.A. Street Sweeper.
> You've got to see this picture starring
> Desmond Williams, the screen's meanest
> good guy. If you see only one picture
> this summer, it's got to be this one.
> It's the law. *John's Law.*"

Just as abruptly the screen switched back to the Channel 11 set with John Roberts continuing his report: "Desmond Williams has been filming the sequel to *John's Law* in San Pedro for several weeks. When police officials notified him early this morning of the murder of his former wife and Adrian Wells, production was immediately shut down . . . And I believe we have footage of the event that had to be very traumatic for Desmond Williams. Yes, we have that tape. Go ahead and roll it."

The television monitor over Roberts' left shoulder dissolved to previously recorded video of the dock area in San Pedro earlier that morning. The view was from a Channel 11 news van that was trailing a police vehicle to an out-of-the-way section of the dock between a group of warehouses where the studio had set up their mobile dressing rooms and stored some of their filming equipment. Pulling in next to Channel 11's crew was a van from another television station.

The cameraman panned the area to give TV viewers the lay of the land. It must have been eight or nine o'clock, but the production people were still fiddling with equipment. The news camera focused on the cops and followed the two officers as they stepped out of their vehicle and were given directions to Desmond Williams' trailer.

The entire side of his huge trailer was painted with the *John's Law* logo. Anybody who was conscious during the past three years knew what it looked like: a black-and-white picture of Williams in partial profile with his .44 Magnum held up beside his tough face. Printed on the blued barrel were white letters that read IT'S THE LAW.

Everybody in the vicinity gravitated toward the trailer. Whether it was the cops, the cameras, or the anticipation of something gory luring them, the people looked like zombies following the scent of the last living body on the planet. The second police officer started directing people away, but the crowd wasn't dissipating with any great speed.

The lead officer knocked on the trailer door and moments later Desmond Williams stepped out of his dressing room with a glass of tomato juice in his hand. He was wearing his famous John Law signature outfit: a black leather jacket, a bright poppy-colored shirt opened to his navel, and blue jeans. He had worn virtually the same outfit during his B-movie career, too. Williams had put on a few pounds since his first silver screen venture, but he was still macho, even with the slight paunch protruding over that gold belt buckle. He was wearing those black lizard boots, too.

There was no audio, but you could tell the police officer was giving him the bad news. Williams' face turned solemn as he was taking it all in. His features went through several contortions before settling on an angry pose. Then, in a move strictly out of a Hollywood movie, he got the glass of tomato juice in a strangle hold and broke it in his hand. Even for an actor this was a little over-the-top. Williams stared at the crimson results. He didn't even flinch. All you could think was: "Just a flesh wound," as he usually said in his B-movies. He had to have twenty-five or thirty bullet holes in that leather jacket by now.

Ginger changed channels. Every network was doing the same story. After five minutes of channel surfing, she had seen Desmond Williams cut himself seven or eight times and was getting queasy. It was the top of the hour and the news anchors would be changing, so she landed once more on Channel 11.

Myrna Blankenship, back from doing the live shot at murder central, appeared on the screen. With the dreadful news about Marcella Williams, Ginger thought the bubbly reporter might lift her spirits. Myrna was an animated little thing. Her short, dark hair was cut pixie style and she sort of twinkled when she spoke, whether it was called for or not. Every time Ginger heard her speak, she thought of Tinkerbell getting ready to tell a bedtime story.

"And that was the scene this morning when famed television and motion picture star Desmond Williams learned the tragic news that his former wife, Marcella Williams, and her friend and latest companion, restaurant owner Adrian Wells, were found shot to death in her fashionable ocean-front home in the secluded Malibu area."

Behind Myrna were half a dozen small TV monitors: three showing her from three different angles; another screen with a shot of Desmond Williams from one of his movies; another with a picture of Marcella Williams and Desmond Williams at a premiere; and the last screen focusing on the front of the Amphora Restaurant with Marcella wearing another diaphanous gown, doing her Greek goddess vamp with Adrian fawning at her side.

The news director did a side-by-side shot of Myrna in the

studio and Marcella and Adrian at the restaurant. Myrna's eyes widened as she began the description of the late Mrs. Williams. She had been such a beautiful woman and her death was exceptionally grisly. Ginger could feel the media feeding frenzy oozing into her living room. She turned off the television and went to work in her garden for a few hours before it got too hot.

The entire nation was treated to over thirty hours of breaking news on the murders. They had every expert on the subject on TV: former lawyers, former policemen, former judges, and former victims, at least those among the living. By midafternoon on day two they were trotting out the psychics, the squirrel hunters, and other conspiracy theorists. It is amazing how far the media will go for ratings.

Channel 8 had the deluxe assortment of mixed nuts. Ginger poured herself a tall glass of iced coffee and watched for a few minutes.

The Channel 8 *L.A. Hot News* set was slick, modern, high-tech. The studio walls were done in opaque black glass with recessed lighting along the floor. Reporters sat on ultra-modern chrome chairs behind a desktop made of smoked glass set onto chrome legs. A TV monitor was buried in the console so the newsreaders could read their news copy off a screen rather than a piece of paper. The entire set was quite extraordinary. Whenever they had breaking news, a flash of computer-generated flame started burning at the bottom of the screen and then spread out of control until the accompanying musical fanfare faded and the seated reporter began their story. It literally looked like hell.

The topic of their afternoon show was billed as A COM-PREHENSIVE LOOK AT THE MARCELLA WILLIAMS MURDER. The woman was barely cold, for God's sake. Since Ginger and her husband rarely watched that station, she wasn't familiar with their midday newsperson, but Phil Jeffries was a bit of a character. He had sort of a Snidely Whiplash thing going on with his mustache and patent leather hair. He sneered when he talked and you expected the whole thing to be a joke because nobody could be that funny without it being a gag. It was distracting at first and Ginger missed what he was saying. Before too long she could tell it didn't matter. It was the co-anchor and the guests who were making headlines.

Young black reporter Gary Johnson was having a field day asking, or rather prompting, the guests. First to answer questions was the well-known defense lawyer, Jonathan Bloomberg. Since there wasn't a perpetrator in the picture, this ersatz Clarence Darrow was basically putting out his résumé.

"Is it true that the bodies of Marcella Williams and Adrian Wells were badly mutilated?" asked Gary.

"I haven't seen the autopsy report," answered Bloomberg, "but I've been told by reliable sources it was bloody. Very bloody."

"Bloody, like in satanic ritual killings?" asked the reporter.

"Signs point to a very bizarre murder."

"Is it easier to defend someone who hacks people up instead of just, say, shoots them?"

"You have to assume your client is innocent, first," said Bloomberg.

"Yeah, but—" started Gary.

"Your 'Yeah, but' costs you clients, Gary. To a lawyer, the client is innocent, and everybody else is trying to hang him."

"How hard is it to maintain your conviction?" asked Gary, not getting his own pun.

"That's good," smirked Bloomberg, getting it. "Actually, it's easy. As a defense lawyer, you sit back and contest everything the prosecution brings in."

"Even if it's real evidence?" questioned Gary.

"You go over everything with a magnifying glass. If they miss anything, you call them on it."

"Like not reading the suspect his rights or not getting a

warrant?" asked Gary. "That's kind of Mother-May-I justice, isn't it?"

"We keep the prosecution on their toes," said the lawyer. "They go by the book or our guy walks."

"Do you go by the book?" asked Gary.

"I wrote the book. My clients know if they let me do my job, they go home."

"You sort of play God, don't you?"

"God doesn't get paid as well." Bloomberg laughed.

"There are rumors . . ." Gary leaned toward the next guest, a former New York City police detective. "The police know who the murderer is, but they're afraid to leak it to the public for fear of a racial backlash."

Thomas Mullins was guest number two. He was now billed as a "police consultant." He had moved to Los Angeles because the TV possibilities were nearly endless in Tinseltown, but there was no soft spot for his newly adopted city. Mullins answered, "This wouldn't be the first time a police department tried to keep a lid on possible riots by leaking small pieces of information to the public to soften them up before releasing the identity of the actual perp."

"Are you saying that the police would conceal evidence in a murder case?" asked Gary.

"With the reputation the LAPD has been getting lately, I wouldn't be surprised what they might do. This isn't the way we did it in New York."

"Have they determined the murder weapon?" asked the reporter.

"My sources say it was a shotgun," said Mullins, glancing over at Bloomberg.

"Could the police be covering up the actual weapon so there won't be copycat killings in Hollywood?" prodded Gary.

"This is California. People will do anything out here. The only time you have weird killings in New York is when it's in a Hollywood movie," said the displaced New Yorker.

"Do you think the police have hushed up other savage

murders like this one?" asked Gary.

"Cops can be bought off. You don't find this kind of stuff in New York," said a cop who should talk with Frank Serpico. "That's why I want to look at the police report. I'm writing a book that—"

Cutting him off, Gary continued, "Is it true there are numerous witnesses to the actual crime?"

"The police are keeping that under wraps, for now," said the ex-cop. "But my sources say they have a few credible leads."

Phil Jeffries finally got in a question. After all, it was his show. "What kind of profile would the police have on the murderer right now?" he asked.

Mullins dispensed his wisdom. "Psychotic. Loner. Somebody who hates people, but loves notoriety," said the ex-cop. "He will no doubt get off on all the publicity. It makes him bigger than he really is."

"Has he done this before?" Jeffries asked Mullins.

"This wasn't the first time he's inflicted pain. The other victims were probably nobody. This time he hit the jackpot. A real high-profile victim. I'm writing a—"

"What about Desmond Williams?" Gary Johnson interrupted, directing his question to the resident psychic, Sasha Dove. "How is he feeling right now?"

The psychic consulted her crystal ball. "He be goin' through a great deal of personal pain by and by."

Gary leaned toward the woman who wore a brightly colored muumuu and a matching scarf wrapped around her head. "Is it true you saw the deaths of Marcella and Adrian in a vision prior to the murders and no one in the police department would listen to you?"

Sasha Dove was trying to launch the Psychic News Network. Meanwhile, this jelly brain was becoming a hot commodity on the regular cable channels whenever anything out of the ordinary happened. She was a "person of color" though it wasn't clear what color that was. She claimed both Haitian and Jamaican heritage, but critics said she sprang from Mississippi. Her accent wandered from calypso to Cajun to Hattiesburg.

"Me have assisted da po-lice in many da murder an' da kidnappin' case, but dis be da first time dey ignore da vision I seen."

"What exactly did you see, Sister Sasha?" asked Phil.

"I seen da bodies of da two kilt peoples on da waves. Like dey be floatin' in da wata an' da blood be all 'round, don't ya know. It be one terrible sight."

"You offered your vision to the authorities and they refused it. Is that right?" asked Gary.

"Like, they told me to beat it . . . Dey not be listenin' to one dat know da truth."

Gary looked intently at the woman. "You know who killed Marcella Williams and Adrian Wells, don't you? Are you afraid you might be next?"

A worried look flashed across Sasha's face before she spoke. "I seen many t'ings and me knows what be da truth. Just ask Sister Sasha da questions."

"Who killed Marcella Williams?" asked Gary.

"It be dark forces working in da night."

Ginger couldn't stand it anymore; she found other things to occupy her time. Since the bodies remained dead and no suspect was in the media's crosshairs, she got a lot of weed pulling done that afternoon.

Fred, her tall Texan husband of nearly nine wonderful years, came home from the office a little after six that evening. He turned on the television in the great room and picked up the newspaper. Ginger was still in the midst of preparing dinner. Time had gotten away from her while working in the flowerbeds, so she was rushing around trying to get dinner on the table.

She caught the Channel 12 *L.A. Comprehensive News* logo as it flashed on the screen, followed by the bright red banner letters reading SPECIAL BULLETIN, accompanied by their musical fanfare. She stopped mid-tomato slice and watched. The picture cut to their evening news set.

The Channel 12 set was modern, slick, high-tech, but the anchors sat in comfortable leather chairs. That was as close to conservative as the station went. The demographics of the six o'clock news program were the thirty-five-to sixty-year-old crowd. That usually meant more discretionary money, so their set made a token gesture to those who understood comfortable furniture. Ginger noticed their ads ran more to teeth-whitening products than to Baby-Wipes. Their young reporter, Steve Gonzales, was at the news desk.

"This is Steve Gonzales, Channel 12 *L.A. Comprehensive News*, with this special bulletin on the double homicide discovered early yesterday morning of Marcella Williams and her latest companion, Adrian Wells, at her exclusive beach-front home. It has been learned from sources close to the Los Angeles Police Department that Desmond Williams, television and motion picture star and the former husband of Ms. Williams, has been brought in for questioning in that double murder.

"A spokesman for the actor said the questioning is just routine, and Mr. Williams is cooperating fully with authorities in the investigation. We're going to roll footage taken earlier this afternoon when Mr. Williams was brought into Parker Center. Go ahead and roll tape."

The screen cut to a remote shot taken by a telescopic lens of Desmond Williams being helped out of a police vehicle. Cops were everywhere. Ginger thought they looked more like groupies gawking at "John Law," but then she realized nobody was smiling. That's when she noticed something else.

"Look, Fred! He's handcuffed!" she exclaimed to her husband, who was more interested in his newspaper than the television. "They must have a new definition of 'cooperation' in L.A."

Fred started clicking to other news channels to see if

any other station had picked up on that little newsflash. He switched to Channel 10. It was your typical "All Hollywood, All the Time" news show.

The Channel 10 *News & Entertainment* studio was modern, slick, high-tech. It reminded Ginger of a 1950s sci-fi movie envisioning the future with its cheesy frosted glass panels on the back wall and several large television monitors housed within recessed areas. The scene always began in black and white before bursting into vivid color. It wouldn't surprise her if Michael Rennie turned up at the console one night repeating those famous words: "*Klaatu barada nikto!*"

The space cadets that evening were Tina Lake and co-anchor Mark Parsons. Rumor had it Tina was the role model for the girls in *Clueless*.

"Mark, we have late-breaking news in the ongoing murder investigation of Marcella Williams, the ex—I mean, former wife of movie star Desmond Williams, and Adrian Wells, the owner of the fashionable Hollywood eatery the 'Ampora.'" [*She still couldn't pronounce the name of the restaurant.*] "Police have confirmed that Desmond Williams has been taken into custody and is being held for questioning in the double homicide. Mr. Williams' spokesman and close personal friend, Larry Tabor, has given a statement saying that this is all a misunderstanding and Mr. Williams will be released shortly. Mark—"

She handed the baton to her co-anchor. "Yes, thank you, Tina. Los Angeles District Attorney Frank Fallen called a press conference at this hour to give details in the arrest of Mr. Williams. I believe we are going live to Parker Center. Yes. The news conference is just getting under way."

The screen behind the news team changed from their logo of a stylized television set with its jazzy antenna sticking out of it to the media room at Parker Center. At first the scene looked like an old *Charlie Chan* movie before it burst into color. D.A. Frank Fallen walked to the podium as the last microphone was being set up. He wasn't smiling. God! Ginger thought. What was this all about? She went into the family room to watch with Fred, who had put down his paper.

Fallen was a distinguished-looking man in his midforties. Hollywood casting couldn't have picked a better D.A. He cleared his throat to get everyone's attention, but most media tongues were already hanging out.

"Ladies and gentlemen, this will be very short. This afternoon at 3 p.m., an arrest warrant was issued for Desmond Williams in connection with the double homicide of Marcella Williams and Adrian Wells. Mr. Williams was picked up in San Pedro where he was filming a movie. He was taken into custody by the Los Angeles Police Department and will be arraigned in federal court no later than Monday, July seventeenth. That's all we have to say at this time."

Hands and voices were immediately raised. One reporter yelled, "What evidence do you have, Mr. Fallen?"

Another reporter called out, "Were there witnesses?"

Yet another, "Are you worried about riots?"

One last reporter chimed in. "Have L.A.'s black leaders been notified of his arrest?"

Fallen had already walked away from the podium. He hesitated for half a second and you could tell he had thoughts on the subject, but he closed his mouth and continued walking.

Ginger was stunned. "Only in L.A.," she said to Fred. "I can't believe a big movie star like that would have anything to do with murder. It's so . . . Hollywood."

Later that evening while they were relaxing, Fred switched to Channel 12 with Steve Gonzales. He had just finished showing a repeat of Frank Fallen's press conference when they joined the news show in progress.

"And that was the scene earlier this evening at Parker Center when Los Angeles District Attorney Frank Fallen made that brief statement. It has been learned here at Channel 12 that sources close to the investigation have said there is an eyewitness to Mr. Williams being near the home of his former wife, Marcella Williams, at the time of the murders, but Larry Tabor, publicist and spokesman for Mr. Williams, has stated that Mr. Williams was on the set of his new movie, *John's Law II*, when the incident happened."

The scene dissolved to a prerecorded video outside Parker Center. Larry Tabor and entourage were leaving the building. Tabor had the air of a union boss right out of *On the Waterfront,* and his staff looked like they knew which kneecap to break first. All were wearing concerned faces straight from Acting Class 101 as they stormed out, but Tabor wasn't all that anxious to dodge the reporters' questions.

Myrna Blankenship, doing a little moonlighting from the Channel 11 *View on L.A.* morning show, got in the first question. "What can you tell us, Mr. Tabor? Are the rumors true about an eyewitness?"

"That's all they are. Rumors. Mr. Williams was in his dressing room on the set of his new movie, *John's Law II*, when the tragedy occurred."

Mark Parsons with Channel 10 asked, "The murders happened sometime Tuesday night, Mr. Tabor. Was Mr. Williams with anyone in his dressing room?"

"The police haven't determined the exact time of death. As for Mr. Williams, there were a hundred people around the set Tuesday evening. No one saw him leave or return. The police have made a grave error. We should have Mr. Williams released by tomorrow morning. This was just a terrible mistake."

Tabor and company rushed off, leaving Parsons and the rest of the media circus speechless—until the next newsflash. The station went back to its live coverage.

Fred changed channels, wanting to hear if Channel 10 had any follow-up to Mark Parsons' previously aired question. The camera focused on Tina Lake, Mark's Stepford Wife co-anchor.

" . . . was the press conference at police headquarters earlier this evening," she was saying.

Tina stopped reading her lines off the teleprompter and was waiting for Mark to continue. But she didn't look over at him. She didn't say anything. She just sat there with a blank look on her face. It was as if somebody turned off her switch. Finally the screen went to Parsons' face. He was hurriedly reading through the lines on the prompter to see where Tina had dropped the ball, and trying to play catch-up. He continued.

"Thank you, Tina. Sources close to the investigation have stated that evidence was found in Mr. Williams' trailer linking him to the crime scene. Further details were not available."

"Yes, Mark," Tina began reading Mark's lines. "It has also been learned that famed defense attorney Malvin Shepherd has been retained by Desmond Williams and is arriving at LAX this evening from his summer home on Martha's Vineyard to represent the television and motion picture star. Mr. Shepherd is known around the country as a hard-hitting, no-nonsense defense attorney, having represented such notables as plastic-pipe heiress Paulette Conrad, financier Maxwell Peterson, and two of the Hillhaven Seven in the 1980s."

"Didn't he *lose* all those cases?" Ginger asked her husband.

"Maybe he forgot to mention that in his press kit," said Fred.

The screen shifted to a black-and-white view of the arrival area at LAX. The scene burst into color just as Malvin Shepherd and his crew came trudging toward the outer doors to face the flock of news cameras and reporters standing on the sidewalk.

Shepherd and his minions pushed their way through the crowd of fellow travelers exiting the airport, none of whom had the slightest idea who he was. His people were loaded down with all kinds of luggage. They had been in too big a hurry to stow it in cargo. Shepherd didn't carry any of his own stuff. That's what you pay minions to do. But they were all doing a really good job playing VIP while the clutch of reporters was circling ever closer.

"If he was that all-fired important, he would have had his own plane," Ginger said.

"He should have borrowed Maxwell Peterson's jet. He won't need it for another five to seven years," said Fred.

The goon squad stormed out through the airport doors, and then they did the funniest thing. Each one of them reached into a pocket and pulled out a pair of sunglasses and put them on. It was damn near choreographed. A few steps more and the reporters blocked their way. The news conference began.

Gary Johnson was first. "Mr. Shepherd, is it true you're here to cut a deal with the district attorney on behalf of Mr. Williams?"

Shepherd was indignant. "I'm here to protect my client from injustice."

"What about the witnesses who saw Mr. Williams at the beach house?" asked Gary.

"Mr. Williams has witnesses of his own who will testify he was nowhere near the house at the time of the murders. If I were you, I'd be skeptical of any evidence to the contrary."

Myrna Blankenship followed with her query. "But Mr. Shepherd, the police say they found blood in Mr. Williams' trailer."

That caught Shepherd off guard momentarily. The information hadn't reached him in flight.

"I am not aware of *anything* 'allegedly' found on my client's private property. Since Mr. Williams did not have counsel present at the time of his arrest, we should all be a little dubious of any so-called evidence presented so far. Just wait 'til my independent analysis team gets hold of it. After all, they don't have an ax to grind or a reelection to think about. I would be surprised if any *supposed* evidence was allowed to escape the scrutiny of the news media in this city. We have our work cut out for us, my friends."

It was going to be a long evening in News-Land.

At ten o'clock, Fred tuned the TV to Channel 12 *L.A. Comprehensive News.* The anchors, Warren King and Christine Mack, were two decades older than their counterparts on the six o'clock show. They were bumped to the late night gig after Christine's latest face-lift didn't pan out. The advertising ran toward cemetery plots and supplemental insurance so the demographics of the news broadcast must have been those lingering in God's waiting room.

Warren King began the news hour: "Topping the news this evening is the press conference being held momentarily outside the Criminal Courts Building. Malvin Shepherd, defense attorney for screen actor Desmond Williams, has called this conference to answer questions regarding the allegations made against his client. Amanda Hill is our reporter on the scene and I believe we're ready with her report."

The scene switched to a remote shot in front of the downtown court building. Amanda Hill, microphone in hand, was waiting for her cue. She adjusted her earpiece and then looked into the camera. Amanda was usually the five o'clock co-anchor with Steve Gonzales. Tonight she was going solo.

"That's right, Warren. I'm here in front of the Criminal Courts Building waiting for Malvin Shepherd to start his hastily called press conference." She was distracted by the noise around her. "I think we're about to get under way. Yes, Malvin Shepherd is walking to the microphones."

Again the scene changed. The camera focused on Malvin Shepherd and the forest of microphones growing out of a single metal tree, lip high in front of him. Shepherd wasn't using notes. He did his act from memory. His face was carved into that serious demeanor used for describing airplane crashes, while his people standing around him looked more akin to bodyguards than merely assistants.

Shepherd was a specimen. He should have gone into politics because he knew how to demagogue and pontificate with the best of them, but there was more money in lawyering, if you had the reputation. And Bulldog Shepherd had the rep. And he had the look. Not quite stocky, but he was solid. Think Edward G. Robinson, but taller.

"Ladies and gentlemen. For those of you who don't know who I am, my name is Malvin Shepherd. I'm lead counsel for Mr. Desmond Williams. There have been some rather damaging rumors about my client that I wish to dispel at this time.

"First, the only witnesses in this case are those who saw Mr. Williams in his trailer at the time of the murders. Second, the blood taken from Mr. Williams' trailer was from a cut on his hand from a glass Mr. Williams was holding when a police officer rather callously told him about the death of his wife. I believe you have all seen that on television. There really isn't any more to it than that."

Amanda Hill was the first reporter out of the starting gate with a question. "Mr. Shepherd, do you think Mr. Williams will be released on bail?"

"After the arraignment on Monday, we will ask for a bail hearing and I expect Mr. Williams to be released at that time."

Amanda asked a follow-up question. "Do you think Desmond Williams might be considered a flight risk?"

"I'm glad you asked. Desmond Williams is a celebrity. Where in the world could he go where he wouldn't be recognized? I'd say his release is a no-brainer."

Gary Johnson with Channel 8 asked, "Why did the police take Mr. Williams into custody if they didn't have any real evidence against him?"

"That's a good question. My client is a very famous person. There are certain people in this city who would do anything to discredit him, to cause him embarrassment. He is currently filming a big budget motion picture and there are those who would find it in their best interest to see that investment lose money."

Amanda asked, "Are you saying that money could be the motive for the killings?"

"I really can't comment on that particular aspect of the investigation at this time."

Myrna Blankenship spoke up. "Do you think Mr. Williams' own life might be in jeopardy?"

"We are working closely with authorities to make sure nothing happens to my client."

Gary Johnson got in another question. "Mr. Shepherd, is Mr. Williams in a private cell?"

"We insisted on it, for his own protection."

Nikki Holt, a reporter with a daily paper, elbowed Gary out of the way and got in a query. "Is it true Desmond Williams is actually under police protection and not really under suspicion for the murder of his wife?"

"I'm sorry. I can make no further statements at this time. Thank you."

Shepherd and staff left in a flurry of unanswered questions, leaving the media speculating which direction to take their late-night news programs. The anticipated bombshell was a bit of a fizzle, but boy, were the trial balloons floated.

Channel 12 got a close-up of their own Amanda Hill as she improvised and appended. "Well, as you can see, Warren and Christine, the press conference is over as fast as it began. Malvin Shepherd is known as the Stealth Lawyer, and I think we just saw an example of that.

"Recapping what he said: The only witnesses are those who saw Desmond Williams in his trailer the night Marcella Williams, the former wife of Mr. Williams, and Adrian Wells were brutally murdered in her Malibu beachfront house. And it has been proven that the blood found in Desmond Williams' trailer was from the glass he was holding when told by officers from the Los Angeles Police Department his wife and her friend had been shot to death.

"And the most surprising news is that Mr. Williams might be a target in a high-stakes movie deal. But Mr. Shepherd did say that his client would be released from jail in the near future. That's all from the Criminal Courts Building downtown. This is Amanda Hill, Channel 12 *L.A. Comprehensive News*. Back to you in the studio."

Ginger looked at her husband. "Wait a minute. How did we go from Desmond Williams, murder suspect, to Desmond Williams, victim in high-stakes movie deal?"

"Maybe Amanda got hold of the defense counsel's talking points," grumbled Fred.

"Or they were handed to her. Why do they always lap up this stuff?"

"The media likes flash and dazzle. Look at the computer graphics they use to sell the news."

"You're right. Commercials for their news shows look more like music videos."

"Flash and dazzle," said Fred, again. "And Malvin Shepherd is all flash."

"So the D.A. has to turn up in drag before they'll listen to him?" questioned Ginger.

"That would probably work. And remember, old Malvin says there's no evidence against his client," said Fred.

"Malvin Shepherd doesn't have access to any evidence yet. The ink's still wet on the lab results."

"Don't let the facts get in the way of a good story," said Fred.

"That used to be called 'jury tampering,'" said Ginger.

"It still is," said Fred.

The television screen switched back to the studio at Channel 12. Warren and Christine had been listening intently to Amanda's breathless skewering of the facts. Warren King was up first.

"Thank you, Amanda. We will be watching the situation closely as this fascinating story unfolds here on Channel 12. Christine . . ."

"Thank you, Warren. Channel 12 has obtained exclusive interviews with several of Desmond Williams' close, personal friends who were shocked at the allegations leveled against the television and motion picture star. First, we have Desmond Williams' barber, a man who has known Mr. Williams for more than six years and who has gone on the record to say that Desmond Williams is the greatest living actor."

The scene switched to a close-up on a small barbershop. It was a far cry from Beverly Hills. The next shot was of a black man wearing a white smock, holding a comb. It looked staged.

The man basically read his lines: "Desmond Williams has been coming in here for six years. He never said anything about killing his wife. And guys like to talk in here. I say this is nothing more than the D.A. trying to get things stirred up 'cause he is running for reelection. It looks likes a high-toned lynching to me."

Fred turned off the television. "Let's go to bed."

For a solid week the public was regaled with every so-called expert on everything from murder to moviemaking. Most were fringe players, but after a fortnight on local and cable TV, the news media started thinking they might have insight. Their evening assumptions became the morning headlines. Their words became gospel even if their very next guest repudiated not only the news show's initial premise, but also their conclusion. Before the second week, so-called experts were debating so-called experts.

Most of the analysis was half-baked, some was wishful thinking, and a smattering was sheer poppycock. Then the rumor mill kicked into gear and the public was treated to analysis of the poppycock. You had to wonder how much was leaked from the D.A.'s office and what sprang forth from the defense counsel's well-oiled machine.

Mark Parsons with Channel 10 *News & Entertainment*

had a guest on Sunday night who captured headlines for another week. Too bad the dead can't sue. The man was billed as an expert on Hollywood, an insider who knew all the dirt. This guy was a walking compost heap.

"So you knew Marcella Williams?" Mark asked Terry Calla, a thin man with a very pointed nose and eyes that popped out of his head like somebody was squeezing him.

"Everybody knew Marcella. And I mean *everybody*. Desmond Williams didn't just divorce her, he ran for his life."

"Did she threaten him?"

"She didn't have to. She had friends who did the job for her," said the Hollywood gadfly.

"Was Marcella involved with organized crime?" asked Mark.

"A lot of this was covered up, you know. She was a celebrity, being married to Desmond. She didn't have any talent of her own, anyway anything you could show on TV. Desmond tried to protect her while they were married. But finally he had enough.

"I've been to parties at Marcella's house where so much coke was snorted, you could get high just inhaling what you could vacuum out of her carpets."

The interview ended. The station went to commercial.

Ginger and her husband were watching open-mouthed. "I wonder how much that set back Desmond Williams and his defense team?" she said after Fred turned off the TV.

"I think I saw that plot in a movie," said Fred.

"If you didn't, you will."

Back on the news set, after the camera was turned off, Mark leaned over to Terry Calla and said, "Marcella Williams didn't have carpets."

Terry looked at the cameras and made sure the lights were off. He covered his microphone and whispered, "Who's gonna know?"

CHAPTER 4

The next day, Ginger was painting some old pieces of furniture she had picked up at a garage sale, doing the work in the guest cottage next to their house where there was more room to make a mess. Both a coffee table and a dry sink were getting a coat of antique ivory paint. Her plan was to decoupage fruit designs on the tabletop as well as the doors of the sink. It would look "cottagey" and since she was going to use the pieces in the cottage, it made sense.

She heard the mailman coming down the street. All the dogs in the neighborhood, including her pair, began their clarion call to announce his arrival. She needed a breather so she pulled off her surgical gloves and closed the lid on the paint can. Walking over to the wooden mailbox made to resemble a little house, she opened its front door, pulled out the wad of mail, and flipped through the letters and catalogs and junk mail. That's when she saw it.

"Oh, expletive deleted!" she said out loud.

She looked up and down the street thinking if no one saw her, she could tear it up and forget about it. But she knew she couldn't get away with it. She sighed.

The envelope was the official pink-and-gray California jury summons with her name on it, **GINGER CAULFIELD**.

As she was preparing dinner that evening, she turned on the small television suspended under a kitchen cabinet to catch the news. She had the volume turned down while she pulled salad makings out of the refrigerator and began creating a mixed-green beauty, but she couldn't help notice that Channel 11 *View on L.A.* was running an extensive story on

Desmond Williams and the murders. It would be just her luck to get on *that* jury, she thought.

She decided to take out her irritation on the vegetables. She tore the spinach to shreds, then grabbed a zucchini and cut both its ends off in a very hostile manner and began slicing the thing with a vengeance. Next, she put a green pepper on the cutting board and started hacking away at it.

"Is it dead yet?" asked Fred.

He startled her. She hadn't heard him drive up nor walk in the kitchen. She was still holding the knife and brought it up in a defensive manner.

With unintentional disdain she said, "Oh. It's you."

Fred set down his briefcase and walked over to her. She put down the knife and wiped her hands on her apron.

"Who did you expect? Freddy Krueger?"

"No. He comes on Wednesdays."

"What's the matter?" asked Fred.

"I got a stupid jury summons."

In mock pity, he said, "Aw. Too bad."

Ginger was still pissed at getting the notice and wasn't buying his concern. "I'm sure you're all broken up."

"Better you than me." She went for his throat. Fred grabbed her hands and held them tightly. "Now, now. Remember, it's a privilege and your civic duty."

"Like your civic duty?"

"Can I help it if my company can't live without me?"

"Write a letter to the court and say you can't live without me."

"But honey, your civic duty—"

"Remember, I won't be here to cook, or clean . . . or iron," she said.

"Where's that phone?" he started to say as he loosened his grip and reached around her for the wall phone.

"You rat!"

Ginger made a lunge toward him, but he grabbed her again, bending her down in a sweeping gesture and then had the audacity to kiss her. Men! Fred gave her that look he gets when he knows he is being a perfect swine.

"But I will miss you," he added.

He brought her back upright.

"There is a good side," Ginger said. "We can meet for dinner, then you can drive me home."

"What will you do with your car?"

"I'll carpool with you. My summons is for superior court in L.A., not here in Pasadena."

His demeanor changed. "Aw, honey. I don't want you to go downtown. All the bums that hang around down there; the rats—"

"Present company excepted," she added.

"—and the perverts. It's not safe and—"

"Yeah, I know."

He gave her a heartfelt and concerned squeeze. Over his shoulder the television was still showing scenes from the "murder of the century." John Roberts with Channel 11 *View on L.A.* was on the small screen. The picture dissolved to shots of Desmond Williams, and then the infamous beach-front house, and finally to Malvin Shepherd.

Ginger got so wrapped up in what she was watching, she stopped her side of the hug.

"What if I get on the Desmond Williams case?" She pointed to the small screen.

"Oh, God! That one will be a killer."

"Do you think he did it? Can you imagine John Law, the screen's meanest good guy, murdering anybody?"

"Some of the experts say he really does have witnesses. Anyway, why would anybody kill an *ex*-wife?" said her adoring husband.

"Cynical, but true," she said. "And he's rich. He would have hired someone to do it."

"Now who's being cynical?"

CHAPTER 5

The next day in the paneled office of the Los Angeles District Attorney, D.A. Frank Fallen stood at the head of a large table. He was visible through the partially open door. In front of him were neatly piled folders. Seated at the table was Bill James, his right-hand man.

Frank and Bill went back a long way. Some said the only reason Frank ended up D.A. was because he photographed better. Frank looked good in a suit. There was just enough gray in his slicked-back hair to make him look erudite. And the hair went with the Armani suits and the expensive shoes. He was beautifully packaged and that velvet baritone voice was right out of a late night movie.

Bill James was brighter, knew the politics of the job better and kept Frank from stepping in too many cow pies. And he was always around to clean Frank's shoes if things got too deep.

Bill was broader than Frank, in both girth as well as experience. His hairline had not only receded, it had left the building. He'd laugh about it, but he better be the one making the joke. The only person he took crap from was Frank, and that was because he knew the man's limits. They went way back.

"This one's going to be a bitch, Bill," said the D.A.

"Has Shepherd said anything about cutting a deal?"

"Not yet. I think he wants to see how far he can push the media."

"They're damn near kissing his butt now," said Bill. "I haven't heard one local news channel even hint that the schmuck might be guilty, and the 'experts' on cable TV are coming up with so many alibis, I'd use one or two if I were defending Williams."

"I bet Malvin Shepherd is taking notes," said Frank. "I liked the one about the stunt double myself. Did you hear that the guy hired a lawyer?"

"It isn't true."

"That he hired a lawyer?"

"No. That Williams has a stunt double. He hasn't used one since his last series. He likes doing the fight scenes himself."

"You're kidding? Then why the—oh. Trial balloons," Frank surmised.

"Shepherd floated the damn *Hindenburg* at his first press conference: Somebody in Hollywood is out to get Williams. The media's been feeding off it ever since."

"They're still asking if we're doing enough to protect the son of a bitch," said Frank.

"Remember, Shepherd said he's the one who insisted we keep Williams in protective custody. Yeah, right. A six-by-nine-foot luxury suite in the maximum-security wing of the L.A. County Hilton. Give me a break," scoffed Bill James.

"I thought Shepherd was saying *we* were out to get Williams," questioned Frank.

"Is that how you heard it? I guess I have too many friends in Hollywood. They're all over me to make sure nothing happens to the fucking prima donna. If it were up to me, I'd push him in front of a bus and end this circus right now."

Frank laughed. "I was thinking of dropping the case."

"What?" said Bill, leaning forward in his chair.

"I won't get reelected no matter how this goes down."

"I can get you reelected, Frank."

"Not if we screw this up."

"Frank, you could have a snapshot of the pig blowing those two away and Shepherd could still find a jury who wouldn't believe it."

Frank was thinking about something else. "Do you think Shepherd might cut a deal?"

Before Bill James could answer, an attractive woman came pushing through the door with an attaché case in her hand. She was quite trim, thirty-two, dressed in a charcoal gray suit that hit just above her knees and her makeup and hair were perfection. Her name was Debra-John Greer, called Johnnie by her friends. She was one of the best attorneys Frank had on his team. Her credentials were impeccable as well as impressive. She was professional to the letter and she was black.

Following closely behind her was Matthew Simms, only a few years younger, but he was years younger in savvy and drive. A handsome guy, Matt's parents were Boston area bluebloods with enough money to make college, and then law school, easily affordable. His uncle was a partner in a prestigious Los Angeles law firm and young Matt was able to clerk there every summer. After graduation he worked for Uncle Albert two years before he passed the bar exam and then he was offered an even bigger office at his uncle's firm. Matt decided to work for the city instead. His parents flew out to California and tried to dissuade him, so did his uncle, so did the D.A. But Matt thought it was right for his career. He wanted to do something important. He wanted to make a difference. Not to mention, he loved his condo on the beach. Matt could always go to work for his uncle if he got tired of putting criminals behind bars. His uncle was a white-collar criminal defense attorney.

Matt was rather attractive in a shallow sort of way. He was amiable and bright and things fell his way without a lot of effort on his part. His professors gave him special con- siderations because his parents had money and prestige and were involved with many charitable and civic organizations. Tickets and box seats were handed out like trick-or-treat candy to those who helped young Matt with his career.

As they stepped into Frank's office, Matt gave Johnnie's

fanny a discreet pat as they crossed the threshold. Nobody noticed, but everybody knew they were an item. Has it been mentioned? Matt was white. They took their seats.

Frank Fallen was the first to speak. It was his ball. "If anybody expects to get any sleep in the next few months, forget it." Polite laughter was followed by silence. "I have the unpleasant duty of picking the prosecuting attorney in the Desmond Williams case. You know I'd prefer that Arthur was handling this one, but he's still on the Cappelletti case and we've got to let him run with that one."

Matt Simms spoke. "What are the odds we get a hung jury?"

"In Cappelletti? Fifty–fifty."

Matt had a thought. "Maybe if we'd really hang the jurors when they can't decide—"

"Remember, you said that. Not me," said Frank.

"Okay. Tell us the bad news," said Johnnie, crossing her shapely legs.

"You've looked at the charges. You know who the defendant is. His reputation. You sure as hell know who the defense is. You've seen the evidence. And you know what the media is saying about us."

Bill James answered. "They're saying the white guys are beating up on another brother."

"Yes," acknowledged Frank. "And the media, bless their exploitable little hearts, are already pitching their tents."

Bill added, "It would be a lot easier if Art could do this one." He had run the option past Frank, but he wanted it on the table so the team could toss it around.

Frank Fallen was resolute. "If I pull him off the Cappelletti case, we'd lose it for sure."

Johnnie was shocked. "You think we might lose? We have more evidence against that child murderer than we have against Williams."

L.A. District Attorney Frank Fallen answered, "This is a great time to be a murderer in Los Angeles."

Johnnie wasn't happy. "Carol Cappelletti hires a quack psychologist with a degree from a correspondence school and all of a sudden she remembers being molested by her father, and that's supposed to make it all right for her to kill her children?"

"Johnnie, I can't make the jury un-believe what they want to believe. It's easier to say some bastard twenty-five years ago is to blame than to find that woman guilty and send her to death row. And this way the jury doesn't get their hands dirty."

"Frank!" said Johnnie, almost coming out of her chair. "Harold Cappelletti died two years before Carol said he molested her. Why can't the media see that?"

"The media isn't on the jury," said the D.A.

"Like hell they aren't," she said, sitting back in her chair. "Christine Mack interviewed the psychologist a day after his testimony. When he said Carol Cappelletti should have more children to help her cope with her loss, that colossal jewel, Christine, burst into tears and said the prosecution had been too harsh on the poor woman."

"After all, Johnnie," said Bill, putting on a sad face, "she just lost her two 'wittle' kids."

"See what I mean?" said Johnnie. "They aren't even looking at the evidence."

"I'd like to say it was defense counsel's brilliant tactics twisting the truth, but Johnnie, the *public* wants her to get off," said Frank. "They're taking polls out there. She's running in the high seventies for being innocent."

"Who runs a poll like that?" asked Johnnie.

"Channel 8," said Matt. "I swear, Phil Jeffries is on some kind of super guilt trip."

"The only thing Jeffries is guilty of is low ratings. If he could film her execution, he'd be singing another tune," said Frank.

"We could go for a mistrial," said Bill.

Frank looked at him. "On what grounds?"

"The 'judge not' juror."

"The *Times* is Bible-bashing again," said the D.A.

"They keep quoting their unnamed source who says one of the jurors is spouting biblical verse," said Bill.

Johnnie said, "A juror quoting the Bible isn't grounds for dismissal."

Bill responded. "But, the *Times* says our Bible-thumper doesn't think we should put *anybody* on trial, in case we make a mistake."

Frank added, "That's not a religious nut. That's just a *nut*. We found the only person in the entire world who didn't hear Carol Cappelletti confess *on television* that she hacked her two children to pieces."

"The media psychics are saying that she dreamed she killed those kids because she was in shock," said Bill.

"I heard one of the kooks say the real killer put us all in a trance and we 'thought' we heard Carol Cappelletti say she killed those two children," said Johnnie.

"How are we supposed to get any kind of justice with crap like that on television?" exclaimed Frank.

"We can just be thankful the jury on the Cappelletti case is sequestered," said Bill.

"What if none of the jurors speaks up about the nut-case?" asked Matt.

Bill explained. "If she's convicted, the defense uses it as reason for a new trial. If we bring it up beforehand, they call for a mistrial, rip us for letting the case get out of hand, and hope we're too tired to try her again."

Matt concluded, "They win either way. The defense might as well have planted the story themselves."

"And don't think they didn't," mumbled the D.A.

"If you ask me," said Matt, "it's the jury pool. We get people who aren't smart enough to lie their way out of jury duty."

"No. We make it too easy to get biased jurors," said the D.A. "When you can cherry-pick a jury panel, justice loses."

Matt said, "You don't think Art can handle both cases?"

"Come on, Matt," said his boss. "This isn't a one-horse town. We do have a few good prosecutors lying around."

"Frank, we know what we need," Bill James said.

"Yeah. A little less publicity. They've already found Williams innocent on Channel 12."

"What do you expect? He's a movie star," said Bill.

"I would *like* the media to stop doing my job," said Frank. "They aren't very good at it."

"They're not paid to be good," said Johnnie. "They're paid to bring in the ratings."

"And I'm paid to see that justice is done," said the D.A. "How the hell can I do that with Christine Mack teary-eyed over an effing movie star?"

"She's not the only one," said Matt. "Did you see Warren King last night? He—"

"—That's exactly what I mean," Frank interrupted. "He gets on the tube and starts analyzing *me*, for chrissake. He doesn't know me from Adam and he doesn't have a clue what I think. Yet he sits there in his off-the-rack suit and tells everybody in Los Angeles what's going on in my head."

"Well, at least you don't have to pay a shrink," Matt added.

"I'd like to shrink him . . . and the horse he rode in on," said Frank. "The media distorts, misreports, and makes up the facts in this case. And I use the term 'fact' loosely. The only way we can get justice is to ignore the bastards."

"Potential jurors can't be sequestered," said Bill.

"I wonder if the media knows their meddling could end up putting a murderer back on the streets?" said Frank.

"Just gives them something else to report if he does it again," said Bill.

"That's why I want to get this into court before the media completely muddies the water," said Frank.

"I thought that was the defense attorney's job," said Johnnie.

Frank smiled. "That's why Shepherd is paid more than I am. He can get somebody else to do his dirty work."

Johnnie looked at Frank with her steady, reassuring eyes and asked, "What are you going to do, Frank?"

"Huh?" He had lost track of the conversation.

"Who gets the case?" she asked.

His smile vanished. "It's a shame, the games we have to play. The only way we can win is to outmaneuver them. I should be able to pick an attorney just because they're the best, not because of their skin color, or sex, or public profile. This should be a simple job. Find the killer, then give him a fair trial before we hang him. What happened?" He let a snicker escape his lips.

Bill James said, "It isn't possible anymore, Frank. It's all politics . . . and showbiz. Who are you going to pick?"

Johnnie Greer could see the handwriting on the wall. So could everybody else. She pursed her lips and shook her head slightly. The district attorney did roughly the same as he studied her.

"The lines are drawn, Johnnie. I'm going with you."

Johnnie was no fool. She knew exactly what the politics were, especially in L.A. She looked up at Frank Fallen, who was starting to pace. He did that when he had to bow to politics instead of justice. She caught his eye and smiled. "Hey, Frank. Am I supposed to be the token black or the feisty feminist in this movie?"

Frank let down his guard and laughed. "You're my second best lawyer, Johnnie. And thank God you're black."

"Anything for you, Frank."

Feeling a little sorry for her, he added, "You know what the media is going to do to you?"

Johnnie had seen the race card played before. It pissed her off, but not enough to back out. And more than that, she wanted the case. She wanted it badly. And she wanted to win it. "Hell, Frank. If we get a black judge and make sure half the jury's black, it'll look like an NAACP convention out there."

He laughed again. "See, Johnnie, that's why I want you on this one. You make me laugh, even if I'm watching my career go down the toilet."

"Frank, I don't know why you're worried," said Bill. "We have enough evidence to fry him."

"Do we have a motive?" asked Matt.

Bill James said, "We don't need motive, son. The evidence, even though it's circumstantial, is overwhelming."

"The media wants a motive, Bill," said Frank. "And I'm damn sure Malvin Shepherd will be screaming for one."

Johnnie said, "I think we know the motive, gentlemen."

"Nobody will buy jealousy. Adrian Wells was gay," said Frank.

Johnnie shook her head. "You don't know much about black men. I dated an African. I mean a *real* African. No African hyphenate. He was born in Uganda. Raised there. Brainwashed there. He thought I was his property. His woman. He wanted me to wear his dashiki and cornrow my hair. I made it quite clear what he could do with his dashiki and told him to take the next boat back to Africa. That was one brother who learned he couldn't pull the Kunta Kinte crap on this girl."

"You think Desmond Williams is the same type?" asked Bill.

Johnnie looked him in the eye. "I'll tell you this: Marcella Williams was his possession as long as they were married. If she was dating some jock or stud, Williams wouldn't have cared, but when a macho guy like Williams sees his ex dating a gay guy, and it's in all the papers—"

"Why would he care?" asked Frank.

"He knew that every black man who looked at him saw a brother who lost his woman to a homosexual."

Frank said, "We can't bring that up in court. Malvin Shepherd would have a field day. They would paint us as the biggest bunch of racists, homophobes, and bigots in the world."

"Because we say Williams hates gays?" asked Matt.

"No. For mentioning that Adrian Wells *was* gay."

Matt persisted, "But how could his lawyer manipulate the jury that way?"

"You've never seen Malvin Shepherd in action."

CHAPTER 6

A t the same time the D.A. was going over his game plan, Malvin Shepherd was sharpening his knives. And his chief of staff picked a great place to do it. Lots of client money was used to rent and furnish the office in Century City. Shepherd wasn't used to cutting corners, only throats—in court—with a vengeance, and an audience. His minions took care of the messy little details.

The big guy had been chatting with Williams over the speakerphone about the basic strategy the defense would employ while his staff was running in and out of the office setting up equipment, but now Shepherd needed to talk with Desmond privately.

"Everybody out! I'll buzz if I need anything."

People disappeared and soon Malvin was standing in the room alone. He picked up the receiver and switched off the speakerphone. He remained standing even though his client had no way of knowing, but Shepherd's tone of voice told Williams who was running the show. For his part, Desmond Williams, the screen's meanest good guy, was scared.

"I don't care what evidence they have, Williams. My job is to blow holes in it, through it, over and under it, and show that the prosecution has zilch."

"But it doesn't look good," muttered Williams.

"It'll look the way I want it to look. But you're gonna have to do something."

"What?"

"Make people think you're broken up over your dead

wife."

"How am I supposed to do that?" said Williams, a little testy.

"You're an actor, for chrissake. *Act* like you're broken up. Every time that camera is on you, cry."

"Wait a minute. John Law doesn't cry."

"John Law isn't facing a murder rap, Williams. You are. Do what I say and I'll get you off."

Williams listened to the pompous ass calling him from the high-priced *rented* suite of offices, rented on his nickel, and thought about it. He knew the meter had started ticking the minute Shepherd picked up the phone on Martha's Vineyard and took his case.

"What are the odds?" asked Williams.

"Good. The prosecution has zip. It's all circumstantial. Frankly, it's all guesswork."

"Their guessing could get me the electric chair," said Williams.

"They don't use the electric chair anymore."

Williams heard the man's matter-of-fact delivery. "Is that supposed to make me feel better?"

"They won't go for capital murder, Des. You're a movie star, for God's sake."

"I don't want to spend the rest of my life in jail, either. I want you to do whatever it takes to make damn sure I get out . . . and stay out."

"Look, Williams, if I get a whiff that we might lose this case, I'll see to it you disappear."

"And just how are you gonna do that, with me locked up in this fucking birdcage?"

"You'll get out after the bail hearing. Trust me. Another thing. I want your bank to put another fifty grand in my account for spreading around money. Call your guy."

"How much is this gonna cost me?"

"What's your life worth?"

CHAPTER 7

The last Saturday in July, Ginger and her husband went to a barbeque and beer bash at the estate of Herbert and Elizabeth Mandrake. It was billed as a swim party, but the first time the couple had gone to one of these things, in swimwear, nobody else dipped toe into water. In fact, no female showed up in a bathing suit, except Ginger. She felt like a fool for not knowing the quirks of the hostess any better.

Elizabeth Mandrake was old money with new ideas. Since her assets were starting to sag, she wore nothing but ankle-length dresses, and any woman who knew better did the same. Elizabeth also liked younger men. Her husband didn't seem to mind. So if you were young, male, and built like Mr. Universe, you wore your Speedo.

Ginger wore a black floral gauze skirt with a tank top. The way Elizabeth's eyebrow arched over her piercing brown eyes warned Ginger to wear a blouse next time, unless she could twist Fred's arm into never attending one of these functions ever again.

As for Fred, the Mandrakes were important clients, and Fred's boss had twisted his arm first and with more force. Most of the time Robert Knight failed to appear at these shindigs, letting his senior management team earn their keep by filling in for him. As long as the investment firm earned their clients a nice return, Robert didn't have to show up.

Elizabeth Mandrake eyed Fred. Her eyes wandered over his tight jeans, looking for a visible Speedo line.

"Don't you two look barbequey tonight," Elizabeth said. "Oh, Ginger. Why didn't you wear your swimsuit? I have this lovely pool and it's just going to waste." Ginger started to answer, but Elizabeth wasn't interested. "You two enjoy yourselves." She buzzed over to the next batch of guests.

"What were you going to tell her?" asked Fred when they were out of earshot.

"That I'd like to strip off and jump in her stupid pool. Let's get a drink. I'll drown in her well-stocked liquor cabinet instead."

"Martini?"

"Sure. Two olives. Elizabeth never serves much food."

"I've got some MREs in the trunk."

Ginger looked around. "Don't say that too loud. Everybody knows you could starve at a Mandrake party."

The Caulfields had several drinks and one small plate of barbeque before the sun finally set. The potato salad was made without sweet pickles and the baked beans were boiled. It was very frugal fare for such wealthy folks. By the time they got to the dessert Ginger was thinking about those Meals Ready to Eat in Fred's trunk.

"Can you get me one more cookie?" she asked.

"Here. Take mine." He handed her the last chocolate chip cookie on his plate.

"Sure you don't want it?"

"Go ahead. I'll play the martyr."

"And you do it sho swell . . ." she slurred. "So well."

"How many drinks have you had tonight?"

"The two you got me and the two Herb Mandrake plied me with."

"The old reprobate," said Fred.

"If they had a little more food, it'd soak up some of the gin." Her voice was going up an octave so Fred moved her to a quiet spot under some trees.

"Liz is watching her weight—" Fred started to say.

"—and everybody else's," added Ginger.

"Maybe she can go for one more tummy tuck."

"If she gets another one, her knees will be stapled to her chin," said Ginger.

"She's just trying to turn back the hands of time," said Fred.

"She'd be better off watching her husband's hands."

"He does like the ladies. I saw you two dancing together."

"He wanted me to teach him to samba."

"He uses that line every time he sees you."

"That's why he tries to get me drunk," she said.

"You and every other good-looking babe," said Fred.

"If he gets us plastered, maybe we won't remember it's the same old line. Let's walk. I need to cool off."

"I'm not taking you anywhere near that pool."

"Why not? This skirt is drip-dry." Ginger gave her husband a playful hug.

They walked down a lighted path on the Mandrake estate. It was edged with flowers and there were wooden benches along the way for quiet moments in the tranquil setting. The house was located high in the hills above Pasadena. Ginger and Fred had been there one Fourth of July and got ringside seats for the fireworks display exploding from the Rose Bowl.

They could hear voices ahead of them in the dark. Raised voices. Heated voices. They looked at each other and grimaced. The Caulfields slowed their pace to catch a few choice words.

"The media is providing a public service," said Jack, a defense lawyer.

"Not when they shape public opinion on the six o'clock news, they don't," said Simon, a corporate attorney.

"They cut through the crap," argued Jack.

"Not if they only give one side," countered Simon.

"It depends whose ox is being gored, Simon. If Channel 12 ran a story about one of your largest holdings and the stock went up, don't tell me you wouldn't profit from it."

"Who says it's going to be favorable. Remember what they did to Michael Milken?"

"The 'junk bond king?' He was guilty," said the lawyer.

"He pleaded guilty after the government leaked a ton of trumped-up criminal allegations against him and the press crucified him," said the attorney.

"They had a ninety-eight-count indictment against Milken," said Jack.

"The Feds only charged him with six felony counts. The media made it sound like Teapot Dome."

"So he had a good lawyer," said Jack, chuckling.

"No, he was railroaded in the press," said Simon. "Ask anybody on the street what they think about junk bonds today."

"Everybody knows they're fishy, Simon," said Jack.

"You're a lawyer, Jack. You know they're good as gold. The press made it sound like making money was a crime."

"They just reported what the government told them."

"They're reporters. Why didn't they check it out themselves?" asked Simon.

Hearing all he wanted to hear, Fred nudged Ginger to leave. He headed back toward the main house. He got twenty paces before he realized Ginger wasn't following him. By the time he made it through the trees, Ginger had entered the debate and was giving her two cents worth.

"I can tell you why," said Ginger. "It's a lot easier to stir up a hornet's nest than to calm one down. And it plays better on the nightly news."

"Hi, Ginger," said Simon. "Your husband's in the mergers and acquisition business. What did he say about junk bonds?"

"The restructuring that went on in the '80s led to wealth creation for society as a whole, Simon. Companies became more competitive."

"You should know about that," Jack said to her. "Didn't your firm work in that field?"

"On the fringes, Jack," Ginger said. "But the press did hype the class envy angle. I thought what Milken did was illegal at first, until Fred explained how it worked."

"Some of it was illegal," Jack said.

"Come on, Jack," said Simon. "When Congress passed the Insider Trading Sanctions Acts in '84, they deliberately made them vague. They could set up their pigeon in the press, let the media ruin his reputation, and then hang him."

"Only if you believe the press can actually influence the public that much," said Jack.

"We see it every day," said Ginger. "The bully pulpit now comes with a microphone and a TV camera."

"Come on. Washington still has that monopoly," Jack contradicted.

"The media can say anything it wants," said Simon.

"There are laws in society. I should know," said Jack.

"Laws aren't a deterrent. Nobody enforces them," said Ginger.

"Don't you think the media helps us get to the truth?" asked Jack.

"Not when they let people on their shows to lie and they don't refute that lie," said Ginger. "First, do no harm."

"They aren't doctors," said Jack.

"They're supposed to report a story or uncover the truth about one," said Ginger. "Not perpetuate a lie."

"Unfortunately, Ginger, we can't get rid of them," said Simon. "They're like the poor; they're always with us."

"And I think there's an amendment somewhere protecting them," Jack smirked.

"There is an inherent problem here, gentlemen," said Ginger. "Let me try an experiment. Stand over there by the lights around the pool. Jack, you play somebody the media loves to hate—a rich guy. Simon, you're his lawyer. I'll be the media. Jack, close your eyes. Simon, spin him around a few times. This will show Jack he is in your capable hands."

Simon grabbed Jack by the shoulders and spun him

around three times.

"Okay," said Ginger. "Now, Simon, you step away. Don't worry, Jack. He won't let you fall in the pool. Remember, he's being paid to save your derrière. Simon has set up an interview with Channel XYZ. He told them you are innocent and that the case against you is pure bull. You'll be a rich guy who is merging . . .let's say TV stations. Now it's my turn. I'm Jenny Journalist doing my big interview. Each time I ask you a question, take a step back. You can trust me. I'm the media. First question, why are you an evil rich guy?"

"Huh?" asked Jack.

"It doesn't matter if you answer it or not, Jack. Just take a step backward," said Ginger.

Jack took one step back and fell in the Mandrake's swimming pool. Jack floundered in water before he finally bobbed up to the surface.

"What were you trying to prove?" he sputtered.

"You shouldn't trust everybody in the media," she said.

"But you told me—"

"Okay. I'll tell you the truth. I had an agenda, Jack," said Ginger.

"What the hell was it?"

"To show you that your theory was all wet."

Partygoers had strolled over to the pool area just in time to watch the debate end. Fred took Ginger's elbow and eased her into the woods before the discussion could be revived. Jack tried to find the ladder and get out of the pool while Simon was doubled over with laughter.

Elizabeth Mandrake stood in the doorway to the pool house, elbows akimbo, staring daggers at Ginger.

"I don't think we'll be invited back," Fred said.

He looked at his wife, got a big grin on his face as they both said, "Good."

CHAPTER 8

Four days later Malvin Shepherd and Desmond Williams were in court. Shepherd flashed a sly smile to Williams as he gave instructions to his men. Shepherd was eating it up. A TV camera whirred quietly a few yards away and he played to it like a ham actor clomping through *The Merchant of Venice*. Act I was over and he knew he had won some important ground. Even though the district attorney did go for capital murder, Shepherd had convinced his edgy client it was easier to defend him against that charge because no jury in Los Angeles would let Desmond Williams face the death penalty. Williams wasn't so sure, but he played along, getting into his role, that of grieving widower cum victim of injustice. Los Angeles Assistant District Attorney Johnnie Greer, on the other hand, was busily packing papers back into her briefcase, a little miffed. As for Ginger Caulfield, she just couldn't get away from the Desmond Williams case.

The following day was warm so Ginger turned on the television in the cottage and began another furniture restoration project. A positively gorgeous secretary desk in dire need of refinishing had just happened to follow her home from a garage sale the past spring. After stripping thick layers of old orange shellac off its beautiful oak carcass, she started applying the first coat of tung oil.

She had turned on the TV, but was up to her elbows in tung oil before she realized Channel 10 *News & Entertainment* was doing a special report on the Desmond Williams case, complete with thundering music and high-tech graphics.

She was trying to avoid the whole sordid mess, but didn't want to peel off the gloves to change the channel so she started watching the show a few minutes after it started. Mark Parsons was alone at the news desk, looking very somber. They must have drawn the worry lines on his thirty-something forehead. The station was putting on a two-hour summary of the three-day coverage of the Desmond Williams preliminary hearing.

" . . . And that was how the preliminary hearing ended yesterday when Judge Hartford Bock ruled that the prosecution had presented enough evidence to have Desmond Williams bound over to superior court for trial in the double homicide of Marcella Williams, the former wife of the well-known actor, and Adrian Wells, Ms. Williams' latest companion and the owner of the popular restaurant, the Amphora.

"The three-day long hearing brought revelations from both the prosecution and the defense, as we will see in this Channel 10 Special Report."

The screen dissolved into a montage of publicity stills and their corresponding negatives of Williams to introduce this epic. Canned music right out of *Dragnet* echoed through the room as the title appeared: **THE CASE AGAINST DESMOND WILLIAMS**.

The TV audience got another look at the crime scene: from sea level, camcorder level, helicopter level, and through the window of a news van. Mark Parsons was doing the voice-over as the camera kept switching from vantage point to vantage point. Viewers would be looking for the Dramamine or a barf bag before he was through.

"The tragic story began one cold gray morning when the bodies of Marcella Williams and Adrian Wells were discovered . . ."

A somber mix of dirge music accompanied an anthology of photographs taken of Marcella Williams' now infamous beachfront abode and environs. They ranged from old postcards from the Sixties to shots taken with a long-range zoom lens. Next, there were views of the actual crime scene leaked by the prosecution, followed by pictures taken by reporters of the covered bodies.

The program then turned its attention to Desmond Williams. They ran the clip of Williams being told about his wife's demise and the breaking the juice glass photo-op. That was followed by stills from several of his movies, then video of Williams being booked at the police station, and finally the triumphant arrival of Malvin Shepherd.

All of a sudden, the music stopped. The scene switched to a black-and-white still picture of the courtroom and the title of the first episode appeared: **THE PRELIMINARY HEARING—DAY ONE.**

The still shot broke into glorious color as Channel 10 showed previously recorded video from the courtroom. There was a man on the stand, a guy named Pete Loomis, who was one of the three prosecution witnesses who said he had seen Desmond Williams on the highway around the time Marcella Williams was murdered. The prosecutor, Johnnie Greer, was first at bat.

"Would you please tell the court, Mr. Loomis, what you saw on the night of July eleventh on Pacific Coast Highway?"

"I saw Desmond Williams' car on PCH before you make the turn up Malibu Canyon Road."

"Are you sure Desmond Williams was driving?"

"Sure. Everybody knows John Law."

Shepherd raised his hand. "I object, Your Honor. The witness hasn't positively established that it was my client whom he allegedly saw. The witness called the man John Law, and my client's name is not John Law."

Johnnie said, "Your Honor, Desmond Williams has made a career playing characters that have gone on to have an identity of their own. One of those characters is John Law. Many people know him only as John Law. Mr. Loomis recognizes Desmond Williams as John Law. To him, they are one in the same."

Judge Bock spoke. "Objection sustained, Ms. Greer. The court must insist on only one name per person. Please instruct your witness to properly identify the person he saw that night."

"Yes, Your Honor. Mr. Loomis, please correctly identify by one name only, the person you saw on the night of July eleventh."

"I saw Desmond Williams in the car. That man." He pointed to Williams.

"Thank you. Mr. Loomis, what make of car was Mr. Williams driving?"

"A 1993 or '94 Volvo, dark green or blue."

The news show cut abruptly to Malvin Shepherd's cross-examination. "What kind of car do you own, Mr. Loomis?"

"I have a Ford 4x4," said Loomis.

"Is that a four-door sedan or a kind of sports car or what?"

"It's a truck."

Shepherd condescendingly said, "Oh. A truck. Do you own . . . a car, Mr. Loomis?"

"No. I own a truck."

"A Volvo is an expensive automobile, isn't it, Mr. Loomis?"

"I guess so."

"You guess so? Could you afford one?"

Johnnie raised an objection. "I object, Your Honor. Where is counsel going with this line of questioning?"

"Mr. Shepherd?" questioned the judge.

"Your Honor, I am endeavoring to show that this witness comes here with several predispositions that might prejudice him against my client."

The judge replied, "The kind of vehicle Mr. Loomis drives is irrelevant, Counselor. You will have to prove your point another way."

"Yes, Your Honor. Mr. Loomis, what were you doing on the highway that night?"

"I was driving."

"Driving where?"

"I was driving home."

"From where?"

"I'd been out."

"Mr. Loomis, I'm not your wife. You can tell me where you had been."

A few titters went around the courtroom.

"I was at a bar."

"Which bar?"

"The Union Jack."

"What kind of bar is the Union Jack?"

"A beer joint. A few pool tables. You know."

"Mr. Loomis, what kind of clientele do they have at the Union Jack?"

"Mostly guys. A few women. The regulars."

"How many blacks—African-Americans—go to that bar?"

"I don't know. Some." Loomis was getting flustered.

"Some? Does that mean half of the—what did you call them? The regulars. Half the regulars are black?"

"Well, not half."

"A quarter? Twenty-five percent of the men at the Union Jack are black. Is that what you are saying, Mr. Loomis?"

"Maybe not twenty-five percent."

Shepherd kept pounding. "How many then? Fifteen percent? Ten percent? Five percent? Do any African-American men frequent the Union Jack?"

"I—I don't think we get any of them in there."

"Any of *them*, Mr. Loomis?" said Shepherd.

Johnnie rolled her eyes. This witness was dead. She drew a line through Loomis's name on her yellow legal pad.

The defense continued. "Do you drink, Mr. Loomis?"

Loomis started getting defensive. "That's why I go to the bar."

"You go to bars to drink," stated Malvin Shepherd in a superior tone. "Do you drink *a lot*, Mr. Loomis?"

"What do you mean by *a lot?*"

"What do you think is a lot, Mr. Loomis? How many drinks are too many?"

"I don't know. 'Til they eighty-six you, I guess."

"Eighty-six you?" Shepherd questioned. "That's a bartender's term when a customer has had too much and they refuse to sell him another drink, isn't it? How many times have you been eighty-sixed, Mr. Loomis?"

"Uh . . ."

"How many times have you been picked up for being drunk and disorderly?"

"Uh . . . a . . . a few times," the man stuttered.

"A few times? How about nearly a dozen in the past five years? Were you completely sober the night you *allegedly* saw Mr. Williams?"

"Look. I may not be a fan of Williams. I don't remember the last movie of his I saw, but I know what he looks like. And I saw him on the road that night."

"If you never saw any of his movies, how can you be sure you saw Desmond Williams?"

"He's on television. Hell, his face has been plastered on TV for weeks."

"Was the first time you saw Mr. Williams *after* he was arrested, and you decided to—"

"Objection, Your Honor. Leading the witness," said Johnnie.

"Sustained. Ask, don't lead, Counselor."

"Yes, Your Honor," said Shepherd. "Mr. Loomis, you don't live in Malibu, do you?"

"No. I live in North Hollywood."

"Do you like the beach area?"

"Sure. Great houses. I want to live there someday."

"What do you do for a living, Mr. Loomis?"

"I do repair work. Fix things."

"You're a handyman?" asked the defense.

"Yeah, I guess."

"Have you worked in homes along the beach?"

"Yes."

"Did you ever work for Marcella Williams?"

"Not her. But I know where she lived."

"Her house is quite elegant, isn't it?"

"It's okay," said Loomis.

"It's worth three million dollars. Are you sure you were never in that house? Maybe checking it out to see how the other half lived?"

"I've never been in it," snapped Loomis.

"Are you sure you weren't there the night Marcella Williams was murdered and that's why you were on Pacific Coast Highway when you said you saw Desmond Williams?"

"What are you trying to say, that I murdered her? I'm not the one on trial."

"I'm asking you what you were really doing on that road the night Marcella Williams and Adrian Wells were murdered?"

Shepherd's hammering of the witness stopped as the judge's banging of his gavel started. Judge Bock was trying to quiet the crowd. Suddenly the pounding stopped. The picture on the screen changed to a black-and-white still shot of the courtroom with another title plastered across it: THE PRELIMINARY HEARING—DAY TWO.

The picture sprang to life with more previously recorded testimony. This time it was Lenora Williams, Desmond Williams' first wife, on the witness stand being questioned by Johnnie Greer. Lenora wasn't a raving beauty, just an ordinary black woman, nicely dressed; hair straightened, but not glamorously coiffed. She was fashionably thin, not Hollywood skeletal. Her clothes were expensive, designer labels, but she had spent the early years of her marriage shopping off-the-rack at Kmart while Desmond was getting his career off the ground.

"How long were you married to Desmond Williams, Mrs. Williams?" asked Johnnie.

"We were married twelve years."

"Did you have children?"

"We had two children. Treela is seventeen and Kahlil is eighteen."

"How would you describe your marriage?"

"My marriage was a living hell."

Malvin Shepherd rolled his eyes and shook his head like a maraca. He whispered something to Williams, and then shook his head one more time for good measure, dismissing the testimony.

Johnnie went on. "Did Mr. Williams ever hit you?"

"Yes! He thought that was what a man was supposed to do to a woman."

Shepherd interrupted. "Objection, Your Honor. Is Mrs. Williams here as a witness or a mind reader?"

"Sustained," said the judge. "Please answer as to what Mr. Williams did. Don't speculate what he might have been thinking. Continue, Counselor."

"Would you please explain the kind of a man Desmond Williams is?" asked Johnnie.

"Desmond Williams is a bully. Everything has to be his way, or else."

"Did Mr. Williams ever ask you to do something you didn't want to do?"

"Yes."

The producers of this made-for-TV news program had edited out the rest of Mrs. Williams' testimony, and there was a quick fade to Malvin Shepherd's cross-examination of the former wife.

"Did Mr. Williams ask you to postpone your divorce?" questioned Shepherd.

"Yes. That was one of the things I didn't want to do."

"But you did postpone your divorce from Mr. Williams, someone you said you despised and who allegedly struck you. Is that correct?"

" . . . .Yes," she said, hesitantly.

"Why did you do that, Mrs. Williams?" asked Shepherd.

"He was in the middle of a signing deal for his new TV series, *Follow the Sun*, and he said they'd drop him if he was going through a divorce."

"Well, that was very nice of you, Mrs. Williams, to stay with a man you despised and who allegedly beat you. Now you say you pretended you were still happily married so he could get a part in a television series. What did you get out of it, Mrs. Williams?"

"Nothing."

"Didn't Mr. Williams tell you the divorce settlement would be better if you didn't file until after the deal was signed?"

"Yes."

"Are you saying you did it for the money, Mrs. Williams?"

"I had two children to think of."

"And what are you getting out of *this*?"

Lenora got defensive. "Nothing. Nobody's paying me to testify."

"How much money is the *National Examiner* paying you for your story?"

"I'm just telling them the truth."

"How much are they paying you for your version of the truth?"

"They're not paying me for a version of the truth," she said.

"Then how much are they paying you for *not* telling the truth?"

Johnnie gave a halfhearted wave of her hand to object, but she knew it was too late for that witness. She lined out Mrs. Williams' name on her yellow pad as she said, "Objection, Your Honor. Leading the witness."

"I withdraw the last question," said Shepherd, knowing he had won. Then he turned to the ex-wife and asked, "But I am still asking, how much are you being paid by the *National Examiner* for your story?"

"Twenty thousand—but I'm giving a large portion to the church."

"How nice. What other reasons do you have for testifying?"

"Objection, Your Honor," said Johnnie. "This is a subpoenaed witness."

"Sustained."

Shepherd kept up his whittling. "Mrs. Williams . . . You still use that name, don't you?"

"I never remarried," said Lenora, indignantly.

"Why did you keep Mr. Williams' name?"

"Uh—"

"If you despised the man, why didn't you go back to your maiden name?"

"I have two children. They have to have a name. This really is ridiculous."

Johnnie raised her hand. "I agree, Your Honor. What is Counselor's point?"

"I was getting to it, Your Honor," explained Shepherd. "Mrs. Williams, how upset were you when you found out the deal cut by your husband for his second television series included not only a guaranteed two-year contract, but also a movie deal at five times his regular rate, and that figure was kept from your divorce lawyer?"

"I was upset," she said, with no emotion.

"Here's a quote from you in *Probe* magazine, dated April 4, 1982: 'He'll not get away with it, no matter how smart he thinks he is.'"

"Those aren't my words," she said.

"Those aren't your words printed in the magazine?"

"No. Of course not. You know how they make things up in the press."

"I'm shocked. What *did* you tell them?"

"I told them I'd make him pay—" Lenora gasped at what she blurted out.

After a very pregnant pause, Shepherd continued. "What

do you want from Mr. Williams now, money or revenge?"

"Objection," said Johnnie, halfheartedly.

"I withdraw the question." Shepherd smiled at his colleague. He knew that was game, set, and match.

The audio portion of the program stopped abruptly, and the station went to another black-and-white shot of the courtroom with a title running across the picture: **THE PRELIMINARY HEARING—DAY THREE.**

CHAPTER 9

Johnnie Greer was questioning the police forensics expert, Martin Mayfield, who had come to the stand with drawings and photographs. An easel was set up within arm's reach.

The prosecutor began her questioning. "Mr. Mayfield, as a police forensics expert, would you please tell the court what singular piece of evidence was found at the murder scene the morning the bodies of Marcella Williams and Adrian Wells were discovered at her beachfront house?"

"The crime-scene officer found a footprint near the broken window."

"What was unusual about this particular footprint, Mr. Mayfield?"

"The footprint was in blood. Both victims' blood."

"Objection, Your Honor," said Malvin Shepherd, his face stern. "The independent lab I commissioned to run unbiased tests hasn't determined conclusively that the blood was solely that of the victims."

"It couldn't have belonged to anybody else," the expert witness said.

"It could belong to a passer-by or a stray dog that cut itself on the glass," Shepherd managed to add, unchallenged.

"A dog wearing tennis shoes?" Mayfield replied.

Johnnie spoke up. "Your Honor, who's questioning this witness?"

"What is your objection, Mr. Shepherd?" asked the judge, remembering whose turn it was.

"My experts haven't determined that the blood belonged

to the victims and only the victims. This witness is stating something that hasn't been introduced as evidence."

"I'll rephrase the question, Your Honor," said the prosecutor. "Mr. Mayfield, what was unusual about this particular footprint?"

"It was made by a running shoe."

"Objection, Your Honor. There are hundreds, thousands, probably millions of tennis shoes, running shoes, jogging shoes, walking shoes out there. People buy them, wear them, wear them out, and throw them away. They don't come with serial numbers. You can't tell one from another."

"Your Honor, I believe we can differentiate these particular shoes," said Johnnie.

"Objection overruled. Continue, Counselor."

"Thank you, Your Honor," said Johnnie. "Mr. Mayfield, what differentiates this shoeprint from the others?"

Martin Mayfield flipped to the first photograph on his easel. It was a police photo of the bloody shoeprint found at the crime scene. It had a very discernible pattern.

Martin Mayfield, a gray-haired man with deep wrinkles, but with eyes still clear and alert, had been on the stand before and knew what to expect from the defense. He wouldn't be disappointed in Malvin Shepherd's attempt at spinning his evidence into worthless drivel. He settled his heavyset frame into the witness chair and braced for the attack.

"As you can see," said Mayfield, pointing to the photo. "This print has a specific pattern. There are loops, whorls, and arches just like with a human fingerprint."

"Can you identify the brand name of this particular shoe?" asked Johnnie.

"Yes, I can. It's a Starmate by Frigerio."

Shepherd wasn't having any of this. Obfuscate, obfuscate, obfuscate. "Objection, Your Honor. Frigerio manufactures ten thousand pairs of the Starmate running shoes a year. One is exactly like another. How is counsel going to prove that any particular shoe made this print?"

The judge was getting a bit tired of the defense's ploys. "Mr. Shepherd, you are anticipating the prosecution. Will you please wait until a question is asked before you object to it?"

Not liking the admonishment, Shepherd mumbled, "Yes, Your Honor."

"Continue, Ms. Greer," said the judge.

"Thank you, Your Honor." Johnnie couldn't help but look over her shoulder at the reprimanded counsel. She let the corners of her mouth curl up slightly before she turned back to the witness. "Mr. Mayfield, what makes this particular shoeprint different from any other print of any similar shoe now in existence?"

Mayfield flipped to the next picture on his easel. It was a bold line drawing of the shoeprint showing each arch, whorl, and loop.

"All right shoes of the Starmate have the exact same design. You can see the traction grids that form this pattern and the resulting channels between each grid." He turned to a blowup of the actual shoeprint found in the house. "This is a close-up of the print found at the murder scene. You can see the same design—"

Shepherd wasn't through with his pain-in-the-butt routine. "Your Honor, excuse me. I can't see the picture."

He leaned out of his chair and contorted his large shoulders in an obvious attempt to show how hard it was for him to see the easel. He strained and stretched his neck until he looked as if he would fall to the floor.

The judge watched the performance with fading interest, then responded. "Mr. Shepherd, there is no jury present. You needn't try to impress the court with your diversionary tactics. Now, would the witness please pull the easel out a little further so defense can see all the evidence being presented? Continue, Mr. Mayfield."

Malvin Shepherd's squinty eyes darted back and forth. He covered his embarrassment by scribbling notes on the yellow legal pad and then tearing off the page and stuffing it into his briefcase.

The forensics expert went on with his testimony. "You can see the same pattern in the bloody shoeprint found on the wooden floor near the bodies. But there is one thing different in this picture. Right here," he said, pointing, "near the ball of the foot, there's a dark smudge. Something was partially filling the channel in that spot. We believe it's dirt from several planters on the deck outside Marcella Williams' side window that had been recently replanted. Some of the fresh dirt spilled onto the deck and was picked up by the running shoe. It absorbed blood from where it was splattered around the couch and was carried back to where this print was left, so we have not only the grid pattern in blood, but also this spot left as a track or print. The person wearing the shoe picked up even more dirt in the channel in the toe area. He was probably walking on his toes around the deck."

Shepherd tried tossing in a few monkey wrenches. "Your Honor, I must object. The witness is guessing how the person who left the print was walking. Is he going to guess anything else?"

"No guessing, Mr. Mayfield," admonished the judge. "Just tell us what you know."

"Yes, Your Honor. We know the person wearing the shoe picked up more dirt as he left the living room."

Another wrench was let loose. "Your Honor, we're talking dirt here," said Shepherd. "And not even that much. And there were no other full shoeprints found on the floor or on the deck."

"That's true, Your Honor," explained Mayfield. "But this particular piece of dirt, the piece that made this smudge, was found . . ."

The television screen dissolved into a tableau of newspaper headlines. There were pictures of the bloody shoeprint and the crescent-shaped piece of dirt along with a daily paper's headline reading **BLOODY EVIDENCE FOUND IN STAR'S**

TRAILER. Another reputable paper's headline read DESMOND
WILLIAMS FORMALLY CHARGED IN EX-WIFE'S SLAYING; GLASS
IN DESMOND'S FACE MATCHES WINDOW GLASS FROM CRIME
SCENE.

As the newspapers' credibility diminished, their publishing quality deteriorated. The headlines became more
sensational:

REDNECK WITNESS: A DRUNK AND A THREAT TO PUBLIC SAFETY
GOLD-DIGGING EX-WIFE IS IN IT FOR THE MONEY
SECRET WITNESS SAYS DESMOND WAS WITH HER ALL NIGHT
DNA PROVES DESMOND INNOCENT
DNA PROVES DESMOND GUILTY
TERRIFIED WITNESS SAYS HIT SQUAD KILLED MARCELLA
    AND NOW THEY WANT DESMOND

The Channel 10 *News & Entertainment* screen jumped to
a live picture on the street outside Desmond Williams'
Beverly Hills estate. Several dozen of his most ardent fans
were there with signs that read

WE LOVE YOU, DESMOND
GOD BLESS YOU, DESMOND
JOHN LAW IS INNOCENT
FREE DESMOND NOW OR L.A. BURNS

Milling around the grounds of the movie star's manor
were even more of the terminally curious who were there
in case something *interesting* happened, like a suicide or
murder or riot. And then there were the media types who
were waiting for any of the above.

Other TV channels were not to be outdone. Lo and
behold, Channel 11 was doing its own homage to Desmond
Williams. Myrna Blankenship was interviewing the very
same fans being shown on Channel 10. The viewing public
couldn't escape the spectacle.

"And what's your name?" the bubbly TV news personality asked the equally animated young black woman by her side.

"Laverne," said the eighteen-something fan.

"Where are you from, Laverne?"

"Uh . . . Right here."

"You're from Beverly Hills?" Laverne's outfit didn't exactly scream Rodeo Drive.

"Uh . . . Buena Park."

"You're a fan of Desmond Williams?"

"I seen all his movies and me an' my frien' here watch that *Follow the Sun* TV show whens we can."

Laverne was wearing a brand-new T-shirt with Desmond Williams' face on it.

"Why did you come out here today, Laverne?" asked the newswoman.

"I wants everybody to know that Desmond Williams is the bestest man an' he done no killings of his wife."

Myrna turned to another fan wearing an identical T-shirt. "And your name?"

"Shir-Lee Wilson."

"Where are you from, Shirley?"

"Hawthorne."

"And do you think Desmond Williams is innocent, too?"

"I done seen every one of Des's movies and he never kills nobody that don't deserve it. That's the law." Shir-Lee struck a "John Law" pose with her hand held up to her face like a gun. She was beaming at her actions. "The po-lice is makin' this up 'cause he be black."

Back on Channel 10 *News & Entertainment*, Mark Parsons was winding up his comprehensive report on the Desmond Williams case.

"Attorney Malvin Shepherd stated that his client would be going into seclusion following the bail hearing that was held earlier today. Judge Hartford Bock released Mr. Williams after he posted the half-million-dollar bond.

"Experts, some of whom have appeared on this channel, assumed Mr. Williams would be released because there is nowhere in the world his famous profile wouldn't be recognized."

The picture jumped to the street outside Malvin Shepherd's rented office. Shepherd and company were leaving the building in great haste. The big man was issuing orders while he pulled out his cell phone. He looked too busy to stop and talk to the press, but a photo-op is a photo-op. He parked directly in front of the first camera as it whirred its way toward its next Emmy nomination.

Tina Lake from Channel 10 got in a question. "Where is Mr. Williams now?"

"My client is resting quietly at his Beverly Hills home, said Shepherd. "He's been through a great deal during the past few weeks. He needs time to relax, take a hot shower."

Several voices spoke at once, asking questions. One seemed to catch Shepherd's attention. It was an attractive woman farther back in the crush of media types.

"Why wasn't Williams let out on bail weeks ago?" asked Nikki Holt, the newspaper reporter. She didn't have a camera crew recording her question, but she did have a following in one of the larger L.A. newspapers.

"The district attorney chose not to allow the bail hearing to take place until after the preliminary hearing for reasons of his own. Due to that callous disregard of my client's rights, Mr. Williams has shown signs of acute mental stress and his personal physician wants to give him a thorough exam."

Nikki got in another question. "Why does he need a doctor? Did something happen to him? Was Desmond Williams assaulted in jail?"

You can never say Malvin Shepherd didn't recognize the sound of opportunity knocking. His ears perked up like the cur he was and he turned solemnly toward the cameras. "I prefer not to comment . . . at this time."

Tongues were hanging out over the implications of what he *didn't* say.

The television was abruptly turned off in the D.A.'s office. Frank Fallen, Johnnie Greer, Matthew Simms, and Arthur Haines were sitting around the large conference table, having seen the latest spin from the defense machine.

Art Haines was a huge man with skin the color of brown velvet. He had to top the scales at 310 pounds, but he had a friendly face, unless you were sitting on the witness stand as the prime suspect. Johnnie called him the Black Widow—behind his back. He would start asking questions, quietly, calmly, methodically, circling his prey until he got the suspect to make a mistake. Then he'd rip the schmuck's head off.

Matt Simms had been watching the drivel on Channel 10 and Malvin Shepherd's impromptu utterances. He spoke first. "He's lying about the bail hearing. Judge Bock is the one who postponed it until after the prelim."

"Judge Bock won't be on TV for three weeks telling every potential juror in Los Angeles that I'm not the one who denied bail to Williams," said Frank.

"It makes me sick," said Matt. "What makes a guy sell his soul like that?"

Frank, Johnnie, and Art answered in unison: "The money!"

"But Shepherd lied," whined Matt. "And he said Williams was beaten while he was in custody."

"Did you hear him say that?" asked Frank.

"No. But he's making it sound—"

Walt Haines spoke up. "But he didn't *say* it. You can replay that clip 'til hell freezes over and you'll never hear Malvin Shepherd say Williams was beaten while in police custody. He can make you *think* it. But he didn't *say* it. He's that good."

Attorneys like Shepherd always impressed Haines. Not

for their glib tongue or sly ways, but for their sheer audacity, especially when they tried that crap in front of a judge who could hold them in contempt of court. He wondered what limits a guy like Shepherd had. Or did he have any?

Matt had a thought. "But if he loses the case—"

The D.A. laid it out. "Lose? He already won what he wanted."

"But—" started Matt.

"He still gets paid," said Frank. "And from what I hear, half of Desmond Williams' assets are in Malvin Shepherd's name."

Arthur Haines added, "And the worldwide publicity . . . Malvin Shepherd—hell, Madison Avenue couldn't devise a better ad campaign."

Johnnie Greer said, "And with the media slant, Williams is already going into victim status."

"What? Am I too young to be that pessimistic?" asked Matt. "Or has it really gotten that bad?"

Frank scowled. "The next time the public doesn't like a verdict and the city burns, you'll have your answer."

CHAPTER 10

It was a hot, dry Friday morning. The Caulfields were finishing a late breakfast in the family room. Fred had a luncheon meeting in Glendale so he hadn't left at his usual time. Knowing he would have to brave the midmorning traffic, he turned on the TV to see how the freeways were moving. Channel 12 had the most up-to-the-minute freeway coverage. No sooner had the newsroom appeared on the screen than the picture changed to their banner headline: **NEWS BULLETIN FROM CHANNEL 12 L.A. COMPREHENSIVE NEWS.** It was accompanied by their attention-getting breaking-news musical fanfare.

The logo dissolved and Warren King appeared on the screen.

"This just in to Channel 12. Actor Desmond Williams, accused in the brutal double homicide of his former wife and her companion, failed to appear in superior court at eight-thirty this morning to hear the date scheduled for his trial. His attorney, Malvin Shepherd, was questioned by Judge Bock in the courtroom, but Mr. Shepherd could only say his client must have gotten the time confused and he assured the judge that Mr. Williams would be there shortly. We're going live to the Criminal Courts Building where Amanda Hill is standing by. Go ahead, Amanda."

The scene switched to a corridor outside the courtroom. The hallway was stuffed with reporters, cameramen, and every other news groupie clamoring for a piece of ephemeral history. The camera panned the area and then focused on Channel 12's cute but dim reporterette in the field, Amanda

Hill.

"Thank you, Warren. I'm standing outside the court-room where Desmond Williams was scheduled to appear this morning to hear his trial date. It's now 9:45 and there is no sign of Mr. Williams. According to his attorney, Malvin Shepherd, Mr. Williams must have gotten the time wrong. In light of his failure to appear, Judge Bock has issued a bench warrant for screen actor Desmond Williams."

The station switched back to the studio where Warren King and the hurriedly coiffed Christine Mack had assumed the position of concerned journalists.

"Amanda, did Mr. Shepherd explain why Mr. Williams didn't come with him this morning? Wait a minute—" King held the earpiece closer to his ear. "We're getting this in from the newsroom. We'll get back to you later, Amanda."

A two-shot of the anchors dissolved to a busy L.A. street across from a high-rise building. Warren's well-modulated voice informed the viewers: "We have just learned Desmond Williams was spotted in the Wilshire District. Steve Gonzales with the Channel 12 news van is at that location reporting live as the scene unfolds. Steve, are you there?"

The camera focused on Steve Gonzales. "Yes, Warren. We're on Beverly Boulevard opposite the Kirkland Building in the Wilshire District. Police received a call less than twenty minutes ago from a concerned citizen who had been listening to coverage of the scheduled court appearance of Desmond Williams. When the caller learned that Mr. Williams had failed to appear, he happened to look out his office window and saw a person fitting the description of the movie star enter the building. He phoned Channel 12 and told us he thought he had seen the missing man. Police arrived just moments ago and are planning a floor-by-floor search."

The screen switched back to Christine, who had a worried look on her face. "Steve, have any other witnesses spotted Mr. Williams?"

"Not at this time, Christine, but let me grab somebody coming out of the building."

Steve tried to snag anybody in the vicinity, but the police had barely started their search. He looked around for a warm body when he became aware of movement near him. He turned slightly and saw two young punks edging into his space. Everybody watching the TV broadcast had already noticed their baggy black outfits, the backward-facing baseball caps, and the attitudes. They walked right up to Steve.

The first punk yelled, "Hey, man! Why don't you leave the brother alone? Like you gonna make him cra-zy."

The second guy said, "Yeah, why you dissing the bro', man. He ain't done noth-*thin*'. Like Des-MOND is da MAN. Like he be the law—John Law. You know somebody out to get him, and you ain't tellin' no-*body*."

"Man, he go up on dat roof an' jump, you mess wit' him," intoned the first kid.

Steve picked up on what the punk said. "Jump? Is Desmond Williams on the roof?" He looked up as his cameraman panned the rooftop.

The second punk got decidedly into Steve's face, almost pushing him out of camera range. "Why? Dat whatchu want, man?" The two kids walked off, leaving Steve disoriented.

Warren King could barely contain himself. He asked his man on the scene. "Steve . . . Steve. Is there a sign of anyone on the roof?"

Steve turned to face the commotion behind him. Nearer the entrance of the building, reporters who had gotten front-row seats were grabbing their gear and racing around to the back of the structure. The Channel 12 reporter and his remote cameraman ran after the horde as the police tried to keep them back. Fat chance.

Steve was running with microphone in hand, giving Warren and Christine a blow-by-blow account. Winded, he said, "Warren, Christine, something has sent reporters to the rear of the Kirkland Building. People are shouting something, but I can't—they're saying Desmond. Desmond Williams."

Christine rose to the occasion by expecting the worst. "This might be what everyone has feared ever since Desmond Williams failed to appear this morning in superior court. His attorney already stated that Mr. Williams was suffering from severe depression, and now there has been talk of suicide . . . or worse. We hope the best for Desmond Williams."

Steve broke in, still winded. "Warren, Christine, I'm at the rear of the Kirkland Building with, as you can see, quite a few other reporters. We're waiting for news from police on the scene, but Mr. Williams is not, I repeat, not, here . . . Wait a minute. There are people near the door. Pan over there, Jim. Several police officers are coming out and . . . Yes. They have Desmond Williams. Desmond Williams is okay. I repeat; actor Desmond Williams is alive."

Christine clutched her highly augmented breasts and heaved a sigh. "Thank God. How does he look, Steve?"

"Christine, Mr. Williams looks fine, but . . . Yes, he *is* handcuffed. The police have taken actor Desmond Williams into custody."

"How does he *look*?" exclaimed Ginger, who was watching the same scene on her TV. "He's accused of murder and they put out a bench warrant on him. Where has she been the past month?"

Fred punched the remote control and brought up Channel 11 *View on L.A.* with John Roberts. He muted the sound as they watched Roberts discussing the same scene running behind him on the monitor of Williams being led away by the police. That's when Ginger noticed the same two punks in baggy pants being interviewed by another reporter within view. They were going through the identical routine they had done on Channel 12. The entire scene looked choreographed.

"Who are they? A new rap group?" she asked.

Fred took a drink of coffee and said, "They'll keep us entertained during intermission."

"It is a show, isn't it?" said Ginger.

Fred nodded. "This isn't going to help Desmond's innocent act."

"To tell you the truth, there have been so many versions of the story, with the leaks and the denials, and the experts and the soothsayers, I don't know who's on first."

"We were watching some of the news coverage yesterday—" Fred started to say. He grinned, knowing his wife would get a kick out of him and rest of the white-collar workers at Knight Investments taking time off from the stock market to watch TV in their executive dining room. "Anyway, we caught some of Gary Johnson's noon report. It made that headline in the *Daily Journal* look like last week's weather report." Fred switched to Channel 8 while adding, "They have to run it again today. It was so *hot*." He winked.

L.A. Hot News had its camera in front of the Kirkland Building, too, and Gary Johnson was doing a live shot. The police had escorted Desmond Williams away and the crowd was dispersing. Ginger happened to notice those two punks in baggy pants still loitering in the background, but Gary wasn't interested in them. The camera went in tight and Gary continued with his top of the hour report.

"Yesterday, this reporter was granted an exclusive interview with a new witness in the Desmond Williams case. This person, who asked to remain anonymous, swore they saw something, something that would exonerate Williams. But the witness was warned not to repeat the information to anyone. And let me tell you, this individual was scared. I've covered other high-profile murder trials, but this time, even I was getting worried.

"I told the witness we should take this to the authorities. That's when the interview abruptly ended and I was asked to leave. We here at Channel 8 will keep on top of this story. Stay tuned for further reports. This is Gary Johnson,

Channel 8 *L.A. Hot News.*"

"I bet the D.A. loves that," said Fred. "Wait 'til this mystery witness shows up on *Larry King.*"

"Then he's useless to either side," said Ginger.

"What do you mean?"

"By the time the defense gets him on the stand, the testimony will have been sliced and diced by every so-called expert the TV stations have in their guest lineup. The prosecution will play up the sensationalism angle and the testimony will be worthless. The sad truth is: It would work the same way even if the mystery guest were a prosecution witness. Why does everybody run to a reporter?"

"They have the cameras," suggested her husband.

"Live by the photo op. Die by the photo op."

Fred finished his cup of coffee, turned off the set, and left for work. Ginger went back to her refinishing job in the cottage. She kept the television off and listened to music.

After dinner that evening Ginger and her husband retired to the living room. The small television fitted into the media center was on with the sound turned down low. Fred had tuned into the Channel 12 *L.A. Comprehensive News,* but they were both reading. Her husband could have eighteen televisions blaring and still be absorbed in his book. Ginger, on the other hand, could have the TV turned down to a mere whisper and be reading the most exciting book in the world and still be distracted. She put down the *Washington Times Weekly* and watched the screen, becoming disgusted with the continuation of the show they had been watching earlier that morning. She was just about to launch into another rant against the news media when Fred turned off the set. He gave her a knowing smile and went back to his reading. Ginger breathed a deep cleansing breath, picked up the paper and read about the other circus going on in Washington.

There are about fifty small Mexican restaurants near

the Los Angeles *Daily Journal*'s downtown offices. By 6 p.m. the accounting staff, the classified personnel, and the secretaries have split. The daily reporters are finishing their stories while editors are poised at their computers to slice and package the words between print ads and dispatches from Reuters and the AP.

Since nobody actually lived in the rundown area except those who sought refuge in corrugated townhouses, most of the restaurants had a better lunch crowd than dinner guests. But a few of the establishments closest to the newspaper offices kept their doors open for the night owls, especially on Friday night. The bar at the El Diablo restaurant did a land-office business, but late-night lovers, errant spouses, or somebody looking for the next big headline preferred the cozy corners of the restaurant, out of the limelight.

Sitting at the farthest booth was an attractive woman wearing a summer-weight suit in a soft shade of blue. Her hair was long and blond and dyed, but it looked marvelous. Several men in the restaurant couldn't keep their eyes off her. She felt them gawking. Looking up, she didn't quite smile at them, but she continued staring in their direction until they looked away. Then she smiled.

A petite Mexican waitress laid a menu on her table and immediately returned to the bar. Nikki Holt, a reporter with the *Daily Journal*, lifted the menu slightly, tilted it toward her, and opened it. She felt the envelope full of money fall into her lap.

A moment later someone left the bar. Mission accomplished.

CHAPTER 11

The next morning while fixing breakfast, Ginger turned on the small TV in the kitchen. Habit. She aimed it toward the breakfast nook so Fred could watch while she was fixing two bowls of cereal. The tiny screen was full of Brian Coleman, the weekend anchor on Channel 11, doing the morning report.

"We have an update this morning on the rather bizarre episode yesterday involving famed actor Desmond Williams and his failure to appear in superior court to hear the date set for his trial in the double homicide of his former wife, Marcella Williams, and her companion Adrian Wells.

"Channel 11 has received a copy of a video taken inside the Kirkland Building during the capture and subsequent arrest of Mr. Williams. The tape shows Mr. Williams in the lobby of the high-rise and his eventual surrender to police officers. Is the tape ready? Okay. Roll it."

The tiny screen suspended under Ginger's kitchen cabinet displayed a miniature view of the Kirkland Building from the day before. The news producer turned down the volume on the video so Coleman could do the voice-over.

"As you can see, Mr. Williams enters the lobby near the elevators where police officers spot him and order him to halt. Mr. Williams, no doubt distraught over the events of the past few weeks, panics, and you can see here, he fights against incredible odds."

Ginger watched the same thing Coleman did, but she saw it differently. The guy with the video camera must have been standing near the main entrance because he got a wide-angle view of the area. A stream of people was coming from the rear of the building. It looked as if Desmond Williams sort of appeared in their midst near the bank of elevators. He mingled with the crowd as they entered the main section of the lobby.

No sooner had the other people dispersed than police officers entered from three sides: behind him from both directions of the hallway and from the main lobby. As they approached, one officer seemed to be yelling at Williams to hold it. The officer aimed his gun and his jaw was going a mile a minute. That confrontation went on for some time. Other officers took up positions along the corridor leading away from the main entrance.

Williams hesitated for a second to assess the situation. You would swear he looked around the lobby to make sure everybody was in position. That's when he went into a crazy man's act.

Even though the sound on the video was turned down low, a few words made it to the surface. The police officer had been yelling at Williams to stop and get on the floor. Then Williams mumbled something about "ga'bage," but the bulk of the tirade was inaudible to the viewers in TV Land.

Ginger kept watching Williams hunched over as if the cops were beating him, but they were still standing a good ten feet away. They had their guns drawn, but the officers were pointing their service revolvers toward the ground, all except the lead officer who was still issuing orders to the recalcitrant actor.

Williams kept waving his hands in the air as if fending somebody off. At first Ginger thought he was hallucinating, but when the three officers finally approached and took him into custody, Williams instantly stopped flailing and then glanced over his shoulder and looked at the camera.

When the scene ended, the small screen in Ginger's kitchen once again filled with Brian Coleman as he continued with his news story.

"Mr. Williams regained his composure and was taken into custody by police officers at the Kirkland Building. He spent the night in a cell at police headquarters downtown. In a brief court appearance early this morning, Judge Bock set the trial date for November thirteenth."

The station went to a commercial break and Ginger turned off the small set. Somewhere in the back of her mind a bell was ringing, but the telephone jingling on the wall caused it to vanish. It was Fred's mom. She always called early Saturday morning. Fred poured her another cup of coffee before he headed to the garage. Ginger settled onto one of the tall kitchen stools for a long chat. She told her mother-in-law that she started jury duty on—oh, expletive deleted! November thirteenth.

In early November, the Caulfields were getting ready for bed and the TV was on in the bedroom. Warren King was talking with Channel 12's entertainment reporter who was exceptionally giddy. It was ten o'clock at night and Ginger wondered what could be so exciting at that hour.

As the woman on the television was saying, " . . . studios hurriedly released the made-for-TV movie that is to air this Sunday, starring former child star DeLon Thomas as Desmond Williams. Rumor around Hollywood says the movie is cut and pasted, but the producer promised an eye-opening plot with revealing information we have not seen on TV. Actor DeLon Thomas, who has recently gotten out of drug rehab . . ."

Ginger turned off the TV.

CHAPTER 12

Monday morning, November 13, Ginger drove her husband downtown to the Knight Building where he worked as the Mergers & Acquisitions Manager for Knight Investments. She pulled the car to the curb in front of the button-down brown building that just reeked with class and Fred got out. Two stretch limos were letting their passengers off and an elegant new Mercedes drew in behind her to let off its VIP. But none of their drivers got a kiss. She did. Fred waved good-bye and she headed toward the Criminal Courts Building on the corner of Spring and First.

She got one block away and stopped at a red light. There was a row of metal newspaper racks lined up on the corner. Each paper had blazing headlines concerning the Desmond Williams case:

DESMOND WILLIAMS FRAMED
DESMOND WILLIAMS' STUNT DOUBLE MISSING
DESMOND CAUGHT IN LOVE TRIANGLE
"I COULDN'T HAVE DONE IT! I'M GAY!"
SECRET WITNESS FOUND SLAIN
POLICE COVER-UP IN WILLIAMS' CASE

She was still reading the headlines when the light turned green and some impatient guy behind her started laying on his horn. A clenched fist shot through his open window and she vaguely heard some obscenity float in her direction. Then he flipped her the universal gesture of oneness. She moved on.

The jury information packet Ginger received in the mail letting her know how lucky she was to be serving on jury duty—what a civic honor, blah, blah, blah—also gave instructions on where to park. Ginger followed their instructions and got lost. She went around the building three times before finding the magic slot to drive down so she could pay an exorbitant sum to park in their underground facility. Fred said it was better to park there than to search for a cheaper place half a mile away and not know if she would have a car when she came out. This privilege was going to cost $18 a day. Frankly, she never liked parking in those underground tombs fifty floors below L.A. She would probably forget which subfloor she was on and lose the car anyway.

She saw a metal sign pointing to **JUROR PARKING ONLY— SUPERIOR COURT.** There must have been a lot of people called that day because there were no empty spaces in the area. She drove deeper and deeper into the belly of the beast until she spotted one lone slot back in a corner. It was for a compact car only so she pulled her silver Toyota Corolla Deluxe into the space.

She had noticed scads of people getting out of their cars and disappearing into elevators on the upper levels, but she wasn't picking up signs of life that far down. Even the utility lights were dimmer. Probably lack of oxygen.

Ginger gathered her purse and a see-through carryall stuffed with reading material, a bottle of designer water, and a handful of candy bars. She knew how boring jury duty could be, and a sugar rush would help. About the same time, she was getting a rather large adrenaline hit just thinking about getting to the elevator safely.

That's when she noticed the dark purple towel on the passenger seat. Under it was her gun. She seldom left home without it. She looked around the outside of the car for anybody who resembled trouble. Then tucking the towel and her .38-caliber security blanket beneath the driver's seat, she heaved a sigh, got out of her car, and locked it.

Ginger was five-seven, 135 in her dreams, and a strawberry blonde every six weeks. Her fiftieth birthday was still two years away, and most people took her for a good ten years younger. Also, no one would ever confuse her with a shrinking violet. But she was a woman, and that still had the tendency of painting a large red target on her back. Without her gun, even she could see that bull's-eye.

Ginger headed toward the sign that read **ELEVATOR— SUPERIOR COURT ENTRANCE**. Then she saw them. Three hooligans stepped from between two cars, blocking her way to the elevators. They moved toward her.

One of the brain trusts yelled, "Hey! You gotta watch, lady?"

His companion said, "You got money? Whatcha got, huh, lady?"

That's when she saw a man coming from the parking area on the other side of the elevator. She waved at him as if she knew him, ignoring the punks. She ran past the three juveniles and straight up to this stranger.

"Fred! Fred! You're late. Where have you been?" She put her arm around him like they were old friends. "Please, help me. Those little snots are trying to rob me."

The wiz kids sized up this man and woman and figured they could take them. The guy was more than six feet tall, but he was wearing a rumpled black suit coat and had a ponytail. For all Ginger knew he was a bookkeeper or a beekeeper. She was holding him quite tightly and thought he might be wearing a body brace under that old coat because with her arm around him she could feel something rather solid. Then one of the punks pulled a knife.

The kid was flashing his weapon and acting erratically. He must have been on drugs because his eyes didn't seem to focus on anything in particular.

"Okay, man. Gimme somethin'. Gimme somethin'. I want what you got, man."

Ginger's companion didn't bother saying anything. He

moved her out of the way with his left arm, and then kicked the knife out of the punk's hand in a move so fast she almost missed it. He grabbed the boy's wrist and shoulder and dislocated the arm in one howling cry. He spun around to receive hooligan number two as the kid rushed him, but her knight-in-rumpled-suit hit the latter-day desperado with a half dozen rapid-fire chops that knocked the punk off his feet.

Hooligan number three pulled a knife from his baggy trousers and came running at the tall man in black, but her guy stood right up to the punk, grabbed his wrist midslash, and brought the kid to his knees. Her hero broke the kid's hold on the knife, then picked him up and slammed him senseless to the ground. From the way the youngster landed and from the screams coming from where he lay on the concrete, it sounded as if his shoulder was pulverized.

The second punk came back for more. He had retrieved the first kid's knife and was coming toward the ponytailed superhero.

"Behind you!" yelled Ginger.

Ginger's friend swung around and kicked the kid in the kneecap as he charged. From where she was standing, she heard the crack. She flinched at the awful sound as the punk dropped to the ground. He had passed out.

The man said to her, "Let's get out of here."

She didn't have a problem with that, but she did have a question. "Shouldn't we call the police?"

"Why? The police don't pick up trash."

They rode up in the elevator by themselves. She kept looking at this big guy and thinking he was something out of a movie. His coat was hanging open and she got a closer look at the body fitting into a tight black T-shirt. He was six-two or better, and that crumpled coat had been hiding the physique of a football player. They were in the thick of football season, but Fred was spending more time watching the Desmond Williams' case so Ginger couldn't remember off-hand which position he would play, but she thought the man would be somewhere between a fullback and halfback. Not that she was noticing or anything like that, but this guy was quite a package.

"Thank you," Ginger said to him, looking for the big *S* she expected to see on his Superman suit.

He didn't smile or even look at her directly. He just nodded and mumbled, " . . . welcome."

They went their separate ways when they got to the main floor, but ended up sitting a few chairs away from each other in the jury room, waiting for the wheels of justice to roll on. Now she could understand why Justice is always shown blindfolded and not on a skateboard. It took forty-five minutes just for somebody to start calling out names for the first jury panel.

The voice over the intercom read off the chosen: "Maria Lopez, Willie Robinson, Yolanda Sanchez, Janice Rose Pierce, Miles Washington, Ginger Caulfield . . ."

Drat. She gathered her things.

The voice continued, "John Dunbar, Jesus Rodriguez, Dallas Long . . ."

As the roll call continued, her tall friend stood at the name Dallas Long. He looked over at Ginger and a slight grin crossed his lips.

The intercom droned on. "John Za-to-pek and Paavo Stenroos. All of you, please go to courtroom eight on the fourth floor at this time. Thank you."

The list had been long. A great many people filed out of the jury room, far more than the twenty or so for a normal jury selection. They had to go up three floors. Ginger was one of the first out of the communal hall and got the first elevator going up. She noticed Mr. Long headed for the stairs. The crowd packing into the elevator made her think she should have done the same. If the elevator got stuck, they would have to sit on each other until they were rescued, but that might have been preferable to serving on a jury. As luck would have it, they made it to the fourth floor and she was the last out.

Mr. Long was already seated in the visitor area in the assigned courtroom. The rest of the group took their seats. That's when Ginger noticed the man sitting at the defendant's table next to a very animated character making a production of pulling papers and notepads and pens out of a briefcase larger than an overnight bag. The character was Malvin Shepherd. The defendant was Desmond Williams.

Oh, *expletive, expletive, expletive* deleted! she thought.

A group of twelve people was called to the jury box and questioned. Many were dismissed by the defense and a few by the prosecution. Three state employees were accepted with no challenge. A man who owned his own company didn't have a prayer. Dismissed. Thank you for your time.

Three down, nine to go. More names were called, and then another bunch. Ginger's name was number four in the third wave. Joy. With her in the jury box were Willie Robinson, Janice Rose Pierce, Dallas Long, Jesus Rodriguez, and a big man in his fifties named John Dunbar. Also with the group was a young man named Bryan Lainey, and lastly, Paavo Stenroos.

Judge Bonita Cherry was presiding. She was one of the first black judges to receive national notoriety for being exactly what she was: a black female judge. After the first patronizing write-up she stopped giving interviews to the press. Now on the first morning in court, she was questioning potential jurors and finding Mr. Stenroos difficult.

"Where were you born, Mr. Stenroos?"

"I Finland born."

"Do you now have American citizenship, Mr. Stenroos?"

"—I Finland born."

"Do you speak English, Mr. Stenroos?"

"No good speak English."

Mr. Stenroos didn't make the cut. Next, the judge questioned Mr. Long.

"You're retired military, Mr. Long?"

"Yes."

"What branch?"

"Marines."

"You're not working at present?"

"No."

Mr. Long wasn't a big talker. He finished the obligatory twenty questions and then Judge Cherry called the young Mr. Lainey.

"Mr. Lainey, you are aware there are two charges of first-degree murder against the defendant. If, at this time, with no further statements by either side, I asked you and the other members of this panel to go into the jury room and come back with a verdict, what would your verdict be?"

This guy was trying very hard to be "fair." "I would have to hear more from both sides before I could make a proper verdict."

"Mr. Lainey, what if I told you this was all you would hear? No evidence of any kind would be presented and you would have to render a decision on just the statements presented to this point."

"Well, I couldn't make any decision without knowing all the facts in the case."

He was dismissed.

Ginger was next on the hot seat. A chart was on an easel near the jury box with a series of questions written in block letters that all prospective jurors were to answer. The bailiff swore her in and she answered the pop quiz.

"My name is Ginger Caulfield. I live in Pasadena. I'm married, no children. I'm a housewife. My husband works for an investment firm. I was on a jury ten years ago. It was a civil case and the jury was hung."

The judge asked, "Do you know or are you related to any of the people involved in this case?"

"No, Your Honor."

"Do you have any friends or relatives on the police

force?"

"I have a cousin in Nebraska who is a police officer, but I see him maybe every ten years. I used to know a few of the local police officers in my neighborhood."

"Are you familiar with the aspects of this particular case?"

"There have been so many stories on television, I can't tell what's going on."

"Did you watch the TV movie based on the Desmond Williams' case?" asked the judge.

"No. Did I have to?" asked Ginger.

"Will you explain your response, please?"

"If Hollywood is the arbitrator of truth, society doesn't need a judicial system."

"Thank you." The judge made a note, and then continued. "Mrs. Caulfield, if I was to stop the case right now and ask you and the other members of this panel to go into the jury room and come back with a verdict without any further statements from either the defense or the prosecution, what would your verdict be?"

"In a court of law, you're innocent until proven guilty, so, with no evidence presented, I would have to say he was innocent."

"That is the correct answer," said the judge. "I hope you all understand that," she admonished the people in the jury box.

Ginger happened to glance over at Desmond Williams. To her surprise, he was staring at her. She looked away, but she could feel his eyes going over her face like a scanner beam. He leaned toward Malvin Shepherd and whispered in his attorney's ear. The thing that got her was the lack of emotion on his face. She had a strange feeling he didn't want her on the jury. But there was an older woman sitting on the first row who had been glowering at Williams ever since she sat down; Shepherd, with only one peremptory challenge left, would probably kick her off and Ginger, unfortunately, would end up on the jury.

A guy in his midforties was questioned after Ginger. He worked in a pizza parlor as cashier. The judge began her questions after he went through the questionnaire on the easel.

"Do you personally know any of the people involved in this case?" asked Judge Cherry.

"I know Desmond Williams."

"You personally know Mr. Williams?"

"Well, not personally, but I've seen all his movies."

"That doesn't count. Now answer this question. You have heard statements by both the defense and the prosecution regarding this case. If I asked you and the rest of the jury to go into the jury room and render a verdict with no evidence being presented, what would your verdict be?"

"I'd have to hear more before I could make a proper decision," he stated quite succinctly.

"Do you remember what the woman next to you said?" He looked at Ginger as if he had never seen her before in his life. "In a court of law a person is innocent until proven guilty. Do you understand that?" asked the judge.

"Yes."

The judge continued, "So, if no evidence is presented and I asked you to render a verdict right now, what would your verdict be?"

"I'd—I'd need to hear more of the case and see what evidence was presented before I could issue an accurate verdict."

"But I'm telling you, there is *no evidence*," intoned the judge. "According to the law, a person is innocent until *proven* guilty. So is he innocent or guilty?"

"Well, if you're not going to show anything, and knowing about the evidence police planted in the Desmond Williams movie, I'd have to say . . . he was innocent."

"No evidence has been presented," said the judge. "A person is innocent until proven guilty *in court*, not on television. You do understand that concept?"

"Yes." He actually looked indignant.

"Tell me what that means."

"Well, it means . . . a person is innocent until somebody says he's guilty."

"And who determines if someone is guilty or not?"

"The judge?"

It was surprising he didn't say Warren King on Channel 12. Nevertheless, he was dismissed. Willie Robinson was next. He went through his list of questions. Mr. Robinson was a young, single black man who worked as an accountant in downtown L.A.

"Let me ask you my questions, Mr. Robinson. Have you formed any opinions in this case?"

"No, sir—ma'am—no, ma'am. Like the lady said, I've seen too much on TV."

"Did you watch the movie based on this case?"

"Yes. I'm sorry. I didn't know I was going to be on the jury."

"What did you think of the movie?"

"It wasn't very good." The people in the courtroom laughed. "DeLon Thomas can't act and the plot had too many holes in it."

"Do you believe you can keep an open mind even with all the publicity on this case?"

"Yes, ma'am," said Willie Robinson.

"And my last question. If I stopped the proceedings right now, with no evidence presented, and asked you and the other jurors on this panel to go into the jury room and render a verdict, what would it be?"

"Like the lady said, you're innocent until proven guilty. I'd have to vote not guilty."

It took three more hours for the jury to finally be impaneled. Then, after the lunch break, the jury and the alternates milled around the corridor, waiting for the next phase. Two officers from the sheriff's department were keeping them secluded from the few other people walking to various courtrooms on the same floor.

Ginger was trying to read the paperback novel she had brought with her, but people-watching was far more entertaining at the moment. She saw Dallas Long standing by himself. Two young women were chatting. A few of the men were talking to each other. One woman was knitting.

Then she noticed something curious. A man was standing near the entrance to another courtroom. He was doing some watching of his own. He was studying the two sheriff's officers posted on the floor. As one of the lawmen walked away and his companion turned to look in another direction, the man pulled out a camera with a zoom lens and snapped a few pictures.

Ginger got up slowly and strolled over to the officer and said in a quiet tone, "Excuse me. The man in the dark jacket in that doorway just took pictures of the jury." She indicated the man with the camera now hidden by his side.

The officer turned in the direction she was looking, spotted the thinly framed guy and stomped after him. Ginger walked over to see if she had to do anything else. She was also curious to hear the creep's sorry excuse.

"What do you think you're doing?" asked the officer.

"Aw, come on, man. I'm just doing my job."

"Who do you work for?"

"I'm a journalist," said the creep.

Ginger looked at the officer, shaking her head, and said, "No reputable paper would print pictures of a jury."

The officer eyed the camera bug and asked, "Which paper do you work for?"

"I'm a stringer. Look, I'm just trying to get a story."

"You know you can't use those pictures," said the officer. "Hand 'em over."

"Oh—I thought—can I get a picture of you, Officer?"

The deputy wasn't buying this. He put out his hand. The little man rewound the roll of film before opening the back of his camera. He handed the roll to the officer.

"What were you doing in that courtroom?" asked the cop.

"Just checking out what's happening," said the slack journalist.

"Not anymore. This area is off limits to you."

The little man slunk away. Ginger shrugged. The officer wasn't happy.

"Stupid guy getting caught like that," he mumbled, mostly to himself. "We'll have to block off the whole floor."

Ginger walked back to a bench and sat next to Willie Robinson. He was going through his briefcase. The heavy gold nugget ring on his finger flashed in the light as he took out a shiny metal cigar case, opened it, and then pulled out a long, dark cigar. He held it up to his nose and took in a long, satisfying whiff.

"I quit cigarettes a couple years ago," he said. "Started smoking these things. Love 'em. And now they outlaw smoking in public buildings. You don't even inhale cigar smoke."

"Are they really good?" Ginger asked.

"Yeah. Smell that baby."

He held it under her nose and she took a deep sniff. She thought it was glorious.

"Oooh. That smells wonderful. What kind of cigar is it?"

"A Hoyo de Monterrey Excalibur, Maduro wrapper, forty-six ring size. I get the five-and-five-eighths size. The big ones take too long to smoke and you have to keep relighting them."

"It has a *menudo* wrapper?"

He laughed. "No, that's Maduro. It's a dark tobacco leaf."

Ginger laughed at her mistake. "That's better than menudo. And it really smells great."

"I've become a real aficionado. Want to try one?" asked Willie.

"Maybe later."

"I make it a rule to have one after lunch, rain or shine.

I work with a couple of guys who've become real fanatics like me. Even on a rainy day, you'll find the three of us standing outside the building with an umbrella, smoke pouring out. It's great."

Ginger was going to tell Willie she'd join him the next time and just inhale that splendid smelling secondhand smoke when the same guy with the camera entered the hallway and tried again to take pictures of the jury. She noticed him the same time the officer did. In fact, the deputy looked over at her and gave her one of those "what-the-hell" shrugs before chasing down the reporter.

The officer snatched the camera from the man and put a hammerlock on him. "Okay, pal. You've just taken your last 8x10."

The guy with the camera tried putting up resistance. "Hey, wait a minute. You can't take that."

"I just did. Now give me your name and the name of any paper you ever worked for."

The jurors watched the bum being led away and then went back to their waiting.

At 1:30 p.m., they were called into the courtroom. It had undergone a bit of a transformation. By popular demand of the viewing public and the acquiescence of the judge, the media was allowed a presence in court, this time in the form of a one-eyed monster. One pool camera was set up to record for posterity this current "trial of the century."

Television stations around the globe were covering the spectacle. Each got their live feed from the solitary camera set up on the jury side of the room. The ground rules stated that the jury wasn't to be photographed at any time during the proceedings, so a black screen blocked them from the television's roving eye. The only views allowed were those of the judge, the witness stand, the ultra-modern high-tech video screens for viewing evidence, the defense table, the prosecution table, the podium in between for the lawyers to state their cases, and finally, a shot of the spectators that changed at every break. Take a number, please.

Johnnie Greer was first at bat. She wore a tailored black pinstripe suit, white V-neck blouse, and a gold necklace—just like female lawyers do in the movies. Dramatically thin and with a skirt a little too short for court, the courtroom sketch artist was obsessing on her outfit. Even Johnnie's designer shoes with the four-inch heels were drawn for posterity.

Her hair had been straightened, lightened, and blunt cut about shoulder length, but again, it was what you would have expected had she been cast for the part. She started her opening statement after the audience settled into their seats and the bailiff read the house rules.

Ginger was taking in all the new gadgets set up around the room and the notsoamateur theatrics being tried now that the camera was turned on. Malvin Shepherd was in his element. He played to the camera even if it wasn't trained on him. He'd roll his eyes or yawn or shake his head. It was so distracting that Ginger missed the first few words out of the prosecutor's mouth.

" . . . will prove that Mr. Desmond Williams did willfully and with malice aforethought, murder his ex-wife Marcella Williams and her friend Adrian Wells on the night of July eleventh. The prosecution will bring witnesses that can place Mr. Williams in the area the night his wife and her friend were murdered. We have a specific piece of dirt and blood found in Mr. Williams' trailer that matches a bloody tennis-shoe print found at the murder scene, and we have a piece of glass taken from the face of Mr. Williams that matches the broken glass in the picture window at the beachfront house of Marcella Williams."

She finished and Shepherd was up. He was wearing a similar black suit with slightly wider pinstripes, but Malvin Shepherd was a meaty man. He had on a soft lime green shirt and yellow tie covered in black swirls. His hair was thick, black, and a little long. Shepherd was in his midfifties, but he must have thought the coif made him look a bit more "hip" or "with it" or whatever it was being called this year, this generation. Again, Ginger was watching instead of listening. She finally turned her attention toward what the long-winded man was saying.

" . . . will show that Mr. Williams couldn't have been at the beach house when Mr. Williams' wife—*former* wife—and her friend were killed. There are at least twenty people who will testify that they saw Mr. Williams in his trailer in San Pedro the night of the murders, and he couldn't possibly have been in two places at the same time.

"As for the so-called witnesses, each has a serious credibility problem. There is only one man who 'alleges' that he saw Mr. Williams on the highway. A second witness, and I use the term loosely, has admitted on two different talk shows that he hates Desmond Williams. He has made several racist remarks against African-Americans and he has been paid for relating his, shall we say, 'eyewitness' testimony. The third witness has a police record, and we will show that this person has a history of providing questionable testimony during other trials.

"The 'alleged' piece of dirt miraculously found in Mr. Williams' trailer could have been carried there on one of the police officer's shoes. There are actually several ways in which that bit of dirt—and we are talking dirt here—could have found its way into Mr. Williams' trailer.

"The tennis shoes have never been found, nor any bloody clothing, nor any powder burns, nor any other evidence linking my client to this crime.

"As for the glass in Mr. Williams' face, everybody in the country saw Mr. Williams' reaction to the news that his wife—*former* wife— was murdered. He broke a juice glass in front of twenty million people. Shards flew everywhere. The entire world has seen that video. The fact that the District Attorney's Office *doesn't* have any pieces of that glass, but they *do* have a sliver from Mr. Williams' face, says a lot about the selective evidence gathered by the prosecution.

"My client has suffered from the adverse publicity surrounding this case. He was denied—*denied*— his right to attend his wife's funeral. What kind of country do we have when a man who has given so much joy and entertainment to his fellow man is denied the simple right to say his last good-bye to his wife? That's all I have to say, Your Honor."

Malvin Shepherd hung his head in shame for what passed as justice in this country. He turned toward the camera and sighed. Judge Cherry managed to withhold any facial expression. You wouldn't want to play poker with her. Johnnie Greer sat stone-faced. Then Shepherd took a quick look at the jury to see who bought what he was selling. He looked directly at Ginger. She turned away, but she could see Williams whisper something to Malvin Shepherd. This time a slight chill went up her spine.

CHAPTER 13

Malvin Shepherd and a group of his more pernicious minions were sitting around their rented Century City office in deep shadows later that evening. A few table lamps were burning. Malvin's face was the only one that could be seen with any clarity. He was reading from notes scrawled on a yellow legal pad.

Across the desk from him was P. J. Henderson, his media man. Henderson was tall with dark, deeply hooded eyes that perpetually squinted. Pacing behind Henderson's chair was Curtis Lee. Built like a professional boxer, Curtis wasn't the kind of guy you argued with unless you could out punch him or you carried a gun. He provided the necessary muscle when Shepherd needed an obstacle removed. The third man was Walter Blue. Blue was short and twitchy, like a loose pin on a hand grenade. He acted as general factotum. He had been with Shepherd long enough to know when to say yes and when to duck.

Shepherd looked over at P. J. "I want the *Daily Journal* to run a story about evidence the D.A. is hiding. Get that to your contact in the next twenty minutes. I want this front page tomorrow. Tell her the D.A. has fingerprints of a known felon, twice arrested for suspicion of murder with a shotgun, found on a piece of that broken window."

"Where's this guy supposed to be now?" asked P. J., his face still in the shadows.

Shepherd had to think about it for a minute, then said, "Missing. He was brought in for questioning the same night Marcella was killed and has disappeared."

The tall man stood and slowly made his way to the door. He was hesitant to bring up something he knew he had to mention. He started to leave, then turned back and faced Shepherd. "She wanted to speak to you the next time she ran one of these . . . stories."

Incensed, Shepherd snapped, "I don't want my name anywhere near this. That's what I pay you for. If you can't handle—"

"No. I'll get on it, but—"

"But *what?*" Shepherd's short fuse was burning.

"She—she wants a little more money."

"Oh, for chrissake, pay her." He waved P. J. Henderson to go. As the door shut, Shepherd turned his attention to Curtis Lee. "I need a witness to call Channel 12 and say they saw somebody else along the beach that morning, running away from the scene in a panic. The witness didn't put it together until they saw the news coverage of the murders. When they went to the police, the cops told them to forget what they saw. Have them do their interview in silhouette. The witness is scared . . . of the police.

"Isn't that the story that Sambo reporter is running on one of the local stations?" asked Curtis.

Shepherd thought about it. "See what he has. Maybe the D.A.'s office is tossing him a bone they can discredit later and then blame on us."

"I don't think so, Boss. They're hardly saying anything. We've put out most of their leaks."

"What's the matter with the people in this town?" Shepherd tore off the top sheet of his legal pad containing his notes, wadded it up, and tossed it into his wastebasket. "Doesn't anybody know how to play the game?"

"The D.A. has a force shield up or something," said Curtis Lee. "I can't get a whiff off him."

"He didn't get where he is without burying a few bodies. Dig 'em up. And Curtis, if the prosecution does leak stories about their evidence, I want you to flood the press with propaganda *against* Williams. I want you to plant a story from 'sources close to the District Attorney's Office' quoting that slick-haired bastard using every fucking racial slur you can think of against Williams. I want that black, fat-assed judge to seriously consider investigating Fallen and *his* office."

"Yes, sir."

Changing the subject, Malvin asked, "Is Channel 10 still running Desmond's movies?"

"Yes," said Curtis. "But they want an exclusive. Something nobody else has."

Without missing a beat, Shepherd said, "Tell them there's a chance Desmond Williams will plead insanity."

No one blinked. They knew how their boss worked.

Shepherd added, "But they can't use the story until we give them the okay."

Walter Blue, a wiry weasel of a man, spoke up. "Mr. Shepherd, some of Williams' friends are coming around here, asking questions, wanting to know why we haven't gotten him off yet."

Shepherd looked at him like Blue had told him to go screw himself. "When did this start?"

"A couple days ago. They're—they're getting kind of pushy."

"Push 'em back. Tell 'em if they don't get the hell out of our way, they could ruin it for Williams."

"That's what they're worried about. One of 'em told me if we didn't get Williams off, he'd break my legs," said Walter.

"He said *what?*" Shepherd wasn't used to someone else doing the pushing.

"And he knows where I live."

"What the hell's going on here? If the son of a bitch comes back, shoot him! Plant a gun on his dead ass and say it was self-defense. What kind of operation does Williams think we're running? We don't take shit from anybody's flunky."

"Yes, sir," said Walter.

Shepherd abruptly stood up. He turned off the desk light and hesitated half a second for Walter and Curtis to stand and head out of the room first. Malvin locked the door securely behind him. Curtis had a couple of hours' work to finish before he left for the night, so he went into his own office across the hall while Shepherd plodded down the carpeted hallway after Walter. It had been a long day.

Walter called for the elevator and pushed the button to descend. When they reached the ground floor he held the elevator door for Shepherd, and then opened the heavy glass door at the entrance of the building to let the big man pass through first. Walter used his cell phone to call for Shepherd's car. That's what flunkies are for.

The Lincoln Town Car made its way around the block to the curb where Malvin Shepherd and Walter Blue were waiting. Walt held the car door for Shepherd, who settled his heavy frame onto the seat, and got in after him.

"We have reservations at Ah Fong's," said Walter to the driver. "The one on Beverly Drive."

"Jeez, Walt. Not Chink food," said Shepherd.

"It wasn't my idea. When I called Pulaski's secretary, she said the Polock liked the place. Maybe he'll be more inclined to cough up your retainer if he's full of 'flied lice.'"

Less than thirty minutes later a solitary figure walked down the hall to Malvin Shepherd's office, unlocked the door, and went inside. A single utility light was on over Malvin's desk. The figure reached into the wastebasket, retrieved the crumpled notes scratched onto the yellow legal pad. The shadowy figure went out the door and locked it. In the lighted hallway Malvin Shepherd spread out the piece of paper and looked at the instructions he had handwritten. Stuffing it in his pocket, he caught the elevator down to the lobby and went back to the restaurant.

CHAPTER 14

The trial resumed the next day. Actor Van Prescott took the stand. Ginger remembered him from his early TV days, long before he became Desmond Williams' sidekick in *Buddies*. He had guested on every television series running during the Seventies and had two short-lived shows of his own, but his star status came with *Buddies*. He still looked pretty much the same. Strong features. His dark hair was now mostly gray and thinning a bit on top, but she would have recognized him anywhere.

The bailiff swore him in. "State your name."

"I acted under the name Van Prescott. Most people recognize me by that name, but my real name is Charles Berruti. I currently write under the name Berruti."

This confused the bailiff. "Your Honor?"

The judge said, "You were summoned under the name Prescott. The court will recognize you as Van Prescott. Continue, Bailiff."

"Be seated."

Johnnie Greer began her questioning. "Mr. Prescott, when did you first meet Desmond Williams?"

"In 19 . . . 77. We had both signed to do the television series *Buddies*."

"How long did the series last?"

"Six long years."

"Did you enjoy doing the series?"

Prescott hesitated. "I love acting. I guested on a bunch of shows in the late Sixties and Seventies. *Hawaii Five-0, High Chaparral, Ironside, Dan August, Mission: Impossible.* I had two other series of my own, both comedies, before I did *Buddies*. But this one was different. It had action, suspense, gorgeous girls, car chases. I loved everything about it—except King Desmond."

"King Desmond? Why did you call him that?" asked Johnnie.

"Because everybody else did. Usually behind his back."

"Was he hard to work with?"

"Yes. Everything had to be his way. If it wasn't, he'd storm off the set and production would shut down until somebody gave in. It was never Williams. Shutting down production costs money, and the show didn't have that big a budget. Anyway, not the first year."

"What changed? Why did Warner Brothers increase the budget on *Buddies*?"

"Both Desmond and I signed one-year contracts to do the show. Nobody thought it would make it past the first year. I was working on some ideas for a series of my own and I really hoped *Buddies* would be canceled. I showed my first couple of scripts to a few producers and some other people I knew in Hollywood, and everybody was hot for the idea. I wasn't going to renew my contract for a second year."

"What changed your mind?" asked Johnnie.

"All of a sudden no studio in town would return my calls. None of the people I had talked to remembered my scripts and half didn't remember my name."

"What happened next?" asked the counselor.

"Our producer told me the storylines I had developed for my own show would be incorporated into *Buddies*. Take it or leave it. I took it. The show ran five more years."

"What was the original premise of *Buddies*?"

"Williams and I were supposed to be two guys traveling across the country. It was just a rehash of *Route 66* from the Sixties except we were supposed to be funnier. We were always stumbling into other people's lives and telling them how to live. Frankly, it made me gag. I wanted to do an action/adventure series like the old Saturday matinees. You know, Terry and the Pirates Go Hollywood. My scripts had fast cars, slick gadgets, great-looking women, and hot locations.

"The producers told me to write a script that explained the plot change. My idea was that Nick and George had been doing a little R&R, tooling around the country before going back to their regular jobs, which was working for an international organization that scouted out trouble spots around the world and got rid of diabolical masterminds."

"Were these changes what angered Desmond Williams?" Johnnie asked.

"No. He was pissed from the beginning. Originally, he was supposed to be the funny sidekick, the one who got into trouble, the Jerry Lewis part. But he demanded that the characters be switched. The rest of the episodes had to be rewritten so I would play the clown. The staff writers changed some of the dialogue and the original storyline to fit the reversal of roles, but they didn't change the names. I ended up playing George Rivers and Williams played Nick Conti."

"Were you given credit for the rewrite?"

"Yes and no. Charles Berruti was given credit. I wrote half the scripts the last three years, but they would only use my real name, not my stage name."

"Were you given a reason why you, as Van Prescott, weren't given screen credit as the screenwriter?"

"Williams had bought into the production company by that time and said it would be too confusing. Like anybody reads screen credits except people in the business."

"No further questions of this witness, Your Honor," said Johnnie.

Shepherd was itching to get at Prescott. He just about leapt out of his chair when Judge Cherry called him.

"Mr. Prescott," Shepherd began, "Are you familiar with a movie made several years ago called *Nemesis*?"

"Yes."

"Do you know who wrote that movie?"

"Yes. I did. I wrote it."

"You wrote it? What was the storyline of that movie, Mr. Prescott? That is what you call it, isn't it, 'storyline?'"

"Yes. It was the story about two actors who starred in a television series. One actor ruined the career of the other by spreading lies about him around Hollywood, getting his agent to drop him, breaking a few arms."

"Was the storyline based on your own experiences in Hollywood, Mr. Prescott?"

"Loosely."

"Were both lead actors in your movie white, Mr. Prescott?"

"Yes, they were."

"But it's obvious Mr. Williams isn't white. Why didn't you make the second character in your movie black?"

"Williams isn't the only actor I ever worked with. And there are plenty of white S.O.B.s in Hollywood."

That elicited several chuckles from the audience. Even some of the jurors laughed. Judge Cherry didn't crack the least hint of a smile.

Shepherd carried on. "But do you agree that you based one of the characters, the one you called Leo, on Desmond Williams?"

Prescott thought about it for a moment, and then said, "No. When I wrote the outline for *Nemesis* a few years after the series ended, I made Leo the spitting image of King Desmond. I vented my spleen on paper for two years. I knew he got the studio to cancel the series I was going to do. It was about a tough teacher in the Bronx. Sound familiar? It's the short-lived series Williams did before he started making movies. The one called *Bronx Zoo*."

"You're saying the Leo character *isn't* Desmond Williams?"

"Yeah. After about five years I really didn't care about

him anymore. I'd been working with other actors and heard some pretty wild tales about their run-ins with some very self-absorbed types. Some of them were kinky, some kooks, some bullies. They all thought they were God's gift, just like Williams. So I threw out my first draft and rewrote the Leo character as a compilation of every bum I'd ever heard about in Hollywood."

"Was this after Mr. Williams had become an international movie star with his first action movie?"

"No. He was still doing schlock B-movies."

"Do you resent Mr. Williams' success, Mr. Prescott?"

"No, but I do resent him stealing everything I worked hard to create."

"Are you sure you don't hold a grudge because his career soared while yours declined?"

"Objection, Your Honor," said Johnnie. "Where is Mr. Shepherd going with this line of questioning?"

"Mr. Shepherd, are you getting to some point with this witness?" asked the judge.

"Yes, Your Honor. Mr. Prescott, do you consider yourself prejudiced?"

"No."

"Then why did you mention that the writers on your television show—I'm speaking about *Buddies* now—why did you mention they didn't change the names of the two leads when they reversed the roles? Mr. Williams played Nick Conti and you played George Rivers. Do you consider the name 'George Rivers' African-American?"

"Not especially. *My* character's name wasn't the problem. It was the name Nick Conti—Dominic Conti. That's Italian. *I'm* Italian. Williams is a lot of things, but, Mr. Shepherd, Desmond Williams ain't I-talian."

Malvin wasn't happy with that revelation. He assumed he was going to expose Prescott as a racist and a bigot, but he hadn't. "That's all, Mr. Prescott," Shepherd said abruptly.

That was short and sweet. Next was the medical examiner who described the condition of the two bodies. That was short, but not sweet. Malvin Shepherd spent his time rustling through his briefcase and sorting papers. Most of the jurors were transfixed by his actions and paid scant attention to Johnnie Greer or the witness. Malvin was a far better show. Court broke for an early lunch.

CHAPTER 15

A fter a quick trip to the powder room, Ginger made her way toward the jurors' private lunchroom. They weren't to mingle with the general public in the main cafeteria on another floor. She was going to grab a quick sandwich and then find a quiet place to read her book.

That's when she noticed her cigar-smoking friend, Willie Robinson, walking up the hallway toward the courtroom. Malvin Shepherd and staff were plowing down the corridor toward the lunchroom. Somehow, poor Willie ran smack into Shepherd who was reading through a handful of papers. The papers and briefcase dropped out of the defense counsel's hands. Ginger was expecting fur to fly. Shepherd's men stood like statues while Willie bent down to pick up what had fallen and hand it to the lawyer, who never blinked. He and Shepherd exchanged several words before Shepherd happened to look in Ginger's direction. Call her paranoid, but she thought Willie looked over his shoulder at her, too. She went for her sandwich.

The cafeteria was compact, for lack of a better word. It was 70 degrees outside, but an oven inside. The dining area was stuffy and the space around the open kitchen was filled with the pervasive aroma of burning grease. The odor was almost tangible as it vied for elbowroom among the jurors crowding in to get something to eat. The air was so thick, Ginger wished she had worn one of Fred's Israeli gas masks. (That's another story.) She would smell like a double cheeseburger before she got out of there.

Ginger noticed a poster of Desmond Williams in his role

as John Law on the back wall in the kitchen area. She was surprised somebody didn't ask to have it removed, at least during the trial. She bought a turkey sandwich and iced coffee and sat at a table with two other jurors, Janice Rose Pierce and John Dunbar. Their seats were at the front of the lunchroom, away from the steamy kitchen, or at least as far away as they could get without sitting in the hallway. A few minutes later Willie, having gotten himself a sandwich, sat down with them. They decided to get to know each other.

Dunbar was everybody's worst nightmare as a fellow juror. He knew everything and didn't mind telling you about it. He also had a laugh that rumbled around his ample gut before it finally made its way to the surface. But for all his laughing, he wasn't a happy man. His wide and persistent smile sat only on the surface.

And Mr. Dunbar had an unrelenting twitch. He sat in his chair, but his left leg constantly bounced up and down, making not only his body jiggle, but also the table shake. Janice Rose's coffee cup tapped out a little tune until she moved her spoon from the saucer to keep it from rattling.

"What happened to the air conditioner?" asked Dunbar. "It's a goddamn icebox in the courtroom and they have the heat cranked up to ninety in here." They all nodded. Before anybody could say anything, he continued. "Do you drive," he asked Ginger, "or take the bus?"

"I drive in with my husband."

"That's handy. I'd take the bus, but it's too damn crowded and it'd take me a week to get here. Do you drive?" he asked Janice Rose.

"Yes, but I hate driving downtown anymore. The streets are all confused with that infernal subway they're putting in. Everything's one way. Back in the Fifties I'd come down here to shop the outlet stores in the garment district and there was always a place to park. No bums on the street. No perverts. A woman could feel safe."

"Those days are long gone, honey," said Dunbar.

"Well, I think it's just awful," said Janice Rose, a suburban housewife in her sixties.

"Why don't they pay for parking?" whined Willie. "That travel allowance ain't gonna cover eighteen dollars a day."

"Park in one of the remote spots," said Dunbar. "I'm paying three bucks."

"Where are you parked?" asked Willie. "Around Dodger Stadium?"

"No. It's only eight blocks from here."

"Eight blocks!" exclaimed Janice Rose. "I can't walk that far. But this garage parking is awful. It's so dark down there. The city needs to put in some more lights."

Willie said, "I drove around for twenty minutes before I found a spot this morning. Jury parking was full. I'm stuck in guest parking. I'll probably get a ticket."

"Look on the bright side," Ginger said. "You won't have to go far to pay it."

Dunbar added, "Maybe you can find a shyster lawyer to get you off the hook. They know all the angles."

Ginger had been pondering whether to tell her luncheon companions what had happened the day before. She couldn't resist. "I've got a story for you. Yesterday, three punks tried to rob me in the garage."

Dunbar was surprised. "You're kidding! How'd you get away?"

"Karate chop." She made the obligatory motion with her hand, and then laughed because they believed her. "No, actually, a guy came to my rescue. He's on the jury with us. That big man with the ponytail."

The two men looked around the room and spotted Dallas Long.

"That was lucky," said Willie.

"Yeah," said Ginger. "He must have learned that in the Marines."

"You see?" said Janice Rose, her worst suspicions confirmed. "We're not even safe in the Criminal Courts parking garage. What if they come back?"

"That guy," Ginger pointed toward Dallas again, "took pretty good care of them. I think he broke a few arms."

"They learn that kinda crap in the military," said Dunbar. "I hate it. Too gung-ho for me."

Janice Rose had other thoughts. "He may have saved your life! They should have guards down there. Did you tell anybody about it?"

"Not much to say," Ginger said. "I don't think they'll be back any time soon."

Willie hadn't eaten half his lunch, but he gathered his stuff and stood up. "Well, I'm going to walk around a little. I can't sit this long."

"Going to smoke one of those Maduros?" Ginger asked.

"I didn't bring one today. Maybe tomorrow." He looked at his watch. The gold ring on his finger flashed under the lights, then rolled to one side. "I can get in a short walk if I hurry." He left.

Dunbar was still in the inquisitive mode. "What'd you say your husband did?" he asked Ginger.

"Corporate mergers," she said. "Stocks and bonds," she clarified.

"Boy, the market's really a mess," said Dunbar.

"It's a roller coaster," Ginger said. "My husband's firm has a lot of foreign investments, too."

"Yeah, Europe, France, Germany. Those are good investments."

"Emerging nation stock looks good," said Ginger. "South America is hot now, except for derivatives." She smiled, knowing what a rat hole derivatives turned out to be recently.

"Yeah, it's hard finding a good derivative," said Dunbar.

"And the Asian market is growing," she added, thinking that old John wasn't the sharpest knife in the drawer when it came to investing.

"They keep making those Toyotas."

"My husband's firm has offices in Paris, London, Hong

Kong, and Tokyo. They have to keep up with all the foreign markets."

"I didn't know we had stock markets over there. That must be new. Does your husband have any good tips?"

"Buy low, sell high."

Dunbar hesitated a second, then laughed. "That's a good one. I'll have to tell my broker."

"He's probably heard it. Who's your broker?" asked Ginger.

"Uh . . . Well, my brother-in-law does most of the buying for me. I let him handle all the technical stuff. What's your husband's name?"

"Don't laugh," Ginger said. "It's Fred."

"Fred?" questioned Dunbar. He didn't get it.

"And Ginger," said Janice Rose. She laughed. "Fred Astaire and Ginger Rogers. You two must be great at parties."

"You cannot imagine the number of jokes we've heard. And people are always asking us to dance."

"Were Fred and Ginger really lovers?" asked Janice Rose.

"I thought they hated each other," said the veritable font, Mr. Dunbar.

"From her biography," Ginger confessed. "I read it out of self-preservation because of all the questions we get asked. But, wow, what a life she had. She knew everybody in Hollywood. And she said Astaire was one hell of a kisser."

"Isn't that romantic?" said Janice Rose. "I always loved their pictures."

"I still do," Ginger said. "I love musicals. I love all the old movies. Even the bad ones. I must have seen every B-movie ever made—twice."

CHAPTER 16

While the jurors were trying to catch a cool breeze in the lunchroom, Johnnie and Matt were working up a sweat in her office. Half the secretarial staff was at lunch, but the ones remaining knew what the locked door meant: Do Not Disturb. The affair had been going on for nearly a year, but Matt never realized he always looked better when he left Johnnie's office than when he went in.

Two briefcases were sitting unopened on the floor near the door. Matt had kicked off his shoes and walked in his stocking feet to the long leather couch. The carpeting was two inches thick and half the time they ended up on the floor, especially if the room was too hot. The leather grabbed at the back of Johnnie's legs and she preferred the plush mauve carpet on a hot day. Today the office air conditioner was pushing out a stream of cold air so the leather actually felt cool against her bare skin.

She had left her blouse on, but it was unbuttoned. Matt had unhooked her bra, but that wasn't his main interest at the time. They had to be in Frank Fallen's office in fifteen minutes, so he didn't have time to make all the usual stops. He hadn't bothered to remove his trousers, either. It had been a long time since he even bothered speaking to her during their noontime encounters. He pretty well knew how to get in, get on with it, and get out in the allotted time.

Johnnie stroked his chest though he hadn't removed or even unbuttoned his shirt. She watched his face as his passion grew, but his eyes were elsewhere. He kept on and on, but never looked down at her. He was a million miles away.

Johnnie closed her eyes and went over her notes from court in her head until he was through. They cleaned up in her private bathroom. Matt used some of Johnnie's hair-styling gel and his own toothbrush before they headed to Frank's office.

The D.A. was on the phone while Bill James was going over a stack of newspapers, writing comments in the margins. Frank slammed down the phone and started to pace. The section of carpet under his feet was actually starting to wear out. He must have walked five hundred miles over the same ten-foot spot since assuming the job of district attorney, and with the way things were going in the media, he wasn't getting any further with them, either.

"The paper won't tell me diddly-squat," said Frank Fallen.

"Who did you say wrote the story?" asked Bill James.

"Nikki Holt."

Bill didn't hesitate in his response. "She was paid by the defense to run that story."

Frank couldn't buy that. "No," he said. "Maybe she's sleeping with one of Malvin Shepherd's goons."

"She only sleeps with women."

"You're kidding!"

"You've heard of Lisa Eban, the actress?" asked Bill.

"Yeah. The brunette in that sitcom about lady truck drivers."

"Nikki was her date at last year's Emmy Award show. They couldn't keep their hands off each other."

Frank still couldn't believe it. "But Nikki Holt is good-looking."

"She still prefers women. Usually brunettes."

"Then why doesn't she care if Desmond Williams killed a homosexual?"

"She's angling for a Pulitzer. And from what I hear, she hates *all* men."

"But this is shit," said the D.A. "We didn't find fingerprints of a known felon at the Williams' house. If we did, you can bet somebody would have leaked it to the press."

"They just did. Even if it's a lie, it has the same effect," said Bill.

"But Shepherd will never be able to prove any of this," said Frank.

"Does he have to?" asked Bill.

Frank was getting defensive. "I'll put out my own statement. Tell them we don't have any exculpatory evidence."

"Prove it!" countered Bill.

"I—"

"You can't prove a negative, Frank."

"What does Shepherd get out of it?" asked Frank.

"The public who reads this crap," said Bill James, picking up the top newspaper, "or watches it on television will see Williams as a victim of some white racist Buford C. Justice out to get da po' black boy. We might as well be living in some jerkwater town down South in the Fifties. Just wait 'til the public gets whipped into a frenzy."

"You're talking another Rodney King riot," said Frank.

"Damn right. Look how easy that was. The right person says the city might burn and voilá, we're watching fire engines screaming into Watts."

"Williams lives in Beverly Hills," said Frank.

"I don't think Shepherd is dumb enough to bus a bunch of rioters into Beverly Hills. But he'll get a rise out of the brothers in the ghetto."

"Why does the public always believe the worst?" asked the D.A.

"Because it's easier to have a mob mentality than for someone to think for himself," said Bill James.

"So what's this to Shepherd?"

"He's waiting for you to panic, Frank. Hoping you think a guilty verdict might start another riot. Then you go easy on a witness. You do a half-assed job presenting the evidence. Basically you fold your cards and he wins."

"Get with your guy at Channel 11 and have him set up

an interview with Johnnie. She can explain why it wouldn't do us any good to muzzle a witness."

"He won't do it," said Bill.

"What?"

"I asked him to get Malvin Shepherd's media guy and a spokesman from your office to debate it on television, but the station wouldn't touch it."

"Why not?" asked Frank.

"You're running for reelection and Channel 11 won't give you the time of day."

"What is this? A preview of campaign finance reform? But I saw Cameron Childs on Brian Coleman's show over the weekend."

"They want him to replace you, so he gets the TV coverage," explained Bill.

"Desmond Williams killing his wife has nothing to do with my reelection."

"Yes it does," said Bill. "You said so yourself. If you win the case, you get reelected."

"The media would scuttle the Williams' case just to kick me out of office?"

"In a New York minute, Frank. That's what happens when they bastardize the First Amendment. To them it's a one-way street and you're going the wrong way."

Frank was trying to think of a rebuttal when Johnnie and Matt walked through the open door. Matt was sweating more profusely than usual. His face was flushed, not to mention his hair was wet and recently combed. Frank exchanged a quick look with Bill, but he consciously avoided making eye contact with Johnnie.

It was time to discuss their war plan, so they took seats around the conference table. Bill James had managed to grab a bite to eat earlier, but Frank was still working on the last of his deli sandwich. The array of newspaper headlines caused him to lose his appetite. The articles ranged from straight news stories from a few reputable rags to absolute fiction from the sleazy ones. Frank stood up from the table and continued his pacing.

He could still see the bold headlines screaming back at him. He reached into his desk drawer for several antacid tablets. A couple of those on top of hot pastrami would keep that ulcer quiet for a few more hours.

The headlines read:

MYSTERY WITNESS FOUND—FEARS FOR LIFE

NEW EVIDENCE THE D.A. WON'T ALLOW

DNA LINKS WILLIAMS TO DOUBLE MURDER

PSYCHIC REVEALS REAL MURDERERS OF
     MARCELLA AND ADRIAN

MURDER WEAPON FOUND IN ANOTHER STAR'S HOME

Frank finally said, "Only two people haven't been accused of these murders, and that's because the Menendez brothers are still in jail."

"Where are these leaks coming from?" asked Johnnie.

"Reliable sources," began the D.A., glancing at Bill James, "say people close to the defense team are leaking information."

Matt spoke up. "Shepherd keeps telling the press he has somebody who can prove Williams didn't do it."

"If he's hiding a witness, I'll get him for withholding evidence in a murder case," said the D.A.

Johnnie said, "But Shepherd can't have a witness, Frank. We know Desmond Williams did it. The blood and dirt we found in his trailer, the glass splinter in his face, the bruise on the side of his hand, and the DNA report all say he's our boy."

Frank picked up one of the newspapers with a blazing headline, then dropped it back on the stack. "Look at this crap. Some psychic sees a blond man in the goddamned tea leaves. What was the one yesterday?" He searched through his memory bank for the story.

Johnnie remembered. "The truck driver was paid by the KKK to say that he saw Williams on the highway. The race card being played again."

"Oh, yeah, and that goes with the one today—" the D.A. started to say.

Matt got an awkward look. "I didn't show her that one, Frank."

"Which one?" questioned Johnnie, thumbing through the papers on the table.

"Oh, hell, Matt. She's going to see it anyway. Where is it?"

Matt pulled the newspaper out of his briefcase. "It's just a background story. It won't affect the case."

Johnnie looked at the picture of herself dancing with Matt at a city function. The headline read **MIXING BUSINESS WITH PLEASURE?**

"What's this?" she asked. "They can't mean I'm a racist. Hell, I'm dating a white man."

"But it can bias a juror who doesn't accept interracial affairs," admitted the D.A.

She turned to her boss. "What the hell are we supposed to do?"

"Get married," said Frank, point blank.

"What?" she exclaimed.

"You're always sneaking around like you two are ashamed."

Matt said, "We were trying to be discreet."

"About what? You aren't having an illicit affair. You aren't kids. It isn't against the law. And it will probably shut up half your critics."

"Frank," said Johnnie, "the media will just find something else to adulterate. They've already made Williams a victim. They're running all his movies on Channel 10. He could run for mayor today, and win."

Bill James spoke. "Ask the judge to sequester the jury before Shepherd buries us in phony leaks and innuendo."

Johnnie added, "Remember what the blond juror said, there has been so much in the news she doesn't know what the truth is."

"We can't trust every juror to keep an open mind. But the blonde is smart," said the D.A. "You can bet your butt Shepherd would have used his last peremptory on her if he didn't have to get rid of that old lady who kept saying, 'I have seen quite enough, thank you.'" He mimicked the old lady's high-pitched voice.

"Why don't we leak some of our own headlines?" asked Matt. "After all, defense tried disproving the DNA results before he even saw it."

"The DNA is solid, Matt," said Frank. "Everything we have is solid. It's the doubt they can plant in just one juror's mind that will get Williams off. That's why Shepherd isn't going for an insanity plea—Yet." He added the last bit after a longer than normal pause.

"How can we stop Shepherd's leaks?" asked Matt.

Johnnie remembered something. "The *National Examiner* admitted they got their headline about the band of Satanists doing a ritual kill on Marcella Williams from some-one *inside* the Shepherd defense team. He doesn't care *who* knows he's the one supplying them with this bilge."

Frank turned to Bill. "If I lose the election, I'm going to run for the state senate. I'll write a law that holds lawyers accountable if they publicly state anything they cannot prove in court. I'm sick and tired of these guys willfully lying in front of a TV camera. If they did the same thing in court, they'd be held in contempt."

"It'll never work, Frank," said Bill. "The Ninth Circuit Court will throw it out just like they overturn any other law they don't like."

"Lawyers," said Frank, laughing.

"Why didn't the *National Examiner* ask Shepherd to back it up?" asked Matt. "Aren't they responsible for what they report?"

Frank answered. "One of my sources said Shepherd gave them the picture of a Bible that was hit by the shotgun blasts, proving it was some kind of satanic ritual. He forgot to mention Marcella Williams used to teach Sunday school."

"What picture?" asked Matt.

Bill James spoke up. "I heard it was from one of those disposable cameras you get in the supermarket checkout line."

"That means it was somebody at the scene. Probably a cop. Oh, great! Just what we need, more bad cop stories," said Frank, becoming more dejected.

Bill James said, "Hey, Frank. It's a way for public servants to make an extra buck, and they don't think it's the same as taking a bribe."

"Jesus!" said Frank.

"Wait 'til the public turns against Williams, then we'll—" Matt started to say.

"The *public*!" said Frank, frustrated. "The public is out there buying Desmond Williams T-shirts. Didn't you watch that pitiful excuse for a movie about him?"

"Yeah," said Matt. "It really sucked. Desmond's buddies in Hollywood must hate him."

"Hollywood!" exclaimed Frank. "They love him. Not because he murdered his wife. Because they can get rich off him."

"Advertisers are throwing money at anything with Desmond Williams' name on it," said Bill. "Maybe they'll wise up before the public turns on them."

"That'll be a cold day," said Frank. "Everything after the fact in a high-profile case is about money," he said instinctively.

"Malvin Shepherd is an old friend of Wilson McKay," said Bill.

"Who is Wilson McKay?" asked Frank.

"The producer of that slick piece of . . . propaganda."

Frank picked up the handiest and heaviest law book on

the shelf behind him. "Why can't somebody write a law that protects the citizenry from crap like that? We bend over and grab the ankles for every lying, murdering cretin out there, but nobody protects the people."

"That's what we're supposed to do, Frank," said Bill.

"How? With these?" He opened the book to a random page. "Rights of the accused. Rights of the accused. Rights of the effing accused. There's nothing in here to stop defense lawyers from libeling the dead or the living in a movie."

"It can't be called libel before the verdict is in, Frank," said Bill.

"Do you think Williams will sue the producers?" asked Matt.

"Desmond Williams won't sue," said Johnnie. "The movie found him innocent."

"Hollywood has come a long way from the days when Louie B. Mayer and the other movie moguls thought they had a responsibility to the public," explained Bill. "Mayer's favorite film was *The Human Comedy*. That's a far cry from *Natural Born Killers*."

Frank wasn't listening. His mind was on something else. He pondered a moment longer then said, "Tomorrow, we move to sequester."

Frank and his wife, Shelley, had dinner with friends that evening at the Century Plaza on The Avenue of the Stars in Century City. Sometime during the salad course Frank noticed a party being seated at one of the larger tables. It was a lively group, a little loud, but attentive waiters were keeping their glasses full of white wine while several tumblers of good Scotch came and went on the table in front of a stocky, gray haired man in his late sixties. Frank's eyes kept wandering over to the other table during his main course of smoked salmon stuffed with shrimp. He ate every bite.

As the evening wore on, Frank lingered a little longer

than usual over his dessert even though he seldom ate sweets. He chatted about his friend's new boat and swore next spring he would sail with them to Ensenada. Frank's wife knew he wouldn't be doing anything of the kind with the election just around the corner, but Frank seemed so sincere. Finally he excused himself and went to the gent's room.

In the hallway leading to the restrooms, Frank spotted Russell Collier, managing director of Channel 11 *View on L.A.*, walking toward him.

"Mr. District Attorney, here with the wife or will I have another lead story for tonight's ten o'clock news?"

"That's a good one, Russell. I'll have to tell Shelley you're in rare form tonight."

"Is she here?" asked the arrogant swine, looking over Frank's shoulder toward the dining room. Frank had seen Collier glance at his table numerous times during the meal, so his ploy was lost in translation.

"I can't afford to go anywhere alone. You know that, Russell," said the D.A.

"So you say, Frank. Anything new on the Desmond Williams' case?"

"How would you like to get an exclusive with Johnnie Greer tomorrow?"

"Your lap dog already tried that one, Frank. Like I told him, I want to see you lose. But I'll make you a deal. Let one of my news teams film you the night of the election. I want to see your fat wife's face when she knows she's married to a loser."

Adrenaline pumped into Frank's bloodstream. Fortunately it ran to his head where he could do some clear thinking before he pounded the shit out of that asshole. Frank looked at the turd and saw a flicker in Russell's eye. Frank knew it wasn't glee. He gave a half turn and saw the camera whirring behind him, the camera's light illuminating what Russell Collier hoped would be his lead story.

"Enjoy your supper, Russell. Try the crow. I heard that was your favorite."

Frank walked over to the cameraman and whispered in his ear. "I'll pay you five thousand dollars for that tape." He looked back at Russell and then walked to his table.

CHAPTER 17

The next day the jurors heard about the sequestration. After lunch Dallas Long, Willie Robinson, Jesus Rodriguez, Janice Rose Pierce, and Ginger were sitting at a table in the cafeteria. None of them was too thrilled about the news.

Janice Rose spoke first. "I swear my husband is glad I'm stuck here. It's going to be wall-to-wall football and beer. The apartment is going to be a pigsty when I get home."

"I think Fred will miss me," Ginger said. "He hates ironing. I think that's half the reason he was glad when I retired."

"You're too young to retire, dear. Where did you work?" asked Janice Rose.

"A private detective agency."

That piqued Willie's interest. "Detective agency? What were you, a secretary?"

Ginger had gotten that response before, from both men and women who thought the job too challenging for the weaker sex. And she also thought Willie had more class than to ask the question. "No. I owned it, managed it, and did most of the legwork."

At least Dallas was impressed. "Good for you! I could have used your help last night. A couple of guys tried breaking into my place."

"Maybe I could have scared them off with my typewriter," said Ginger, looking at Willie. "How did you get rid of them?"

"I—um—made them an offer they couldn't refuse." Ginger had seen the guy in action and she guessed the intruders left with a few broken appendages.

"Did you enjoy your work?" Dallas continued, interested.

"Most of the time," said Ginger. "It's amazing how much people will tell you when they don't know they're being questioned."

Jesus thought it was really cool. "Wow! You know karate, kung fu? Watch out for you, lady."

He threw a few chops in her direction. Ginger looked at Dallas, knowing she wasn't in his league. "I was never very good in the martial arts. I figured if I couldn't think my way out of a situation, or talk my way out, I better not be in the business." She forgot to mention she was licensed to carry a gun. That's not one of those things you bring up unless it's absolutely necessary.

"A detective, huh?" said Willie, sitting forward, interested. "Never met one before. What kinda stuff did you check out?"

"It wasn't exactly *Magnum, P.I.* My agency did a lot of undercover work in factories, small businesses, and some large blue chip companies. We specialized in industrial espionage and internal theft of goods and intellectual properties."

Willie eased back in his chair and glanced over to the row of pay phones on the wall.

Jesus had a question. "You mean like people stealing pencils?"

"Employees stole everything from office furniture to manufacturing equipment. I retired before every workplace had a PC. From what I hear now, hundreds of computers walk out of offices every day. The sad thing is, those people don't think it's wrong. But my agency mainly went after employees who stole corporate secrets and sold them to the competition."

Jesus asked, "Did you send them to jail?"

"That's what courts do," said Ginger.

Willie noticed one of the pay phones was free. "Look, I've got to make a call. Need to borrow a suitcase from a friend. See you guys later. Wonder where we get to eat tonight?"

As he walked away, Ginger noted he bypassed the row of phones and headed down the hall.

"You two ladies are rooming together?" Dallas asked the ladies.

"Yes," answered Janice Rose. "We'll be one big, happy family by the time this is over. How come you got a room by yourself?"

"I asked," said their elusive friend.

They chatted, or rather, Janice Rose chatted about hearth and home, until it was time to resume their seats in court at 1:00 p.m.

CHAPTER 18

Malvin Shepherd was up first when the jury took their seats after lunch. He began his cross-examination of the arresting officer at the Kirkland Building. Officer Boyd Lewis was describing the scene when he and his fellow officers apprehended Desmond Williams.

"He was standing in the lobby of the Kirkland Building, screaming like a madman, telling us to get away from him," said the officer.

"Do you have a degree in psychology, Mr. Lewis?" asked the inquisitive Mr. Shepherd.

This wasn't Officer Lewis's first time on the witness stand. And it wouldn't be his last. He was defense counsel's worst nightmare. His expression never changed. He never blinked. And he had the unpleasant habit of telling the whole truth.

"No, sir," answered Officer Lewis.

"Then how can you make an assumption about the state of mind of Mr. Williams?"

"The guy—Mr. Williams—was ranting just like any other accused felon who had jumped bail and was caught by the police."

"Mr. Lewis, my client has not been charged with failure to appear. It was a clear case of misunderstanding due to extreme stress."

"It looked like bail jumping from where I stood," said Lewis.

"I didn't ask you a question, Mr. Lewis. Please refrain from answering until I have asked you a specific question.

I would like that last remark stricken, Your Honor."

"The jury will please disregard the witness's last remark," said Judge Cherry. Then to the gentleman on the stand she said, "Only answer direct questions, Officer Lewis." Lewis nodded.

"Your Honor, at this time, the defense would like to play the *entire* videotape of the incident at the Kirkland Building when Mr. Lewis and other officers of the Los Angeles Police force confronted Mr. Williams and ordered him to submit to their demands. I was disappointed the public was only given an edited version."

"Objection, Your Honor," said Ms. Greer. "The public is not judging this case."

"Sustained. Rephrase your statement, Mr. Shepherd," said Judge Cherry.

"Yes, Your Honor. The defense wants to play the entire videotape of the incident at the Kirkland Building that involved my client."

"Any objections, Ms. Greer?" asked the judge.

"No, Your Honor."

The viewing screen was already in place opposite the jury box. Another one was suspended from the ceiling near the front of the courtroom. It looked like a sports bar. A remote control was at the podium where Shepherd was standing. Walter Blue handed the defense's copy of the video to the bailiff and it was inserted into the VCR. Shepherd started the tape and provided the color commentary.

"We see Mr. Williams enter the hallway from the rear and proceed toward the front lobby. At this point, one of the officers—which one is that, Mr. Lewis?"

Shepherd didn't just ask the question, he demanded an answer, as if it mattered who anybody was except the poor, pitiful victim of the piece, the now all-suffering Desmond Williams.

"That's Officer Torres."

"Officer Torres enters from the rear and then I believe

this is you, Mr. Lewis, coming from the front?" Shepherd stopped the video and turned toward Officer Lewis. He made a point of waiting for the officer to answer a question, a question Officer Lewis hadn't realized had been asked. "I am waiting for your answer, Mr. Lewis. Is that you?"

"I didn't know you were—"

"Just yes or no, Mr. Lewis. Is that you?"

"Yes."

"Thank you," he said very quickly, very condescendingly. "You enter here and shout at my client to halt. Is that right?"

"Yes, sir."

"Yes. In fact we have the confrontation on tape." Shepherd started the tape again. "You are screaming at Mr. Williams, and what does my client do at that point?" He stopped the tape short of Desmond's next move.

"He threw a fit," said Officer Lewis.

Shepherd repeated the officer's answer as if he was thinking about it clinically. "He threw a fit. Is that what you call this?"

Malvin played the remainder of the tape where Williams basically threw a fit.

The scene was the same one that had been played over and over and over, day in and day out for weeks on end on every television station in the country. But this time they turned up the volume so the jury could hear what Williams had been saying. Ginger had thought that the only audible vocal was that of Officer Lewis yelling at Williams to hit the floor because that was all they ever aired on TV. Actually the police officer called out only four times. Some TV producer had looped the scene for the news broadcasts because they had the cop yelling the same command for seventeen seconds.

Ginger watched the entire scene on the big screen. At first she thought the dialogue had been dubbed like in a Japanese horror flick to make Desmond Williams' words clearer, because the voice coming out of him was high-pitched and whiny. But his mouth was moving and it was definitely Desmond who was acting out this drama:

> "Hold it, Williams. Stop right
> there. Stop. Get on the floor."
> Williams braced himself against the
> wall and then slumped to the floor.
> "Get away from me! All of you! I
> want outta here! You're not gonna take
> me back! I didn't do anything. Why are
> ya treating me like ga'bage? I'm inno-
> cent. Don't you understand?"
> The police officers moved in, guns
> drawn, and Desmond Williams was cuffed.

Shepherd stopped the video as they were pulling Desmond's arms up behind him and slapping on the bracelets. One of the cops had his hand on Williams' shoulder, pushing him down, keeping him off balance. It looked sufficiently brutal and the defense knew it. Ginger noticed Shepherd didn't show the part where Williams was looking over his shoulder at the camera to see if it was all gotten on film. Shepherd was obviously aware of that part of the video, too.

Malvin Shepherd turned back to the police officer on the witness stand and asked, "I repeat, Mr. Lewis, is that what you call a fit?"

"Yes, that's what I call a fit."

"I beg to differ with you, Mr. Lewis. What you witnessed was the cry for help from an innocent man."

"I object, Your Honor," said Johnnie. "Is Mr. Shepherd testifying or doing his summation?"

"Mr. Shepherd," said Judge Cherry, "you will have a chance to summarize when the prosecution has concluded. Do you have any more questions for this witness?"

"No more questions, Your Honor."

That was the first time Ginger had seen the entire tape of Williams being arrested with the full sound and fury. Something as juicy as that should have made every news broadcast from day one. Maybe it ran during the two hundred times she turned off the television when she was getting sick of the media saturation. She kept staring at the screen now frozen in time. Something was familiar about that scene. Ginger kept tossing it over in her head . . . Ah! She took the pen and notebook provided to the jurors by the great city of Los Angeles and wrote a note. She raised her hand to get the bailiff's attention.

The bailiff retrieved the note. After reading it, he handed it to Judge Cherry. The judge read the message, and then paused. She didn't look in Ginger's direction. She did take a slight glance at the video screen.

"The court will take a two hour break. Be back here at two-forty-five," said the judge. "Counselors, I need to see you for a sidebar. This is off the record." Turning to the court reporter, she said, "I won't need you."

Malvin Shepherd and Johnnie Greer stepped to the sidebar and were shown Ginger's note. They both took a quick glance in her direction as the jury was leaving the jury box.

The judge said, "I'll have a copy of that video in my chambers in thirty minutes. Be there." Judge Cherry was steaming under her black robes.

Thirty minutes later the counselors were in the judge's chambers, where a VCR was set up and ready to roll. Shepherd and Greer were seated. Malvin wasn't happy. His face was stone. Johnnie was near euphoric, but she fought to keep a straight face. The judge didn't like being taken for a fool and it showed. Her face was screwed into a fist as she started the tape.

CHAPTER 19

Judge Cherry and the two counselors sat back in their chairs to watch the video in chambers. On the television screen was a movie Desmond Williams had made ten years earlier called *Madman*. It didn't do very well at the theaters and went quickly to video rental stores under the title *Doctor Hope*. It was one of those dogs that ran in the middle of the day when most people were doing something more interesting. Ginger had watched it three consecutive Fridays while ironing one summer when the movie channel was in one of its ruts.

In it Williams played a compassionate psychiatrist, absolutely dripping with the stuff, who worked in a colossal county hospital in the slums or ghetto or project in some big megalopolis. He was so self-sacrificing you expected him to walk on water. He kept turning down a rich white colleague's offer to work in an upscale hospital in Beverly Hills where the nutty patients were wealthy and just needed somebody to hold their well-manicured hands, or so said the white doctor. Williams' character had to refuse in order to minister to people nobody else would help.

The kindly doctor was trying to save Mike, a crazy patient who started out a little jerky at the beginning of the movie, and who then turned into your standard Hollywood psychopath who wasn't responsible for his actions. It was society's fault. The video picked up when warm and kindly Dr. Peters was trying to calm down the frenzied man. The scene was in a hospital corridor. Desmond Williams was dressed in a casual doctor's outfit: jeans, shirt open nearly

to his navel, and a white doctor's coat. His hair was cut in a
modified Afro style. They had set the movie in the Sixties.
The psycho, Mike, was dressed in grungy clothes. He had a
five o'clock shadow sponged on by the makeup department
and greasy hair. He was also a white guy. All the nuts were
white guys back then. It was a low-budget, no-brainer movie.

Williams, as worldly-wise, all-compassionate Dr. Peters,
was doing the tough-love role, saying

> "Mike. Mike! You're all right, kid.
> It's just you and me here. Just like old
> times."
>
> Mike, the lunatic, said, "Old times? Is
> that what it is, Doc? Why is it every
> time somethin' goes wrong uptown, they
> bring in Mike? I may a done some bad
> things before, but Doc, you gotta believe
> me, I didn't do murder."
>
> "Things don't look good for you, kid."
>
> "But Doc, I can't go back inside. I
> can't handle it no more."
>
> "Mike, listen to me. This time you went
> too far. The girl died. You hit her too
> hard. I don't think you meant to do it."
>
> "I didn't. Honest. I didn't mean to do
> it."
>
> "But, Mike, you have to face the demon
> inside you. You've got to face it and
> destroy it."
>
> "What'll they do to me, Doc? I'm
> scared."
>
> "Be scared. I'm here for you." He waved
> for the cops to approach from the hall-
> way.
>
> As the three officers walked toward
> Mike, he turned and saw them. He shrank

back against the wall as if they were
monsters and he slid to the floor.
   "Get away from me! All of you! I want
outta here! You're not gonna take me
back! I didn't do nothin'. Why are ya
treating me like ga'bage? I'm innocent.
Don't you understand?"
   The tough-love Hollywood doc said,
"Face it, Mike. For once in your life,
face the demon inside you."
   Mike looked at the kindly face of Dr.
Peters and straightened at those saccha-
rine words.
   "Okay, Doc. Whatever you say."

Judge Cherry shut off the VCR and looked at Shepherd,
who was contemplating his options.

"We are on the horns of a dilemma here, Counselors.
Mr. Shepherd, you can discuss this video with your client
and see if he wishes to change his plea. Ms. Greer, you, on
the other hand, can run both tapes side-by-side and let the
people on the jury make up their own minds. Mr. Shepherd,
as they say at Wimbledon, the ball is in your court."

Shepherd hadn't earned his reputation without some
effort. He found his option. "What does this prove? My client
was no doubt so disoriented, so distraught over the death of
his wife, he reverted to something subliminal, some bit of dialogue from a very riveting movie that he had made, and his
subconscious brought it to the surface in a time of great
stress. Ms. Greer, if you don't admit the video into evidence
yourself, I will, as further evidence of my client's mental
state at the time of his unjust incarceration."

Johnnie turned her head toward her colleague.
"Remember, Counselor, the loony tune in that movie was
guilty—too."

Shepherd didn't blink, but he did grit his jaw. He left

shortly thereafter. Johnnie exited thirty seconds after he did. Judge Cherry sat forward in her chair. She opened her top drawer and took out a handful of letters. The envelopes were addressed to her at the Criminal Courts Building. She pulled the first letter from its envelope, spread it out on her desk, and reread the brief note:

Judge,
You die if the brother does time. We nos where you lives.
XXX

The judge's secretary entered the room and saw the letter.

"Did you get another one, Your Honor?" asked the diminutive woman. Janey, the judge's five foot one secretary, had been with her for ten years.

"No, it's the same one. The one we got earlier today," said the judge.

"You should seal it in a forensics bag. The police could get a DNA sample off the stamp."

"Janey, if I brought this up now, I'd have to give up the case. That's what they want."

"But Your Honor, some crazy person is threatening you."

"They're not crazy. Whoever wrote these notes is using high-quality bond paper. And in the first one they could spell the word 'know.'"

"Why does someone want to hurt you?" asked the secretary.

"They don't want to hurt me. They want to make me famous."

"I don't understand, Your Honor. Do you think one of the attorneys is doing this?"

Judge Cherry didn't answer. She looked at her confused secretary and smiled. "You go and have your lunch, Janey. Don't worry about this. I'm not going to lose any sleep over it."

Janey started to leave, then turned back to the judge. "What are you going to do?"

"Nothing. As far as I'm concerned, it never happened."

Janey wanted to say something, but she didn't really know what to say. She closed the judge's door and went to lunch. Judge Cherry brought out the handful of letters that had been sent to her over the past few days and ran them through her shredder one at a time.

She happened to glance at a plaque hanging on her wall that carried a quote from Joseph Addison, the eighteenth-century scholar, who wrote: *"Justice discards party, friendship, kindred, and is therefore always represented as blind."*

CHAPTER 20

Barely five minutes later Malvin Shepherd was standing in a private consulting room at the Criminal Courts Building with Desmond Williams. They were in the room alone. Desmond was seated at a table with his head down, while Malvin, standing, had just started his rant. Malvin was fit to be tied, but Desmond was a sleeping volcano.

"What the *hell* do you think you were doing? I am the only goddamned person between you and lethal injection. When I told you to 'lose it' if you were caught at the Kirkland Building, I expected more than you reading the fucking lines from one of your half-assed movies."

"You should have had a better plan to get me out of there," Desmond mumbled.

"My people were outside. We had a plan. You're the one who decided to play *Hamlet*."

"We should have rehearsed it. I knew you'd screw this up," grumbled Williams.

"*I* didn't screw it up. You just better be damn glad I turned this thing around before the prosecutor got her hands on it. Remember, Williams, I run this show. You understand me? I orchestrate it. I choreograph it. And I get the right kind of publicity. I will *not* have you jeopardizing my reputation."

Barely looking up, Williams said, "Your reputation? I don't give a shit about your reputation."

"It's what'll keep you alive, Williams."

Malvin caught a glimpse of Desmond's face and sensed the rumbling deep within that now dormant body. He distanced himself from his client.

His voice rising slightly, Williams added, "You oily son of a bitch. Don't you ever threaten me."

Knowing when to back off, Malvin soothed, "I'm not threatening you, Des. I'm telling you. My way works."

"All your clients have done time." Desmond was now staring at the table.

"All my clients were guilty," Shepherd said matter-of-factly.

"And they gave you every goddamned thing they owned."

"And I saved their goddamned life!"

"I wonder if it's worth it?" said Williams, rather quietly. "I wonder if you're worth it?" Williams was still pondering a thought.

Shepherd sat next to his client, thinking he had calmed him down. "No client of mine has been put to death. So far."

Still studying the table, Williams said very clearly, "And I don't intend to be the first. I'm paying you a hell of a lot of money to get me out of here. I told you I didn't care how you did it. I don't care who you buy off or who you run off. But if you screw this up—if any of your fucking plans back-fire—I'll make sure you pay."

"You're in no position to threaten me, boy."

Williams turned his head slowly toward the lawyer. His eyes took on the look of the family pit bull right before it rips your arm off. "You wanna make a bet? If you think your East Coast bags of shit are tough, you, in your fancy striped suit, you don't know L.A. Guys like you are buried from here to Las Vegas and nobody's even lookin' for 'em. And that ain't a line out of a fucking movie."

"I don't like that kind of talk, Williams. One word from me and you'll never leave this building."

Williams was sitting quite close to Malvin. He reached over with his right hand and grabbed Shepherd's throat. Shepherd froze. The guard posted outside wasn't watching through the small glass window, so he couldn't see Shepherd's eyes go wide with fear.

"I don't have to ask anybody to do my dirty work, Malvin. I can do you right here. What's another dead body? My next lawyer will play that video of me at the Kirkland Building, play it over and over and over until everybody's sick of it. It'll prove I'm a psychopath. They'll put me in a hospital for a few years and I'll be out before the maggots finish chewing your dead white ass."

Shepherd tried finding a rebuttal. "I don't have to—" he stuttered.

"Yes you do. I bought and paid for you, Malvin. Now get me the fuck out of here."

CHAPTER 21

Court resumed thirty minutes later. Officer Lewis had taken his seat on the witness stand, but was dismissed with no further questions from the defense team. The look on Lewis's face said this was unusual. Obviously something had happened in the judge's chambers. Oh, to have been a fly on that wall.

Johnnie Greer was unusually sullen and Malvin Shepherd kept his eyes lowered. Then both tilted their heads slightly toward the jury box and looked at Ginger.

"Call your next witness, Counselor," said the judge.

"The prosecution calls Police Detective Lawrence Patrick."

The bailiff gave instructions to the uniformed officer at the rear of the courtroom. "Call Lawrence Patrick to the stand."

An officer from the sheriff's department opened the rear door to the courtroom, stepped into the hallway, and called, "Lawrence Patrick."

Patrick entered the courtroom wearing a tweed coat and tan slacks. He kept pressing his left elbow against his side trying to feel the shoulder holster that wasn't there. He felt like Jimmy Cagney in an old gangster flick itching for trouble. It was all because the courts had some pesky rule that said you couldn't carry your service revolver into a courtroom if you were a witness. Go figure.

The police detective took the stand and was sworn in. It was established that he was the officer in charge of the investigation on the morning of the double homicide. While the prosecution was eliciting Patrick's job history on the police force, his credentials were being scrutinized by the defense to the point of exhaustion. Shepherd kept thumbing through the pages he had in front of him, checking off or lining out pertinent points. Johnnie was standing only a few feet away at the podium and she was becoming distracted by the noise. Finally, the flapping of pages caught the judge's attention.

"Mr. Shepherd, find your place so your colleague can continue."

Shepherd had been so consumed by his diversionary tactics, he was actually caught off guard.

"Uh—excuse me, Your Honor. I was just trying to keep up."

"Do it more quietly, Counselor. Continue, Ms. Greer."

After a long string of challenges to the police officer's credentials by the defense team, Johnnie went on to another topic. "Detective Patrick, do you have photos taken at the murder scene?"

"Yes."

Next to Patrick in the witness stand was a small computer monitor that showed the same picture being shown on the two large video screens in the courtroom. Detective Patrick brought up photos of the patio area, the broken window, and the dirt spilled from the planters. Using a computerized pointer to highlight sections of each photograph, he was trying to be as thorough as possible against the best-laid plans of the defense counsel, who was waiting for the first opportunity to toss in one of his handy-dandy monkey wrenches.

As the officer was saying, "It had to have been broken from outside. All the glass was found on the living room floor. It couldn't have been broken by the gun blast or else glass would have spread well into the room. The killer broke it with either his hand, the butt end of the shotgun, or some other heavy object."

The prosecutor asked, "Detective Patrick, could a hand have gone through that heavy plate-glass window?"

"Yes, if it was hit with enough force in the center of the pane. The pattern of glass remaining in the frame shows even distribution that would indicate it was broken in the center."

"Would anyone hitting the glass with his hand receive an injury?" asked Johnnie.

"Objection, Your Honor. Calls for a conclusion," said Shepherd, tossing one of those wrenches.

"Your Honor, this witness has already been subjected to a media anal exam concerning his qualifications. Detective Patrick *is* an expert in crime-scene investigations. I am asking what would be the probable result of a person putting his hand through a plate-glass window."

"Objection overruled. Continue, Counselor."

"Detective Patrick, what would be the probable result of a person putting his hand through a plate-glass window . . . wearing gloves?"

"There'd be bits of glass everywhere, most probably from splinters flying in the air and landing on clothes, face, hair, socks, and shoes. Whoever broke the glass would come in contact with pieces at some point. Even if the person was wearing good leather gloves or heavy work gloves, he would probably incur at least one cut or splinter."

"What if he was wearing boxing gloves?" asked the defense, getting some chuckles from the crowd.

"You are out of order, Counselor," said the judge. "You don't have to answer that question, Detective."

"Go ahead, Detective," said Johnnie. "What would happen if the killer were wearing boxing gloves?"

"It would have taken quite a few punches to finally break the glass. Then the killer would have to take off the glove in order to pull the trigger of the shotgun. Marcella Williams and Adrian Wells would have heard the repeated banging and even if the glass were broken quickly, by the time the killer took off the glove and was ready to pull the trigger, the two victims would have been off the couch."

"How were the bodies found?" asked Johnnie.

"Both Marcella Williams and Adrian Wells were found seated on the couch."

Johnnie turned to smile at Malvin, then went back to her questioning. "How many lights were on in the living room when the police arrived on the scene?"

"Every light in the room was on. It was very bright."

"Detective Patrick, if we agree the window was broken quickly with a gloved fist or the butt end of the weapon, wouldn't it still make a lot of noise?"

"Yes, it would have made a great deal of noise, especially on that bare floor."

"Can police experts determine from what point, either on the patio or in the room, the weapon was fired?"

"We know it was fired inside the room."

"How can you be sure of that?" asked Johnnie.

"There was no potassium nitrite, charcoal, or sulfur residue on the curtains that were hanging at the window."

"And what are those chemicals?"

"They are the chemicals used in gunpowder," said Detective Patrick.

"You are saying no chemical traces were found on the curtains?"

"None."

"So the weapon had to be fired from somewhere within the room?"

"Yes," said the officer.

"How many seconds would it take to break the window, make the hole big enough to step through, aim and fire a shotgun, approximately?"

"We ran a test. It took eight seconds."

"How long would it take to jump off that couch?"

"Two seconds."

"Marcella Williams and Adrian Wells had eight seconds

to see who was coming through that big window. You have testified that every light in the living room was on. There was enough light to see whoever was breaking into the house. Is that correct?"

"Yes."

"If the intruder had been wearing a mask, the victims would have had eight seconds to recognize the danger and react. Does that sound reasonable?"

"Yes," said Patrick.

"What would a normal person do under those conditions?"

Shepherd interjected "Objection, again, Your Honor. These couldn't be considered normal conditions."

"Your Honor," said Johnnie. "I specifically asked what would a *normal person* do under those conditions. I did not say the circumstances were normal."

Shepherd wasn't having any of this. "Your Honor, I still must object. We have no way of knowing the state of mind of the two victims that night."

"Your Honor, neither victim had any trace of drugs in his or her bloodstream. Their blood-alcohol levels were consistent with someone consuming less than one glass of white wine. In this case, a Chablis. Neither was undergoing psychotherapy. Between the two victims sitting on that couch, at least one must have qualified for 'normal person' status."

"Overruled. But be careful, Counselor. That ice is getting thin."

"Yes, Your Honor," said Johnnie. "Detective Patrick, what would a normal person do if someone was breaking through their window?"

"They would get up or run or cower or cover themselves."

"How were the bodies found?"

"They were just sitting there on the couch," said the detective.

"Why would they—both of them—just be sitting there?"

"They probably knew the person coming through..."

Jumping to his feet, Shepherd shouted "Objection! That's a conclusion, Your Honor."

"I'll restate the question, Your Honor," said Johnnie.

"The jury will disregard the previous answer. Continue," said Judge Cherry.

"Detective Patrick, was there any sign from the positions of the bodies or the looks on their faces that the victims, Marcella Williams and Adrian Wells, were necessarily afraid of the person who broke through that plate-glass window?"

"None at all."

"Thank you. Detective Patrick, how much noise does a twelve-gauge shotgun make?"

"Quite a bit."

"Could it be heard a hundred yards away?"

"It depends."

"Depends on what?" asked the attorney.

"Wind velocity, baffles, ambient sound, distance," said the cop.

"Explain that, please."

"In high wind, sound can actually be knocked around. It echoes. Inside a building you have baffles. We call them walls. Acoustic ceilings and insulation, even glass, can muffle sound. You also have other noise such as traffic, the ocean, radios, and television that can dampen the resonance of gunfire."

"You also mentioned distance," added Johnnie.

"Yes. Your ability to hear sounds depends how far away you are from the blast."

"How far away is Marcella Williams' living room from her neighbors?"

"Her living room is one hundred ten feet from the house on the right and ninety five feet from the house to the left."

"Would someone be able to hear a shotgun blast from that distance?" asked Johnnie.

"You'd hear something."

"Detective Patrick, did the neighbors hear anything the night of the murders?"

"No."

"Can you explain why no one heard a sound?"

Patrick said, "Yes. I have pictures."

Detective Patrick clicked the mouse on his computer console bringing up an enlargement of Marcella's side yard facing her neighbor on the right. The house in the distance was long and low and wrapped in glass much like Marcella's home. A **FOR SALE** sign was rising out of the ground next to a large, rusty anchor.

The detective continued. "As you can see from the picture, the place next door to Marcella Williams' house is for sale. The real estate agent said it had been vacant for two months prior to the murders. The house on the left is also unoccupied. The owners are on an extended vacation." The detective brought up another picture. "You can see in this photograph, the windows are shuttered and a few weekly newspapers and fliers are piled along the walkway on the right side of their house."

The police photograph of the unoccupied residence appeared on the viewing screen. They must have used a cheap camera on a very sunny day because the areas in deep shadows had turned into indefinable black splotches while the lighter sections lost most of their definition in the enlarged pixels. It looked more like a Cubist painting.

"Thank you. That's all I have for this witness, Your Honor."

"Cross-examine, Mr. Shepherd?" asked the judge.

"Yes, thank you, Your Honor. Mr. Patrick, the Malibu Beach community is your beat, as they say, isn't it?"

"Yes."

"The Escondido Beach area is your jurisdiction? Yes or no?"

"Yes."

"Is there a lot of crime in that area? The beach specifically?"

"Not much."

"Do the residents in that area feel fairly safe using the beach?"

"I would be speculating, but yes, I think so."

"All hours, day or night?"

"Maybe not all hours, but most of the time."

"A lot of people walk on the beach—at night, at dawn, in the early morning?"

"Yes. There's usually somebody on the beach."

"But there was nobody on the beach during the time of the murders. No witness to pinpoint the time of death or perhaps see the killer or killers. Is that correct?"

"No one has come forward."

"Are Marcella Williams' house and her two neighbors' homes the only ones along that stretch of beach?"

"No."

"In fact, there are many houses in that area." Another small computer screen was mounted next to the podium. Shepherd clicked the mouse to bring up a new picture on the large screen. It was a beautiful aerial shot of the coastline. "As you can see, there are dozens of houses nearby." He switched back to the picture of the empty house. "Mrs. Williams' neighbors might have been gone, but can you say nobody else heard the shots that evening?"

"As I said before, no one has come forward," said the detective.

Ginger got a second look at the neighbor's house on the left. She could see the pile of what she guessed were the old newspapers along the walkway, but with the quality of the film resolution she had to look intently at the image on the screen to see anything specific. She was studying the enlarged picture with growing interest when she felt eyes watching her. Ginger turned to see Malvin Shepherd staring at her. His thick eyebrows were knitted across his forehead as he wondered what she was seeing that he missed.

Actually, she wasn't seeing anything too clearly. She handed another note the bailiff.

The bailiff glanced at Ginger's note while several members of the jury wondered what this exasperating woman wanted this time. The bailiff handed the note to the judge. Ginger wanted to review the actual hard copy of the photograph. So much for high-tech computer gizmos. The candid shot was brought to the jury box and passed down the line. When Ginger got to see it close up, she nodded her head. Something did catch her attention.

Malvin Shepherd grabbed his copy of the photograph and studied it. He tossed it on the table and then leaned over to Curtis Lee, whispering something in his ear. Before Shepherd got halfway through with his next question, Curtis was on his way through the rear doors of the courtroom.

"So, Mr. Patrick, you're telling me in an area where there are usually people around, joggers on the beach, cars on the road, people taking long walks, at this one specific time, the evening Marcella Williams and Adrian Wells were murdered by several loud shotgun blasts, nobody—not a living soul—was in the area?"

"It looks that way."

"I want a yes or no, Mr. Patrick."

"No. Nobody. No witnesses."

Shepherd went back to his cluttered briefcase and pulled out one of the weekly rags with a particularly sleazy headline. He held it up.

"Have you seen this headline, Mr. Patrick?"

The item was admitted as a defense exhibit. The headline read **MYSTERY WITNESS FOUND—FEARS FOR LIFE.**

"Yes, I have," said the officer.

"How do you explain a reputable newspaper like the *World Globe* finding a witness while the Los Angeles Police Department can't?"

Patrick didn't bat an cye. "First, the *World Globe* isn't a reputable newspaper. Second, who believes the crap written in a rag like that? And third, I could show you pictures of Elvis being taken aboard a spaceship and it wouldn't make that true, either."

"Are you telling me this newspaper is lying?" Malvin was shocked, shocked!

"I'm telling you whoever leaked this story is lying."

"And do you have any idea who leaked this story?"

Patrick bit his tongue. Lawsuits are so costly and he wanted to keep his job. "No."

"No more questions."

Judge Cherry thankfully called it a day. Everybody was pooped. Malvin Shepherd had driven the court like a maniacal trail boss, and the people on the jury were ready for an early dinner. Then Ginger remembered they were being sequestered. Oh, joy.

CHAPTER 22

Later that evening Johnnie and Matt were in her office going over their notes, preparing for the next day's session. Johnnie had taken off her jacket and had slipped on a pair of flats. Matt was already in his shirtsleeves. He had dropped his tie and coat in his office after dinner and was kicking back. He hadn't taken many notes in court that day and was running out of things to do in Johnnie's office.

Matt started watching the slim woman in her well-fitting skirt with the side slit just above her knee. He noticed the glint of her stockings as they caught the light. He watched her well-rounded backside as she shifted her weight from one foot to the other.

As for Johnnie, she was more than busy. She seemed obsessed with the paperwork. She had taken pages of notes during court and was now flipping through her yellow legal pad, checking off items, underlining certain parts, and circling others. Next, she started pulling papers out of her briefcase and reading through them, making more notes.

Johnnie had kept her back to Matt and he realized she hadn't said one word since he came into her office. She began stuffing papers into her briefcase, still avoiding eye contact.

Matt spoke, "It went pretty good today. Didn't it?"

"Yeah!" came her terse reply.

"I don't think Shepherd is so tough. Maybe they think so back East, but out here, he's just another ambulance chaser." Matt was swinging back and forth in a swivel chair, playing with a pencil he had picked up.

She grunted and went on with her work.

Matt stood up and stretched. He wasn't thinking about work, just that slit in Johnnie's skirt. He walked over to her. She felt him near her and turned toward him. He reached for the button on her blouse and tried unsuccessfully to undo it with one hand. He gave her a playful grin and leaned down to kiss her instead. She turned away from him.

"Is there something wrong?" he asked.

Johnnie reached into her briefcase and pulled out a newspaper clipping. "Damn it, Matt, what's the matter with you?"

"What have *I* done?"

"This." She held up the clipping **MIXING BUSINESS WITH PLEASURE?** "*You* leaked the story to the *L.A. Times.* Why didn't you say something to Frank when he brought it up yesterday?"

"Because I knew you wouldn't like it."

Exploding, she said, "Wouldn't like it! I ought to have you fired!"

"Johnnie—"

"This—this rubs off on me, Matt. People will think *I* condone it. It'll look like the D.A.'s office condones it. Don't you understand? We're held to a higher standard than scum like Shepherd."

"But, Johnnie, I thought—"

"No, you didn't. That's the one thing you didn't do, Matt. You didn't think at all about how this would look when they found out where it came from."

"Nobody knows."

"I know. If I know, Frank knows. My God, Matt, he probably knew yesterday, and you sat there so damn pious and innocent."

"Jeez, Johnnie."

"Frank will think I put you up to it."

"I'll tell him—"

"You sure as hell will. And you'll ask for a transfer when this is over."

"What?"

"Matt, you know how hard I've worked to get where I am. I've had to fight every damn prejudice out there."

"Johnnie, I'll explain—"

"Matthew, it isn't a matter of explaining. It's my reputation at stake. It's my honor. What the hell else do I have? They patronize me for being a woman. They patronize me for being black. I tell them I don't give a shit about being black. Just look at my record. Look at what I stand for. And just to get a conviction on some stinking slimeball who kills his wife, you sell me out."

"I never meant it to hurt you, Johnnie. I wanted to beat Shepherd at his own game."

"It isn't a game, Matt. None of it. We could each lose what we value most."

"I wanted the public to know Frank didn't pick you to prosecute Williams just because you're black."

"It doesn't read that way. It sounds like the *only* reason he picked me was because of the color of my skin."

"That isn't what I wanted," he said.

"It's what you got, Matt."

"But what about us? I don't want to lose you."

Distancing herself from him, she walked behind her desk and said, "You need to put in more time on your own. I'm holding you back."

"But—we work well together."

"You use me, Matt. Like a crutch."

"Johnnie—"

"It's true. I don't want to prop you up. I want you to stand on your own two feet. Oh, Matt, I don't know what I'm saying. I love you, but I want you to *be* more, *do* more— for yourself. Don't depend on me all the time."

"Is that what you think I've been doing? I just admire you so much."

"I know you do. But I want a man—a man who'll run with me, not behind me."

Meanwhile, Frank Fallen was riding the elevator down to the parking garage. He kept looking at his watch, ignoring his fellow passengers. Those who were acquainted with him knew he seldom spoke unless there was a microphone in front of him and then his words were well-chosen. The political ramifications could be costly if the wrong person heard the wrong thing at the wrong time.

The people on the elevator were making plans for dinner. As for Frank, he wasn't hungry. He looked at his watch again as the doors opened. Exiting, he nodded to a few faces he recognized. Since Frank was the only one on the elevator who was parked in the reserved section, he walked alone to his car. **LOS ANGELES DISTRICT ATTORNEY** was stenciled in bold black letters on the wall in front of his Lexus, with a removable plaque with his name on it below.

He stood near his car and rattled the keys for a few moments.

"Mr. Fallen?" whispered a voice nearby.

Frank turned to see the familiar face coming from behind a concrete column. He motioned for the man to stay where he was and then glanced around the area. Frank walked into the shadows. Mark Parsons from Channel 10 *News & Entertainment* was older than he appeared on television. It must have been the makeup and the youthful hairstyle in a modified spike that made him seem younger. But there was definitely something about the eyes that showed age.

"Hello, Mark. How have you been?"

"Fine, Mr. Fallen." Mark grinned as though he had just dined on a fat canary. "The news business has been colorful lately."

"Colorful? I could use a little color right now," said the D.A.

"My source says Malvin Shepherd was really pissed after meeting with his client today."

Frank had watched the television coverage of the trial in his office and he went back over the afternoon's testimony in his head.

"I thought Malvin did a pretty good recovery job after he floated the *Globe* story and their mysterious witness fantasy. If he presented that as fact, I'd hang him for withholding evidence. But as long as he quotes one of the papers he's bought off, we can't touch him."

"I don't mean this afternoon's testimony. It was after they ran the movie in the judge's chambers."

"You know about the movie?" The D.A. was surprised.

"Yeah. Shepherd wants the story in the papers tomorrow and we run the exclusive on television tonight. I'm doing a side-by-side. You know the spin: Williams cracking up at the Kirkland Building and then the movie clip. They want us to play up the mental-anguish angle."

"Ah. That will go with the insanity plea you told me about. Has your guy said any more about Malvin throwing Williams overboard?"

"Nope. But that wasn't the whole thing. I was told—" Mark looked around for other ears listening. "Shepherd looked scared. And—he kept rubbing his throat."

Frank's eyes widened. "Williams threatened him? Whoa. Trouble in paradise."

"That's why Channel 10 got the exclusive on the *Madman* video. Shepherd can't have it look as if his client is lying."

"Desmond Williams will never take the stand, and I don't think lousy acting on a police video can be called perjury."

"May I quote you?" said Mark, smiling.

"No."

"How's it going? Anything new in the case?" asked the reporter.

"I'll tell you this, Mark. It's almost too easy."

"You mean somebody might really be setting Williams up?"

"What are you hearing?" asked the D.A., knowing when

to listen. "I mean from Malvin Shepherd."

"He's leaking like a sieve."

"There's no chance he really has a witness? I mean a legit witness?" asked Frank.

"My source says they have squat," said Mark. "But he doesn't think they'll need anything."

"Then why is he—?"

"What?" asked Mark.

"So damn sure of himself?" asked Frank.

"Isn't that his job?"

"To the cameras and the press. But behind the scenes, he should be sweating bullets."

"Shepherd isn't sweating. Just talking. He's been on every news show in the country."

"That's why we sequestered the jury," said the D.A.

"Yeah. Thanks for giving me a heads-up on that before any other station got it," said Mark.

"Sure. No problem."

"Why does Shepherd do it?" asked Mark.

"What?"

"Play all the angles," said Mark.

"He knows all it takes is one nut job on the jury who buys into that mumbo-jumbo and Williams walks."

"Man, I'd be reaching for the Right Guard. What's up tomorrow?"

"We drop a bombshell. She'll make you some headlines. Here's some background on her. Talk about colorful."

CHAPTER 23

Each juror had been given an hour to go home, pack a bag, and get back to the courthouse. Ginger had given Fred a call earlier in the day and asked him to throw a few things into a suitcase. She hoped he would choose some of her favorite outfits. She feared he would pick something she wouldn't be caught dead in. Ginger knew she should have sent a sack or two of her old clothes to the Salvation Army months ago.

The jury had dinner at a local Chinese restaurant. John Dunbar was the life of the party. The only thing missing was the lampshade. He kept spinning the Lazy Susan in the center of the table, all the while chortling, "Round and around and around she goes, where she stops, nobody knows."

His little joke was not only cooling off the bowls of tantalizing Mandarin and Szechwan cuisine, but Ginger didn't much care for her teacup disappearing as the small tray revolved, so she lifted her cup off midspin. Dunbar finally calmed down. Ginger figured he had run out of pranks, but she was pretty sure he would come up with more.

After dinner they rode through the relatively quiet streets of downtown Los Angeles in one of the buses the police use to transport criminals. That was a thrill. Ginger was not usually claustrophobic, but the bars on the windows and the presence of police guards made her a little anxious. Vehicles pulled up alongside the bus at the stoplights and tried getting a glimpse of the occupants through the white-washed glass. They couldn't have known if the occupants were among the Ten Most Wanted or a rock band, but they kept staring. Ginger felt like a fugitive.

The jury was put up at the Crawford Hotel in downtown Los Angeles. An entire floor had been secured for their motley crew. The old hotel had been a favorite of movie stars back in the Golden Era of Hollywood when it was considered out-of-the-way. Now it was right in the middle of a rather seedy area of urban L.A. Ginger was expecting maybe the Hilton or the Biltmore or the Mayflower. The Crawford didn't even show up on AAA's list of third-rate hotels. Not that it was ill kept or was frequented by those who rented by the hour; it was just well past its prime.

But the old gal had class. The lobby was right out of *Grand Hotel*, the 1932 movie, not to be confused with the Arthur Hailey book/movie, *Hotel*, which came along in 1967. This was a dame from a different era. The Crawford just reeked of mystery and had ambience up the wazoo. The place even smelled of venerable cigar smoke and since nobody was allowed to light up anymore, the scent had to be embedded in its very foundation. It was magnificent.

The lobby's dark interior was all wood paneling and ancient wallpaper that looked tea-dyed. There were soft, cushiony sofas and club chairs tucked into quiet corners for secret rendezvous. The front desk was a long expanse of polished walnut that reached halfway across the fairly large room, with crystal chandeliers illuminating the area instead of a phalanx of fluorescent tubing. In the center of the main reception area was a massive marble-topped table sprouting a gigantic arrangement of hydrangeas. The flowers were dried, but they were still gorgeous.

The hotel covered a fair amount of downtown real estate. It was only eight stories high, but it consumed the entire block upon which it rested. A gallery of stores fronted the street side, but they weren't going to give the Miracle Mile a run for its money. One lone gift shop could be accessed from the hotel's lobby, but it only sold cheap Los Angeles memorabilia, made in China.

There was a restaurant on the ground level, but as jurors, they would be dining in a private room on another floor. The hotel offered room service, but that would be on each juror's own nickel.

They were divided into bunches and took the elevator to the top floor. Since jurors are seldom put up in hotels, elaborate preparations hadn't been made for their security, but there were cops everywhere on the ground floor so Ginger didn't worry about it.

Their floor was laid out in a U shape. There weren't any surveillance cameras in the hallways, just guards placed at the stairwell door across from the two elevators, but those accesses were on the same side of the U. As it turned out, the room Ginger shared with Janice Rose was on the opposite side.

An officer rode up with Dallas Long, Ginger, Janice Rose Pierce, Willie Robinson, John Dunbar—who was still entertaining the group—and two other females who chatted continually to each other. They all stepped off the elevator and started walking down the hall. The cop got back in the elevator to get another bunch. The jurors were left on their own except for another guard manning the floor. Their luggage had already been deposited in their rooms and they had been given their room numbers.

Willie had been grumbling all through dinner. Nothing seemed to please him. He was still griping about the free dinner they had just eaten even though he had more than his fair share of the pot stickers and Kung Pao chicken.

"We're supposed to get room service, aren't we?" he asked.

"Yeah. But you have to pay for it," said Dunbar.

"What? Why do I have to pay for anything? Aren't they supposed to feed us?"

"We just had dinner, for goodness sake," said Janice Rose.

"That wasn't much. I need a couple a burgers and fries."

"You shoulda got that at the restaurant," said Dunbar.

"They had nothin' but tofu burgers. I need real food."

"Whataya expect from the city? Ya get whatcha get," said Dunbar.

"I expected more than this broken-down hotel. There's a TV in the room, isn't there?"

Dunbar said, "They have rent-a-movies, but you can't watch regular stuff. 'Fraid we'll get brainwashed by all the publicity."

"I just wanna watch *Star Trek*," said Willie.

"Have somebody tape it for you," said Janice Rose. "My hubby's taping my soaps."

"Aw, shit," groused Willie. "How are we supposed to live without TV and food?"

"To tell you the truth, I am a little hungry," said Janice Rose. "Ginger, you order us girls something, on me. That'll give Harold something else to complain about when I get home. And if you don't mind, I'm going to be the first into that bathtub for a good soak. This has been a very long day."

"Be my guest. I could really use a cup of coffee," said Ginger. "When do they shut off room service?"

"I don't remember what the brochure said." Janice Rose looked at her watch. "It's still early. We should be able to get coffee and a piece of pie."

They said their good nights. Dallas walked ahead of the group. His room was at the end of the hall on the same side Ginger and Janice Rose were on. Willie and John Dunbar shared the room in between. Dallas gave a little wave before shutting his door, while Willie moaned to Dunbar about getting more food. As for ol' John, he was finally running out of steam.

Willie's carping got lost in the sound-dampening thickness of the carpet and the sheer size of the hallway. It was enormous. You could throw a reception in there with a marimba band. That's the great thing about big, old hotels: lots of space.

Janice Rose and Ginger went into their room. It wasn't

exactly luxurious, but it was spacious and full of early twentieth century furniture that had seen better days though it still had that touch of class. The flowers on the well-worn carpet had faded to khaki, but even the floor covering had an aura, or maybe it was just seventy-five years of vacuuming and spilled late-night martinis.

There was a vintage vanity table near the bathroom similar to the one Ginger's grandmother had, with the round beveled glass mirror and the small tufted, backless chair tucked under the glass-topped table. She could almost smell her gram's perfume and see her beige powder puff sitting in its gold case along with the silver-plated comb, brush, and mirror set. Even the burled walnut beds with the faded chenille bedspreads were from that bygone era. They must have traveled there through a time warp.

Janice Rose turned on a small bedside light while Ginger switched on a standing lamp that stood between two massive chairs. She rubbed her hand over the dark green fabric. It was that scratchy horsehair material that used to make the back of her bare legs itch when she visited her grandparents in the summer. There were antimacassars on the chairs' heavily rolled arms and a gold-veined mirror hanging on the wall. This wasn't a hotel. It was a museum.

Their respective luggage had been placed beside both beds so their territory had already been decided. Ginger opened her train case and pulled out shampoo.

"Are you going to wash your hair?" Janice Rose asked.

"Yes."

"You shower first. That'll give you time to dry it while I soak."

"Thanks. It won't take me long."

Janice Rose pulled out her nightgown, robe, slippers, and a romance novel with Fabio in full throbbing color on the cover. She sat on the edge of her bed and fumbled through her purse for a pair of glasses, then flipped to the page of the book she had been reading while Ginger slipped on a pair of hot pink feather mules Fred had packed for her. Bless his heart, he had bought them for their second anniversary, but she never wore them. They were a size too small and three decades too daring.

Ginger went into the bathroom. After removing her makeup and setting out the shampoo, conditioner and some lavender body oil that had been left in her travel case from a previous trip, she started running the shower. Sixty seconds later the phone rang in the room, but Ginger couldn't make out anything being said.

Janice Rose knocked on the bathroom door. "They're sending up free pizza!" she said.

"What?" Ginger yelled from the shower.

Janice Rose opened the door a crack and tried again. "They're sending up free pizza. I'll save you a slice."

Ginger finished her shower, towel dried her hair, and picked up the blow dryer. She would finish her hair at the vanity table. Opening the door, she noticed the main room was dark. The floor lamp had been turned off and the light on the stand between the beds was off. She hesitated at the door and listened for sounds. Nothing.

"Janice Rose? Did you fall asleep? Aren't you going to take your long soak?"

Could she have eaten the whole pizza herself and fallen asleep, done in by the pepperoni? But Ginger couldn't smell pizza. She turned on the lamp between the beds. Janice Rose wasn't asleep. She was lying across her bed, bruise marks on her neck, her face blue-white.

Ginger's was close to the same color, the blood having drained from her own face. She picked up the phone, her hand shaking. She knew the line went directly to the police officer on duty in the lobby. She told him in as calm a voice as she could manage what happened.

Everybody was rousted from his or her room. They assembled in the hallway at the bottom of the U, clustered into small groups, talking nervously to one another. After what seemed like forever, Janice Rose's body was wheeled out on a gurney. Ginger had been standing with Dallas Long until Willie Robinson and John Dunbar joined them. Ginger noticed that for once Dunbar was absolutely silent.

Several high-ranking police officials were going over the room with that fine-tooth comb along with the city official in charge of the jurors at the hotel, Mavis Price-Jones.

Mavis was forty-something with straight black hair pulled into a tight bun. She wore black clothes and had a pair of black half-glasses perched on her pointed nose. The whole package screamed efficiency. She led the two police officers out of the murder room and marched up to Ginger.

For a second Ginger thought she was to be placed under arrest. Nobody was smiling—not that they should—but they looked so intense.

Mavis spoke first. "Mrs. Caulfield, we will find you another room. We may have to put a cot in one of the other ladies' rooms, but we will get you accommodations."

"Mr. Long has invited me to move in with him."

Mavis's eyebrows shot up into her hairline. She looked at Dallas standing there in a pair of jeans and half-buttoned shirt and shook her head. "No, no, no, no, Mrs. Caulfield. That would be totally unacceptable. We'll—"

"It's acceptable to me—and to Mr. Long. I prefer to feel safe and Mr. Long will provide me with that sense of security."

"But Mrs. Caulfield," said Mavis. "We can assure you this was an isolated incident. Unfortunately, petty thieves prowl hotels and—"

"First, you can't assure me of anything. Second, petty thieves don't kill, or they wouldn't be considered petty. Third, I'm moving in with him. Fourth, I need my husband to bring me some things from home. I'd like permission to call him tonight."

"That would be quite impossible, Mrs. Caulfield."

"I need some feminine protection, Ms. Price-Jones. It

is *quite* necessary. This incident has totally thrown off my cycle and I need my special medication."

The police captain and the other cop exchanged glances. They wouldn't touch that subject with a ten-foot pole. Mavis gave in.

"As soon as these gentlemen are through, I'll go with you to Mr. Long's room and make arrangements for you to call your husband."

"Thank you."

The police captain had some questions for Ginger.

"Did you hear anything out of the ordinary, Mrs. Caulfield?"

"I heard the phone ring after I turned on the shower. Janice Rose knocked on the bathroom door and said something to me. I asked her, What? She said the hotel was sending up free pizza and she said she would save me a slice. I finished washing my hair and then went into the room. The lights were out—and I didn't smell pizza. I turned on the light and saw her. I called downstairs."

"Did you touch the body?" asked the captain.

"No."

Mavis spoke up. "You didn't try to help her?" She was aghast.

"She was blue. That was well past any CPR training I know."

The police captain continued. "Her purse seems to be missing. When was the last time you saw her with it?"

"She had it on the bed when she pulled out her reading glasses. She was going to finish a book—" Ginger got a little choked up. "What a horrible thing." Dallas put his arm around her shoulder and watched Mavis raise those eyebrows once more into her hairline.

The police captain moved on to another juror. He spoke to John Dunbar. "And you heard nothing, Mr. Dunbar?"

"No. I didn't hear a damn thing. How could this happen? What the hell are we paying you people for?"

The captain had the patience of Job. "Mr. Dunbar, let me reassure you, we are doing everything we can. A couple other rooms were broken into on another floor. The occupants were out so no one else was hurt, but it looks like we have a thief working the hotel. Now, if you would please help us out here. Did you hear anything out of the ordinary?"

"Like I said," he growled, "Robinson and I were still awake, but the television was on. How the hell were we supposed to hear anything?"

Willie added, "Our room is next door to theirs." He pointed to Ginger. "I heard their water running. I remember that. You couldn't hear anything else over the water."

"Did anybody here get a phone call about free pizza?" asked the cop.

"We didn't," said Willie.

Dallas shook his head.

"I know this is very upsetting for all of you," said the cop. "We're putting two more guards in the hallway and more officers will be positioned around the hotel for the rest of your stay. You people go back to your rooms and try to get some sleep. The district attorney has been advised of the incident. Judge Cherry is also being contacted. But right now, we have no idea if the trial will be postponed. We'll know more tomorrow."

Ginger headed for Dallas's room to make her call to Fred. Mavis was right on her heels. Willie wandered nervously around the hall checking out who would be guarding them while Dallas waited patiently outside his room while Ginger used the phone.

John Dunbar patted his roommate on the back when Willie finally came to a stop outside their door. "Come on, buddy. Let's get some sleep. We oughtta be perfectly safe tonight."

Ginger was allowed to make the call to her husband, but Mavis listened to every word. Ginger knew someone else was monitoring the call besides Ms. Efficiency. She heard the click-click-click of a tape recorder being turned on somewhere downstairs.

Fred came on the line. "Fred, this is Ginger. Would you mind terribly bringing me a package of my women's things for that time of the month? Be sure to bring the super-maxi kind I keep in the niche on my side of the bed. And the little six-pack of that prescription Midol. You can use my old attaché case to carry them. I don't want you to be embarrassed, honey."

Fred was sitting on his side of the bed listening to his wife's request. He leaned back and lifted the small door in the headboard. Sitting on a purple cloth was her Smith & Wesson revolver and a speed loader with six more bullets.

"Do you really need them, honey?"

"Yes, Fred. You know how I get during this time of the month? The PMS could just kill me. I'll be downstairs to pick it up. Thank you, sweetie. Oh, bring my other slippers. See you soon."

Ginger's hair had dried into a slight frizz. She needed to re-wet and blow-dry it again, but that could wait until morning. She rode the elevator down to the lobby with the ever-present Mavis. Twenty minutes later Fred walked in with Ginger's old attaché case. It was a great ponderous thing, not the trim-line ones that have become the fashion. A police officer started toward Fred, but Ginger got there first, grabbing the case and opening it for the officer. Several brands of sanitary napkins were inside along with a pair of leather-soled slippers. Each package of feminine hygiene products was open and the tops of individual napkins could be seen. Ginger started pulling them out, one by one, and she could tell the officer was more than reluctant to go through the contents on his own. He waved an approving hand over the case and she quickly closed the lid. Ginger blew a kiss to Fred as he left.

"Thank you, Fred. You're a lifesaver."

"Take care, honey. You take care," said her wonderful

husband.

Mavis eyed Ginger as they rode up to the top floor in silence. Ginger knew Mavis wanted to get her hands on the attaché case, but there was no way that was going to happen. The warden stood at the bottom of the U and watched as Ginger entered the room where Dallas was waiting with the door open. He gave a little salute to old Mavis and they could feel a frosty breeze waft toward them.

Ginger's belongings were piled onto a small bed wedged into somewhat smaller accommodations than those she had shared with Janice Rose. She sat on the foot of the bed with the attaché case across her lap and heaved a sigh. Dallas was going through his own suitcase.

"What were you? Force Recon?" she asked, having heard of the enigmatic group.

"Nothing's secret, is it?" he said by way of response.

"That's why you could take on those punks in the parking garage."

"Self-preservation is a great teacher."

"Yeah. And you know something else? I'm not buying the hotel robbery theory. I think they wanted me instead of Janice Rose."

"You're probably right. It takes a pretty smart petty thief to pick a room with two defenseless women in it."

"This one's not defenseless anymore," she said.

Ginger turned toward him. Her .38 was sitting on top of the attaché case.

He didn't bat an eye. "Neither is her roommate," he said, placing his nickel-plated .45 automatic on his lap.

"Yours is bigger than mine," she said, grinning. "How did you get that in here?" she asked.

"Professional secret. This suitcase has many secrets."

"You're James Bond, aren't you?"

"No. I'm just a Texan."

"So is my husband. That explains a lot." She smiled at him.

Meanwhile, District Attorney Frank Fallen and his staff were assembling in his office for an emergency meeting. Frank was in a suit, having just come from a late dinner with friends. Johnnie was in a silk jogging suit. Matt came in late wearing jeans and a T-shirt. Bill James was already seated behind Frank's desk, the phone pressed to his ear.

"It looks like a burglary that got out of hand," said Frank. "The police found stolen items from some other guests in a vacant room a few floors below the jurors. Chief Trotter says it was strangulation. A professional killer would more likely have used a knife or garrote. Whoever it was must have been surprised to find someone awake in the room and killed Mrs. Pierce."

"How could the guard miss seeing a stranger on the floor?" asked Johnnie.

"He was helping two women in another room rearrange their beds and wasn't at his post."

"What will the judge say?" asked Matt.

Bill James had the answer. He hung up the phone and said, "She'll allow the case to continue if the jurors don't have a problem with it. We'll know more tomorrow morning."

CHAPTER 24

The night passed with no more excitement. Dallas got up early, showered and shaved, leaving the bathroom free for Ginger. He stepped into the hallway while she washed up and dressed.

Jurors were allowed room service for breakfast. Ginger had eggs Benedict. Dallas ordered a double plate of sausage and eggs over easy. They were then driven to the Criminal Courts Building in the paddy wagon. Court was convened and Judge Cherry spoke to the courtroom about the incident the night before.

"You are all aware of the tragic death of Janice Rose Pierce. The police discovered evidence that burglars were operating in the hotel. Mrs. Pierce's handbag was among several other stolen items found in an empty hotel room. All rooms were searched and there were no signs of the burglars. My staff has interviewed the jurors and the alternates to see if any are too disturbed by the incident last night to continue. One of the alternates voiced concern and she has been dismissed.

"We will now poll the remaining eleven jurors and the alternates to verify that they are able to continue with the trial. Will you please signify by a 'yes' or 'no' to the following: Are you comfortable enough to remain on the jury, and are you still able to render a fair and impartial verdict in the case before you?"

The vote was unanimously "yes." The replacement juror for Janice Rose was selected.

"With that, Counselor, you may proceed."

Johnnie stood up. "Thank you, Your Honor. The District Attorney's Office wishes to commend the jurors for their decision. I would now like to call Lolita Spring to the stand."

The first witness of the day was named Lolita Spring. No kidding. She was a pitiful soul. Tall, lanky, more sinewy than svelte, dressed in clothes far exceeding her occupation, which would be classified as "sidewalk hostess." The prosecution supplied her tailored outfit to give her some sense of credibility, but they couldn't convince her to do anything with hair that had seen too many bottles of peroxide. On her thin wrist she wore a charm bracelet covered with tinny-sounding little trinkets. Every time she spoke she flapped her arms, making a sound reminiscent of an East Indian temple.

"Where are you employed, Ms. Spring?" asked Johnnie.

"I don't have a regular . . . you know . . . job—like work anyplace, uh, regular."

"Ms. Spring, have you ever been arrested?"

"Uh—yes."

"For what?"

"Soliciting."

"What does that mean, Ms. Spring?"

"Huh?"

"What is soliciting?" asked the attorney.

"You want to know what soliciting is?" Lolita smiled, assuming it was a trick question.

"Yes. What is soliciting?"

Lolita blushed. A quaint touch for someone in her profession. "It's . . . prostitution."

"You're a prostitute?"

"Yeah," she said, as though Ms. Greer was some kind of simpleton.

"Now, where is it you work?"

"Oh, okay, okay. I get it. I work the street."

Lolita was a self-propelled marionette. Every time her hand flailed, her mouth opened and words spilled out.

"Are you on the street every night, Ms. Spring?" asked the

counselor.

"Yeah. I hardly never take a night off. I work hard!"

"Were you on Lincoln Boulevard the night of July eleventh?"

"The night of the murder?"

"The night of the murders. Yes."

"Yeah."

"Did you see the defendant that night?"

"The what?"

"Did you see Desmond Williams the night of the murder of Marcella Williams and Adrian Wells?"

"Oh, yeah. I seen him."

"Would you explain to the court what Mr. Williams was doing that night?"

"He was drivin' around in his big, fancy Volvo. Dark green."

"Are you sure the man you saw was the defendant, Desmond Williams? Take a good look."

Lolita half stood in the witness stand and stared at Williams. She stared for the longest time and then sat down. She thought about it for a while, and then answered, "Yeah. That's the bum."

"No more questions."

Johnnie Greer sat down and Malvin Shepherd got Lolita in his sights.

"Ms. Spring, is Lolita Spring your real name?"

"No. I kinda took the name sorta like a movie star does when I turned pro."

"Have you legally adopted your name?"

"Legally what?"

"Legally adopted," he reiterated. "Have you gone to court to have your name legally changed to Lolita Spring?"

"I spend enough time in court. Why would I want to spend more?"

Laughter filled the room.

"What is your legal name, Ms. Spring?"

"You mean the name I was born with?"

"Yes."

"My momma named me Candy. Candy Tufts. Now *that* sounds like a hooker." More laughter. "I thought Lolita sounded higher class. Didn't they make a movie outta that name?"

"Yes. Thank you, Ms. Spring. Now, Ms. Spring, do you know what perjury is?"

"Huh?"

"Perjury," explained the defense attorney. "The willful giving of false testimony under oath." That went sailing over Lolita's bleached-blond head. "Lying. Do you know it's against the law to tell a lie when you have sworn in court not to? Do you know you could go to jail for a very long time if you are lying to this judge and to these good people?" He pointed to the jury.

"Yeah. I guess so."

"Ms. Spring, do you know it is probably the most serious thing you could do, to lie to this court?"

"But—I'm not—I'm not—" She slouched in the witness chair like a little kid caught with her hand in the proverbial cookie jar.

"Ms. Spring, are you lying about seeing Desmond Williams on Lincoln Boulevard the night of July eleventh? Ms. Spring?"

" . . . Yes."

The courtroom exploded. Matt and Johnnie looked at each other as if somebody just caught them on the carpet in her office. Matt tried to get to his feet in protest, but Johnnie pulled him back into his seat. They couldn't believe Lolita had this sudden epiphany. Johnnie wondered how Malvin Shepherd got to the witness. And she was waiting for the other shoe to drop. But she had no idea the size of that particular shoe.

As for Malvin Shepherd, he couldn't contain the smirk on his face as he walked back to his chair. He didn't sit down.

He just looked at the prosecution and narrowed his eyes, still smirking. Judge Cherry was banging her gavel until the courtroom came to order.

Shepherd was reveling in his mischief making. When the courtroom quieted, he continued. "Ms. Spring, why did you say you saw Mr. Williams that night? Were you honestly mistaken? Did you think you saw someone who resembled Mr. Williams? Did you want the media attention? Why, Ms. Spring, did you perjure yourself? Why did you lie?"

"I—I didn't want to. It's not my fault. I was minding my own business. They picked me up. The cops. Just because I work that street."

"Are you saying the police picked you up on a prostitution charge?"

"No. They weren't gonna charge me with nothin'. They told me I had to talk to this guy who would give me something to say I saw Desmond Williams."

"Ms. Spring, are you saying someone *paid* you to testify that you saw Desmond Williams that night?"

"He sure as hell did."

That got rave reviews from the assembled crowd. Judge Cherry banged her gavel again. Johnnie Greer sat back in her chair, crossed her arms, and waited for the scene to play out.

"Ms. Spring, do you know who the man was?" asked Shepherd.

"No. We weren't into names. But he told me where he worked."

"And where did he say he worked, Ms. Spring?"

"He said he worked for the D.A.'s office."

The courtroom erupted like Mount St. Helens. Matt looked over at Johnnie, but she was staring at the witness, watching to see if Lolita was getting hand signals from anyone in the room. Johnnie knew the woman was bought and paid for by Malvin Shepherd, but it would be hard to prove and even harder to put that genie back in the bottle.

It took a few minutes for the courtroom to quiet. Johnnie

scribbled a note to Matt that read, *"When did Lolita contact the police? When was the last time she was picked up for soliciting?"* Matt hurriedly left the courtroom. The judge made an executive decision and dismissed the jury for a long lunch so everybody could regroup.

While the jury was filing out, Shepherd was pacing back and forth at his table like a prizefighter itching to land the knockout punch. He did a little dance by his chair as he waited for the courtroom to clear. As for Johnnie, she couldn't keep her eyes off him. He noticed her stare and was going to ignore it, but he saw the corners of her mouth curve upward and he felt flattered. He sauntered over to her table and leaned close to her ear and whispered.

"Sorry, but this is the way the big boys play."

Johnnie turned her face slowly upward and looked in his eyes. Then in a tone that came from deep within her, she said, "Watch it, white boy. You fuck up and that nigger's gonna rip off yo' head."

She looked over at Williams, who was sitting at the edge of his seat, trying to overhear the counselors' conversation. He didn't care for Shepherd cozying up to the prosecution. Johnnie grabbed hold of Shepherd's sleeve and pulled him down closer.

Then she whispered seductively in his ear, "What do you value most, Malvin?"

Shepherd pulled away and stood up. He tried laughing it off as if the whole incident was a huge joke, but he was starting to sweat.

"Clever girl, Ms. Greer. Very clever. If you ever want a real job, give me a ring."

Shepherd backed toward his chair, trying to find the grin that had been bitch-slapped off his face. He sat down and did a little damage control with his client.

CHAPTER 25

The jury was anxious to get started when Judge Cherry entered the courtroom after lunch. The lovely Lolita resumed the stand and Johnnie was preparing for redirect. Matt had already returned with the answer as to when the inimitable Lolita had availed herself for questioning.

"That was forty-eight hours after Malvin Shepherd blew into town," she said to Matt when she saw the date. "He doesn't miss a trick. And the last time she was arrested was in January. She was ready for the picking."

"Ms. Greer, your witness," said the judge.

Standing, Johnnie asked, "Ms. Spring, did this man who said he worked for the district attorney take you to his office?"

"No. The cops that picked me up drove me 'round awhile, then we stopped behind this restaurant on Venice Boulevard where this guy was. He got in the back and told me he would put me in jail for ten years unless I said I saw Desmond Williams that night. Then he handed me five hun'erd dollars and told me I better play ball or else."

"Ms. Spring, why did you decide to tell us your rather interesting story now after you had already told us an entirely different version?"

"Well, the man from the D.A.'s office—"

"The *alleged* man," corrected the prosecutor.

"The what?"

"Ms. Spring, there is absolutely no proof that the man to whom you spoke was actually with the District Attorney's Office."

Little Lolita was off in La-La Land. Her mind had obviously taken a detour. "Ain't that cute the way you say 'to whom.' Sorta fancy-like. But—but that's what he said."

"Ms. Spring, the man could have said he was from Mars."

Lolita had to think about that. "He didn't look like he was from Mars. He looked like a lawyer."

That got laughs from the crowd. Johnnie wondered who was writing her material.

"I'll rephrase my original question," said Johnnie. "Why didn't you tell us about your conversation with this man when he threatened you? Why did you wait until now?"

"Well, that's easy. The guy in the car said I'd do hard time if I didn't tell his story and that guy—" she indicated Malvin Shepherd, "said I'd do hard time if I lied. And that guy—" she pointed to Malvin again, her charm bracelet jingling, "looks like he could do somethin' about it."

"What did this man look like, Ms. Spring?"

Lolita pondered the question. For her it was work. "He was taller than me. Maybe this much." She raised her thin arm a foot above her head. "Big. Probably works out. He kinda filled out his suit and it was a cool suit. Sharp like a lawyer, not a salesman. I kinda know how guys dress in my business."

The courtroom chuckled.

"What color hair did he have? Did he have any distinguishing marks?"

"His hair? Dark, but I saw him at night. I don't know for sure. What was the other question?"

"Did he have any distinguishing marks? Scars, tattoos?"

"How could I tell? He was wearing his clothes."

Lolita was turning into a regular stand-up comedienne.

Johnnie clarified her point. "Did he have any marks on his face?"

"Oh." Lolita thought about it. "I can't remember none. But it was dark in the car."

"They didn't turn on the overhead light when you were talking to this man?"

"No. But I remember somethin'. I caught my charm bracelet on the seat cover and lost one of my charms. I asked the cop to turn on the light so I could look for it, but he said the light was busted."

"Are you sure it was an actual police car?"

"Oh, yeah. I been in a few. They kinda have a smell."

Johnnie was getting frustrated. Lolita was sounding too credible. "The two officers who picked you up, did you recognize them? Had they picked you up before?"

"You know, that's funny. I thought I knew all the boys workin' that district, but these guys were new."

"What did they look like?" asked the counselor.

"The one driving, he never got out of the car. I only saw him from the back when I got in. He was a big guy built like a wrestler or somethin'. But I never seen his face real good."

"Was the man white?"

"Yeah."

"And the other man, describe him."

"He was tall and skinny."

"What else?"

"What else?" asked Lolita.

"We'll need a little more description, Ms. Spring."

"Okay. This guy, he came up to me on the sidewalk and had like this real gritty voice and he had like this attitude. But I get that from cops all the time."

"No, I mean, what was this man's race?"

"His race?" Lolita's eyes darted around the room. She started scratching her ear. "Well, I don't like to talk color . . . Like, I go out with all kinds of johns—I mean, men." She was finding it hard to say what color the guy was. "It don't matter to me none."

Johnnie didn't know what to make of this kooky woman. "Ms. Spring, in conventional terms, the man was tall and—?"

"He was tall as the ace of spades," she declared.

People were rolling in the aisles after that remark. Johnnie waited for the laugh track to subside or for Judge

Cherry to gavel everyone to silence, but Lolita was just too funny. Johnnie leaned against the podium until the room quieted.

That was about it for Lolita. She was dismissed. Johnnie was hoping she would walk over to Malvin Shepherd and ask if she did okay. She didn't. Judge Cherry consulted her calendar and watch and made a few notes.

"We will adjourn for the day. Be back at eight-thirty tomorrow morning. Have a good evening."

"All rise," said the bailiff.

The judge left the courtroom, the visitor section was cleared out first, the cameras were turned off, and then the jury was escorted out. They walked between the defense and prosecution tables while Desmond Williams was being taken out a side door. Only Malvin Shepherd with his people and Johnnie Greer and Matthew Simms remained in the courtroom.

Johnnie was still stuffing legal pads into her briefcase when she saw a tiny folded piece of paper in the corner of her case. She looked around to see who might have left it and if anyone was watching her, but Ginger had already filed out the front door. Johnnie picked up the paper, unfolded it, and read the note. She nudged Matt and he read it, then he nodded. They hurriedly gathered their stuff and left the courtroom.

Malvin Shepherd was picking up some of his papers from the podium and called over Curtis Lee.

"Take Vince with you and get over to the movie set in San Pedro. Go through every one of those damned police cars and find that bimbo's charm. If you can't find it, burn 'em all. I don't want that to come back and bite us."

"Yes, Mr. Shepherd."

On the street outside the Criminal Courts Building a lone television news van was still parked at the curb. The other news organizations had packed up and headed back to the barn. Since modern-day news footage is uploaded to satellites and downloaded to the various TV studios and newspapers and magazines worldwide, nobody had to rush film to the lab anymore, but the crews did want to get to their respective home bases for their next assignment or to clock out, grab a bite to eat, and tell everybody they knew what went on in court that day.

One of the men in the van still had his ear glued to his earphones. His companion was chomping at the bit to leave. He had plans for the evening and wanted to get the show on the road. He had no idea what his buddy was doing, but whatever it was, it had grabbed his friend's full attention. Then he noticed the LED panel on the console was lit up.

"Is that mike still—?"

"Shhh." The man continued listening until the conversation was over, then he exhaled loudly.

"What is it?" asked his friend.

"I'll tell you on the way."

They cranked up the news van and headed toward the freeway.

Two and a half hours later . . .

The *John Law II* movie site had been shut down and the location was all but deserted since Desmond Williams' indictment. Desmond's trailer was sealed with crime tape, the equipment sheds were empty, and the chain-link fence surrounding the area was padlocked. Off to one side a light was flickering. With their headlights off, the two guys in the news van had moved their vehicle in closer and parked along the fence in gathering shadows. They were on a side street that ran perpendicular to the main road that curved down to the docks. Their handheld camera was focused on three decommissioned police cars . . . fully engulfed.

Twenty minutes later several police cars, in-service ones this time, came racing to the site, lights flashing. Screeching to a halt at the curb, people piled out like clowns from a circus car. With the men in blue were Johnnie Greer and Matt Simms. They walked to the fence and watched the inferno.

Matt's face was glowing in the light of the flames. "How'd they do it so fast?"

"They didn't have to wait for a goddamned search warrant!" Johnnie said, holding a piece of paper in her hand. "Let's see if there's anything left."

While that was happening, Frank Fallen was trying to put out another fire.

"That wasn't exactly the bombshell I meant, Mark," said the D.A. to Mark Parsons with Channel 10 *News & Entertainment* in the parking garage of the Criminal Courts Building. "I was watching it in my office upstairs when that Lolita character dropped the first one. I swear to God I thought she was kidding. She was starting to sound like a night at the Improv."

"You said you thought the case was too good to be true," said Mark. "But I didn't think you'd put a goofball like that on the stand."

"Believe me, Mark, we had no idea that testimony was coming."

"Do you think Malvin Shepherd put her up to it?"

"That's what I want to find out."

"My contact won't tell me," said Mark. "His leaks to the media only help Desmond Williams."

"His leaks help Malvin Shepherd, but we won't split hairs," said the D.A.

"He still won't tell me anything that will hang Shepherd. What are you going to do now?"

"First, Ms. Spring is going to sit her bony rear end down in front of pictures of every cop in Southern California and see if she can spot at least one of those men."

"You don't really think they were cops, do you?"

"No. But if she says she can't ID anybody, the public

might believe her."

"Funny, isn't it?" said Mark. "They'd believe a bimbo like Lolita, but not a cop like Larry Patrick."

"We're the guys you love to hate, Mark. You lick your chops when one of ours goes to the slammer. Cops put their lives on the line, they die in the line of duty, but you guys just love to nail us."

"It pays the bills, Mr. Fallen."

Frank laughed. "But you go wall-to-wall without commercials when one of these circuses comes to town. How does your CFO explain that to the shareholders?"

"To tell you the truth, Mr. Fallen, I've heard some of the news anchors say they thought the newsroom should have an open budget."

"God help us. I wish you guys would go back to doing a single hour-long news show like they had when I was growing up."

Stunned, Mark said, "An hour? How'd they do it?"

"They told the truth, the whole truth . . . You know the rest."

"There's no money in that, Mr. Fallen."

"Lawyers do it for the money, Mark. For the media, it's strictly politics."

"Speaking of politics, how's your campaign going?"

"Depends who you ask. The networks want to bury me with the Williams case."

"The media's not on the jury."

"Do they have to be?" asked Frank.

"The jurors are sequestered, Mr. Fallen. All that spin falls on deaf ears," said Mark.

"What about the next time? It just gets easier. More TV coverage. More spin. More guilty people walking the streets. See if you can get your guy to give up something on Shepherd."

"I can't lean on him, Mr. Fallen."

"Why not? Don't you want the truth? Or are you satisfied with spin?" Frank looked the young man in the eye.

"Can you give me something?" asked Mark, hoping for a little quid pro quo.

Frank thought about it. "If I can't get a conviction, I'll quit. You can quote me."

"All or nothing. Your competition will be rooting for Williams."

Frank walked toward his car. "They'll be backing a murderer, Mark. Can the media live with that?"

The D.A. got in his Lexus and drove off, leaving Mark alone. As he walked away, the reporter said to himself, "Yes, Mr. Fallen. They can live with that." Mark cut between several vehicles and made his way to his own car parked on a lower level.

For a few moments the garage was silent, then footsteps shuffled across the concrete floor. Curtis Lee stepped from behind a midsize van and lowered the camcorder he had balanced on his shoulder. He walked two rows away to his rented car. As he leaned down to open the door, he felt a presence behind him. He straightened and started to turn. He saw the fist coming toward him, but not much else. The second and third punch knocked him to the floor and turned out his lights.

The burly man who decked Curtis retrieved the camcorder and disappeared into the shadows as the sound of voices and feet came closer. He made it to the parking level one flight below and handed the damaged piece of equipment to Bill James. Bill didn't say a word. He tossed the camcorder onto the passenger seat, got into his vehicle, and drove away.

CHAPTER 26

Back at the hotel, Ginger was sitting on her bed looking at photographs. They had finished dinner in the hotel's private dining room, but it was too early to turn in, so she was still dressed in her black slacks and a red turtleneck sweater. She had taken off the black and gray windowpane jacket. Dallas was in a pair of dark slacks and lightweight crewneck sweater. He had been reading a book, but stopped and was watching her.

"What are you looking at?" he asked.

"You remember I told you about the guy who was taking pictures of the jury? The guard who took away his camera had the film developed. He's our hall monitor."

"I saw you talking with him earlier."

"He gave me a set of prints. For some reason he wanted me to have them."

"He wanted to talk with a good-looking woman," said Dallas.

"Thank you," she blushed. "At first they were just pictures, but then I started looking at them. Here. Tell me what you see."

Ginger handed him some of the photos.

"They aren't very good. No photojournalist took these," said Dallas.

"Too much negative space," she said. She could tell he didn't understand what that meant. "I had an art teacher once who critiqued a picture of mine. I had crammed the drawing way over on one side of the paper and she circled the blank area and wrote 'too much negative space.'"

"Well, this guy doesn't have anything going for him. But he sure had his favorites. There are a bunch of pictures of Jesus and Willie and a couple of guys who didn't make the final cut."

"I'll give this one to Jesus. He'll get a kick out of it." Ginger studied the photograph a little longer and noticed something. "What's wrong with this picture?"

Dallas took it to the desk and examined it under the light.

"You know, that doesn't look like Jesus. Something about the hair. Jesus has more hair than this guy."

"Maybe one isn't Jesus," Ginger suggested.

"Let's pay our friend a late-night call," said Dallas. "I'll bring a few party favors."

He lifted his suitcase onto his bed and rotated the twin locks until they were perpendicular to the floor. A narrow panel separated at the leather binding. It was a little over an inch deep and was fitted with a good thirty pockets that housed all kinds of interesting things. Ginger recognized the surreptitious entry kit. Dallas had a magnificent set with some twenty different lock picks and keys. There were flashlights, scopes, and several types of knives. Some of the gadgets she had never seen before.

"How do you get through metal detectors?" she asked.

He didn't answer.

Her elusive friend pocketed a large multitool and a regular pocketknife. He handed Ginger a smaller version.

"I have a Swiss Army knife," she said, holding it up.

"Good for you. Take this one instead."

Dallas handed her a Kershaw titanium knife with a three-inch blade. It had a little knob that allowed you to open the blade quite fast in one hand with just your thumb.

"So you won't break your fingernails trying to open it," he said by way of explanation. "It'll take you a week to open that Swiss smorgasbord. Too many doohickeys."

He was right. She usually needed a screwdriver to pry

out the main blade. The scissors and the toothpick were easy, but she could never get to the blades without help.

Dallas reached for one more piece of equipment. So did Ginger. They tucked their guns into their belts, put on their jackets, and walked out the door.

The center core of the U-shaped hallway housed the two elevators, plus five small rooms, three on Ginger's side of the U and two on the elevator side. Around the outer section were eleven larger accommodations and the stairwell. Her old room had been in the middle of the left wing. John Dunbar and Willie Robinson were next to her, and Dallas occupied the room at the end of the hallway. Jesus was across the hall in the center core. One guard was at the turn in the U on their side, two guards were stationed at the other turn between the elevators and stairwell, and the fourth guard was at the far end of the right wing.

Ginger expected to see their friendly guard sitting in his chair reading a book. The chair was empty.

"He must be taking a break," said Dallas.

They walked across the hall. There were no rules saying jurors couldn't chat among themselves, as long as they didn't discuss the case.

"Block the view for a second," said Dallas.

He didn't want everybody to know they were making an unannounced visit. Ginger placed herself between Dallas and anyone who might walk into the hall. Dallas used his lock-picking tools to work the mechanism. Ginger thought she would have to mug for a minute or two while he maneuvered the lock. He was tapping her on the shoulder twenty seconds later with the door standing ajar.

They could hear the shower running as they entered Jesus' room.

"I'll do this part alone," said Dallas.

He walked to the bathroom and stepped inside. Ginger took the gun from her belt and held it by her side. She could hear a muffled cry and struggling before Dallas dragged

Jesus out of the steamy room. Jesus had a towel clutched around his waist and a shower cap on his head. His eyes were wide with panic, but he couldn't scream with the soggy washcloth stuck in his mouth. Dallas pushed him onto the bed and tossed him one of the pictures.

"Who are you?" asked Dallas, taking out his weapon and aiming it at the surprised man.

Jesus pulled out the rag. "Say what? You know who I am. Man, what is this? Ginger, what's going on?"

"Who are you?" she asked, tossing him another picture.

He looked at the photo, then back at the two of them. He didn't have a clue what they were talking about.

"I'm Jesus Rodriguez. Who are you, man?"

"You don't look like the person in that picture," said Dallas.

Jesus took another look at the photographs, but he didn't know what the hell was going on.

"If that's you, you just grew a new head of hair," Ginger said to him.

Jesus started to smile. "My hair!" He pulled off the shower cap and pointed to his head. "It's new! I paid for every one of these stinking plugs. I can't get 'em wet for five more days. They won't replace 'em if I get 'em wet."

"Those are implants?" she said, feeling like an idiot.

Jesus was just a bit irritated. "Yes, for chrissake! I started the program before I got on this stinking jury, but had to stop when we were sequestered. They'll let me start up again after we're finished, but I can't get 'em wet!"

"I'm sorry, Jesus. We thought you were a ringer," said Dallas.

"What's a ringer?"

Ginger answered. "A fake. Somebody who looks like somebody else."

It was getting noisy. They all noticed the sound of banging water pipes from the adjacent room.

"What is that?" Dallas asked.

"The plumbing isn't too good. Every time they take a piss—excuse me, ma'am. I mean every time they use the facilities next door I can hear it. That's why I traded rooms with Dave. He said he couldn't sleep. It doesn't bother me. Sounds like home."

"Ours isn't much better," said Dallas. "We must back up with Robinson and Dunbar's bathroom. I can hear them all night long."

What he said made Ginger think. "Dallas, we *can* hear them, can't we?"

"Yes. Does it bother you?"

"Not the noise. But when Janice Rose was killed, Willie said he didn't hear anything because our water was running. My old bathroom doesn't back up to his. Yours does. And you don't shower until morning."

"But he knew somebody in your room was going to take a long, hot bath because Janice Rose made a big point of it," Dallas remembered.

"But she let me go first," said Ginger.

"You said you thought the murderer was after you," said Dallas.

"What's going on here, you guys?" asked Jesus. "Somebody's replacing jurors, murdering jurors—hey! I'm a juror!"

"And there's something else about good ol' Willie," Ginger added. "The first time I spoke to him, he told me how much he loved cigars. He was a veritable encyclopedia. He said he made a point of having one after lunch every day. How many times have you seen this guy light up a stogie?"

"He had a pack of cigarettes in his shirt pocket today," said Dallas. "I think we should have a talk with Willie Boy."

Dallas tucked his gun in his waistband and Ginger did the same. He cracked open the door to see where their resident watchdog was. "The guard's still gone. Let's go."

Dallas motioned for Ginger to follow. She stopped for a second to say good-bye to Jesus. As soon as she stepped toward the partially opened door, a blinding flash of light and a thunderous explosion knocked her backward. She landed on the floor. Dallas threw himself on top of her. Jesus leapt over his bed and dropped to the carpet.

By the time they got to their feet they could see the flames. The interior of their old room was an inferno. The door had been blown off its hinges and was hurled across the hall. Dallas cautiously peered outside. Their guard was standing near the gaping hole, looking at the destruction. The other security men came racing around the corner. Doors flew open up and down the hall.

Willie was standing in his doorway, still in his street clothes, assessing the damage. Dallas saw him and waved him over.

"What happened?" asked Willie, all innocent.

"Maybe it was a gas leak," offered Dallas, watching every twitch on Willie's face.

"It sounded like a bomb," said Willie. "Man, it knocked me outta bed. Were you in there?" he asked, noticing the scorch marks on Dallas's jacket. Dallas hadn't realized the flame had shot that far into Jesus' room and had partially melted the sleeve of his jacket.

"No. I was talking to Jesus."

"Lucky for you. But, Ginger—Jeeze."

"Sounded like a bomb, huh?" continued Dallas. "Maybe somebody really is trying to kill her."

Willie heard the word "is." "She—she wasn't in your room?"

"No. She wasn't, *Willie*," Ginger said, as she stepped into view. "Or whoever the hell you are."

"Ginger! You're okay! Thank—"

Dallas pulled Willie into Jesus' room and shut the door to the confusion outside. He gave the man a cursory patdown to see if he was carrying a weapon and relieved the guy of a knife he had in his waistband.

Fire alarms were sounding and there were shouts from

the guards for everyone to prepare to leave the building. Jesus had pulled on a pair of jeans and was stuffing a few things into a gym bag. The rest of the jurors were in a royal panic.

Dallas brought his gun under Willie's chin. "Who are you?"

"What do you mean? You know who I am."

"You aren't Willie Robinson," said Dallas.

"You're crazy! That explosion must have—"

"That explosion is going to be your last job for the defense."

Willie's eyes did a little dance as he tried thinking of a way to escape.

The commotion in the hall was getting louder. Someone was yelling.

"Pull that hose down here! Hurry!" said the voice.

Dallas looked around the room. "We need to get out of here so I can get some answers from this piece of shit."

"Why don't you turn him over to the police?" asked Jesus.

"The police can't make him talk. I can."

"We can walk him out when we're evacuated," Ginger suggested.

"He might squirm loose. Isn't there a window in your room?" Dallas asked Jesus.

"No." Jesus had a thought. "Hey, man, there's some kind of door in the bathroom."

"Show me," said Dallas.

Jesus led the way while Dallas wrestled Willie into the bathroom. Ginger brought up the rear. In the back wall of the small room was a half-sized utility access door. Jesus slipped the bolt and opened the hatch. A narrow passageway ran between the rooms and the two elevators in the center core of the hotel. There were a few utility lights illuminating the space that dead-ended to their immediate left. There were access doors at the backs of both elevators for servicing and a regular sized door exiting to the main hallway at the bottom of the U.

Dallas shoved Willie against the shower stall and snapped a handcuff on his right wrist.

"Hey! You can't do this," said Willie. "You aren't the police."

"I've got a gun, asshole. Shut up."

That calmed him down. Dallas grabbed Willie's other arm and yanked it behind him, clasping the other bracelet in place. Then he pushed Willie through the small opening and climbed into the utility area after him. Ginger followed.

They were able to stand up and walk down the passageway to the door. Ginger slowly opened it and checked out the hall. Jurors in pajamas and bathrobes were crowding around the corner watching the fire. She motioned to Dallas that they had to wait. That's when they heard the rumble of the elevator as it landed on their floor. Mavis Price-Jones was leading a cadre of cops to ground zero. Her shrill voice was issuing orders for everyone to stay calm.

Dallas whispered, "We won't get out that way. They'll have cops on every landing to make sure they evacuate everybody."

"Can we get through the back of the elevator and take it down to the basement?" Ginger suggested.

"We can try. Watch Willie."

He spun Willie around and pressed the guy's face into the wall. Ginger pulled out the small knife Dallas had given her, flicked it open, and placed the point at Willie's throat so he could feel it.

Dallas opened the access door, then loosened the bolts holding the panel to the back of the elevator and then lifted it out of the way. The main doors to the elevator were standing wide open. He stepped into the small compartment first and released the stop so the doors would shut. Ginger shoved Willie inside just as Dallas punched the down button.

A second later the lights went out. Utility lights switched

on, but the elevator wouldn't be moving until the fire was out.

"Some Boy Scout turned off the juice," said Dallas.

"Knock him out and we can carry him downstairs," said Ginger.

"I'd have to take off the handcuffs. If he comes to, he'd tell the first cop he sees we're kidnapping him."

"Just let me go. I haven't done anything," said Willie.

"We know you aren't Robinson," said Dallas.

"But—?"

"Where's your stogie?" asked Ginger.

"Huh?" said the guy they were calling Willie.

"Let me put it this way," said Ginger "You're close, but no cigar."

"We need another way out," said Dallas. "Did any of the other rooms have a utility door?"

They stumbled back into the passageway but there were no more utility doors.

"What's that?" Ginger asked, pointing to the far end of the passage next to Jesus' room.

She squeezed past Dallas and his charge and walked to the dead end that didn't look dead after all. There was the faintest outline of a doorway that had been plastered over before the wall was repainted.

"What's the matter?" asked Jesus, sticking his head through the half door.

"We're trying to find another way out," Ginger said.

"Do you want me to do something?" asked Jesus.

Ginger was busy sizing up the barrier. She tapped in its center and it echoed back with a hollow tone.

"I know why there's no window in Jesus' room. There's more hotel on the other side of this wall." She tapped even louder so Dallas could hear. By that time, the noise level from the firemen, Mavis, and the evacuating jurors was starting to ring through the entire floor. So was the smoke.

Dallas shoved Willie to his knees and rapped the barrier himself. "I thought our floor looked a little abbreviated. The hotel covers a square block. We need to get through this wall."

"I'll get you something, man," said Jesus.

Jesus pulled his head in and was gone before they could find out what his plan was.

"We can't wait," said Dallas. "The firemen won't let him back in his room anyway. We've got to get out now."

Ginger turned sideways and gave the wall a kick with her high-heeled shoe, then gave it a few more bangs before Dallas moved her out of the way. He was wearing thick-soled boots right out of the Army surplus store. He cocked his leg and jabbed three or four times until the plaster wall crumbled. He broke away pieces of the partition with his hand until the opening was large enough for them to slip through.

He yanked Willie up on his feet and spun him around so he could take hold of the handcuffs as they squeezed through the opening. Ginger was right behind.

They found themselves in another maintenance passageway. This one hung a right and led to the exit door. There were two utility doors along their route, but they didn't know if they would end up in somebody's bathroom or find themselves face to face with a cop evacuating people on that side of the hotel. They opted for the regular exit.

Ginger cracked the door and found the floor unoccupied. The entire area was undergoing major renovation. It was lit with only a handful of recessed lighting fixtures and green exit signs, but there was just enough light to still see the peeling wallpaper and where the carpet was worn right down to the wooden subfloor.

"We head down," said Dallas.

"Where do we take him?" Ginger asked.

"We find a vacant room on a lower floor. If the building starts coming down around our heads, we don't want to be too far from a fire escape."

The opposite side of the hotel was not a mirror image

of its other half. First, the newly discovered side was larger and resembled a rabbit warren with its nooks and crannies. There were small hallways off what must have once been large apartment-sized rooms. And there were back stairways, carpeted, that led, unfortunately, nowhere.

Dallas propelled Willie down the first flight of narrow stairs they located, holding onto the handcuffs to keep him from bolting. They descended two floors only to find a plastered wall with no exit.

"Reconstruction," said Dallas, slightly frustrated.

"Why don't you kick through the wall, macho man?" said this guy they were still calling Willie.

"I'll ram your head through first if you don't shut up, smart ass."

They got back to the top floor and noticed smoke had entered the area. They made their way along the main hall until they came to a huge hole in the floor. As Dallas peered over the edge, Ginger saw Willie Boy make a move.

"Don't do it, Willie," she said, raising her gun. "You push Dallas and you follow with a bullet in your spine."

He backed off.

"They have to get up here somehow," said Dallas. "Where the hell is another stairway? That smoke's getting thicker."

"There's a fire hose on our floor. Why aren't they putting out the fire?" she asked, coughing.

"Mavis is probably reading them the fucking instructions," Dallas said. "Let's see if we can get to the other side of this hole."

The opening was a good twelve feet across. They couldn't get to the other side without walking the wooden plank that straddled the abyss or jumping over it. Ginger wasn't in favor of either idea. She aimed her flashlight into the hole. There was a pile of debris, mostly old carpeting and chunks of plaster, scattered about.

"They're probably cutting through the floors to install an elevator," she said.

"The construction crew has to have a way to get up here," said Dallas. "Let's see if one of the other rooms has a stairway."

They tried the next door. Nothing was locked, but the room was filled with furniture almost wall-to-wall. All the old hotel furnishings were stored there until they finished the reconstruction job. The next room was empty. They checked doors until they found an exit through an area that had once been somebody's private kitchen. It led to a narrow stairway akin to the one across the hall. This one looked more promising. They descended two floors and then hit another barrier. Everything stopped on the sixth floor.

"Maybe you should try kicking it in," Ginger suggested. "We've got to get out of here."

Dallas reared back his leg and side-kicked the wall. He didn't even make a dent.

"Firewall," he said.

"Oh, great," said Ginger. "And we're on the wrong side of the fire."

"Go back up," said Dallas. "We'll walk across that plank. If Willie here is that damn anxious to die, he can jump."

They turned around and climbed the stairs. Dallas had Willie by the arm with his gun in the guy's back, forcing him to move. They got nearly to the top when they heard someone call out. Dallas took a firmer grip on Willie and shoved him against the wall to keep him in place until he could see who their surprise guest was. Ginger had already looked up and recognized that stupid John Dunbar standing there with a dopey look on his face.

"Where have you guys been? I've been lookin' for you," said Dunbar.

He took a few steps down the stairs, and then stopped. From his vantage point he couldn't see Dallas's gun in Willie's back, but Ginger noticed Dunbar's right hand was lodged deep in his jacket pocket.

"They're evacuating us. Come on," Dunbar continued,

but he didn't make a move up the stairs.

Both Dallas and Ginger could see his eyes watching Willie.

"Is somethin' the matter?" Dunbar asked.

Dallas pushed Willie in front of him. Right then the imposter was more useful as a human shield. That's when Dunbar got a glimpse of the gun aimed at Willie.

"Hey! What's going on? Did—did Robinson have something to do with the explosion?"

"That's what he's gonna tell us. Aren't you, Willie Boy?" said Dallas.

"My God!" exclaimed Dunbar, taking another step down the stairs. "And I was rooming with him."

All eyes were still on Dunbar. That's when Willie decided to make his move. He lunged up the stairs, jerking out of Dallas's grasp. Dunbar pulled the gun out of his pocket and started to raise it, but Ginger already had her .38 pointing directly at him. He stopped, momentarily confused, and then tried to act insulted because she could possibly think he was a threat. He must have forgotten she could see the 9 mm clutched in his hand.

While Ginger was preventing a Mexican standoff with Dunbar, Dallas made a dive for Willie. He grabbed him by the arm and dragged him down several steps with relative ease and then pushed him to his knees. Dallas put the gun against Willie's neck.

Dunbar, still playing dumb, even with a gun in his hand, looked at Ginger with a hurt expression. "Ginger?" he tried.

"No sale. Drop it!" she said.

"What are you doing? I'm trying to help. I'm not part of this."

"You were his alibi," she said. "Drop your weapon."

"I'm not gettin' paid to do that. Sorry, sister."

He tried raising his gun. She fired two shots into his chest. He dropped where he stood. Dallas hoisted a very surprised Willie to his feet and shoved him toward Dunbar's body just in case Ginger hadn't finished him off. Dallas managed to lean down and feel for a pulse, but Dunbar's time had expired. They continued up the stairs.

They made their way through the smoke that was pressing into the area, Dallas propelling Willie forward until they were at the edge of the twelve-foot hole.

Looking down, Dallas said, "The only way outta here has to be on the other side of this goddamn hole. We've gotta go across." He said to Willie, "You screw up and you know your options."

"I think you're runnin' out of them pretty quick, man," said Willie. "You better go back the other way."

"We go across," said Dallas. "You're not getting away. And you're gonna talk."

He studied the plank. It was nailed to the exposed floorboards on either side of the hole. He spoke to Willie. "Don't try anything funny. Ginger is a good shot. Just ask Dunbar."

Dallas put all his weight on the end of the board and tested its stability. "Seems sturdy enough. There's a 2x4 nailed along both edges to keep your feet inside." He grabbed his prisoner by the shoulder. He unlocked one of the metal bracelets, which had to delight ol' Willie, and then clasped it on his own wrist.

"Hey!" exclaimed Willie.

"If you want to try something, I'll be beating the shit out of you all the way down."

They started across the plank. Ginger stood on the one end to keep it stable, but it felt secure. She trained her flashlight along the plank so Dallas and Willie could see their way. Looking into the blackness gaping a few inches from her toes, she took a deep breath. Her lungs clogged with smoke. That was just the incentive she needed.

Ginger placed both feet between the wooden guardrails on the walkway and took two hesitant steps before a shot rang out. She heard someone shriek. She was going to drop to her knees and grab onto the plank, but she hadn't realized she had turned in the direction of the gunfire and was facing the wrong way when she squatted down. She pitched forward. There was nothing but air under her right arm, but her left arm hooked around an exposed floor joist and she lay there sprawled over the pit, her toes on the plank the only thing keeping her from swinging like a pendulum. She could just manage to look over her right shoulder to where Dallas had been standing, but he had disappeared along with Willie. Now she was really worried.

Ginger was trying to figure how she could move without losing her toehold or just plain falling. She heard footsteps. Someone was walking along the narrow strip of flooring near her head. They stopped. With the position of her arm around the beam, she couldn't turn her head far enough to the left to look up, but she could see and almost taste the boot polish so close to her mouth. She tried getting a better grip on the joist when two more shots rang out. This time they came from below. The shoes scraped backward in a hurry and they receded into the blackness and smoke coming from the jury side of the hotel.

Ginger heard movement somewhere below her.

"Dallas?"

"Ginger! You okay?" he asked.

"Watch out. I'm hanging by a thread here. Just a minute."

She was very close to the flooring around the big hole. She managed to straighten her body and roll herself onto the joist and then inch her legs along the plank until finally landing butt first on solid wood. Sitting up, she realized she had nearly dislocated her arm, but she could still move her fingers.

"I'm okay. How are you?" she said into the darkness below.

"Me?"

"You're the one who fell."

"Willie broke my fall."

"How is he?"

It took a moment for the diagnosis.

"I won't be getting anything out of him."

"You're lucky you didn't break *your* neck," she said, now standing at the opening and aiming her flashlight at the two figures below.

"He didn't break his neck," Dallas said, aiming his flashlight at the bullet hole in Willie's chest. "That's from a gunshot."

Ginger didn't speak for a few moments. "Dallas, was the shooter aiming at you—or him?"

"When we find out who did the shooting, we'll know the answer."

"Whoever it was went back the way we came in," Ginger said.

"Let me find a way up there. We'll go back that way," he said.

"Dallas, before you do that, would you mind looking for my gun?"

He found her gun in the carpet debris as well as locating an unblocked stairway on that side of the hole. It led to one of the huge suites on the top floor. The once plush apartment occupied a quarter of the far right wing of the hotel. Pretty fancy. They were tearing down the walls, making the new accommodations much smaller. Pity.

"Maybe Jesus saw our perp," Ginger said as Dallas was walking across the plank to her side.

"They probably told him to get the hell out. But one of the cops or a fireman might have seen whoever it was."

They went back to the service corridor and walked through the opening to the other side of the hotel. The smoke was dissipating, but its residue hung heavily in the air. There was an acrid smell of burning wires and smoldering furniture. Ginger went through the half door into Jesus' bathroom and stood at the doorway until Dallas joined her. Jesus wasn't waiting impatiently for their return. Ginger was actually surprised.

"I thought he'd still be here," she said.

"He is," said Dallas, looking over her shoulder into the bedroom. "You stay here."

Ginger turned in the direction he was staring and saw a pile of linens crumpled on the bed and a growing stain of dark red seeping through the top white sheet.

"Jesus!" she whispered.

Dallas went to the body. He pulled back the sheet. Jesus was laying face down and Ginger could see a horrible gash along the side of his head. A fire ax was next to the body. That's when she saw his hand move slightly.

"God, he's alive. I'll get medical help."

She didn't have to go far. Firemen were still in the hall and they were just a little astonished to see the woman walk into their midst. She asked one of them to summon a doctor. The medical personnel had to carry the stretcher up the stairs, but by the time they arrived, a doctor had already started working on poor Jesus. He had lost a great deal of blood and was in deep shock. But he was alive. God and Time were his only allies.

CHAPTER 27

A ll hell broke loose after that. Mavis, the police, and the hotel people weren't at all happy with the explosion, the fire, and the attempted murder of yet more jurors, and they were positively unreasonable about the two dead bodies Dallas and Ginger provided.

The next day the jury was dismissed and a mistrial was declared.

Not long after that news, in a private consulting room at the jail, a nervous Malvin Shepherd was alone with Desmond Williams. The defense attorney was pacing the room while his client was thinking of a way to kill him before he could be stopped. Shepherd was trying hard to appear in charge of the situation, but the sweat beading up on his forehead and running down his neck was a dead giveaway.

Williams was seething and he couldn't keep his anger contained. "I knew you'd fuck this up. You find a way to get me released and out of the country. Now!" He pounded the table with his fist.

"I haven't fucked anything up," offered Shepherd.

"If they trace the money, I won't have a chance—"

"It was all in cash. Not one withdrawal was made from any of our known accounts," explained the lawyer.

"What about the double? Who the hell are they gonna think planted him on the jury?" asked Williams.

"They'll think what I want them to think."

"You can't guarantee that. You can't guarantee shit!" screamed Williams.

"The media is already running a story that's going to

turn you into the biggest victim of racial injustice since
Rodney King. I've got them eating out of my hand."

Malvin held out his open hand only to have Desmond
spit into it.

"Why, you black son of a bitch!" blurted Shepherd.

"Let me tell you somethin', white boy. You and your
fancy suit and leather briefcase—" Williams knocked the
case off the table. "I bought you. I *own* you. I put those
clothes on your fat, white back and I can get somebody to
take them off you, *and* your wife *and* your kids, and they'll
keep picking at you 'til there's nothin' left."

"You can't threaten me."

"I'm *telling* you! Do something to get me the hell out of
here! Now!" Desmond slammed his fists on the table again
even harder.

"I'll see to it you aren't allowed any more visitors," said
Shepherd, trying a few threats of his own, but he was keeping his distance from his client.

"My people know where your children live."

Desmond reached into his jail uniform and pulled out
a pretty hair clip made of ribbons and plastic toys. Malvin
tried to snatch it out of his hand, but failed.

"If you do anything—" Malvin said with the faintest
quiver in his voice.

"Just get me out of here." Desmond threw the hair ribbon across the room.

CHAPTER 28

That same morning Ginger got word at home that the trial had been dismissed. Within thirty minutes she received a call from Johnnie Greer and was asked to come downtown and talk with the D.A. She put on a business suit and drove into the city. She parked in one of the open-air parking lots and walked three blocks to the Criminal Courts Building. She wasn't worried about a reprise of the incident with the three hoodlums. This time she was concerned about a different element lurking in the bowels of the building. This group wanted more than her money. But there are different types of muggers. Ginger got to the main entrance and was accosted by that other contingent.

"Ms. Caulfield! Ms. Caulfield!" screeched Myrna Blankenship. She must have beamed off the Channel 11 starship, but Ginger recognized her high-pitched voice. "Are you being brought in for questioning? Who's your lawyer?"

Myrna jammed a microphone in Ginger's face, and she was lucky another news ferret confronted Ginger from the opposite side because Myrna was just about to get it jammed down her own inquiring throat.

"Ms. Caulfield!" yelled Tina Lake. She was much shorter in person. "Tina Lake, Channel 10 *News & Entertainment*. Is it true you knew the two dead men? What was your connection with them?"

The sun wasn't *that* hot. Maybe the camera lights had fried their brains. Ginger tried to squeeze past them and get into the building. Another reporter stuck a microphone in her face.

"Gary Johnson, *L.A. Hot News*. Are the rumors true that you belong to the Aryan Nation?"

Her first reaction was that he was kidding. She grinned. She forgot for a moment why she would go months without watching the news. They made her crazy. They'd believe anything and verify nothing. Ginger wanted to get in his face and tell him he was a moron, but she did remember the first rule of self-preservation in L.A.: Don't Say Anything.

"Do you have anything to say, Ms. Caulfield?" asked Johnson.

That's when she remembered the second rule. Ginger grabbed his handheld mike, much to his amazement, and started singing. She had been a detective in her former occupation, not a singer. Her range was somewhere between a mashed cat and fingernails on a chalkboard. The audience cringed.

"Feelings, nothing more than feelings. Feelings, feelings, feelings . . ."

She tossed the microphone back to the guy with the surprised look on his puss and went inside the building. Dallas Long was standing inside the door laughing his head off. He applauded politely and they caught an elevator up to the D.A.'s office. Nobody in the elevator gave her even so much as a sideways glance though they had all seen her act on the sidewalk. Welcome to L.A.

They were walking toward Frank Fallen's office when Malvin Shepherd came charging down the hall. He was so lost in thought he didn't see them. He looked panicky. Ginger thought there was another fire somewhere.

"What's with him?" asked Dallas.

"I've seen that look before. Somebody just scared the hell out of him."

"Who?"

"Just a minute," Ginger said.

She reached in her handbag and pulled out a small notebook and pen and put on her tinted glasses. She pulled out the combs holding up her hair and shook it loose. She ran after Shepherd, stopping him in the hall. He was still disoriented.

"Mr. Shepherd! Mr. Shepherd! I'm Amy Winters with the *Globe*. Were you with your client?"

He didn't recognize her. "Uh—yes." He must have been on autopilot.

"Are you preparing for the retrial?"

Shepherd was coming out of his haze. "What retrial?"

"Do you still think your client is innocent, Mr. Shepherd?"

"Innocent!" His voice went up an octave. Ginger thought he was going to bite her head off. "I have nothing to say at this time. Excuse me."

He literally pushed her out of the way and dashed off. Ginger smiled at Dallas who had walked up behind her.

"What the hell was that all about?" he asked.

"We do think Malvin Shepherd is behind this, don't we?" Ginger looked at Dallas like maybe she was losing her grip.

"Yeah."

"He should be the happiest guy in Los Angeles," she said. "Everybody he bought off is dead."

"Okay." Dallas still didn't understand her point.

"Why did he look like somebody just killed his cat?"

They went to Frank Fallen's office. He was there with Johnnie and Matt. Bill James was sitting at Frank's desk going through some papers. Nobody was doing handsprings. They sat around the large conference table and tried to figure out what the hell the prosecution was going to do next.

Frank spoke first. "With the two of them dead, we don't have anything."

"When will you call another jury?" Ginger asked.

"Thirty days. Maybe more," said the D.A.

She continued. "How is Shepherd spinning how John Dunbar and the guy who assumed Willie Robinson's identity got on the jury?"

The room suddenly got very quiet. Frank finally said, "He's saying that you," he pointed to Ginger, "were the plant and you were trying to influence the other jurors to hang Desmond Williams."

The full impact of that statement didn't register at first. She was still putting the run-in with the TV people in perspective. "So that's why the media was asking all those stupid—" She finally got up to speed. "Don't they know the real story?"

The D.A. continued. "Ginger, there's no proof John Dunbar did anything wrong other than have a gun. Shepherd's people are saying he was trying to protect Willie because he thought Willie was in trouble."

"But the money? They found twenty thousand dollars in Dunbar's house," said Ginger. "I heard that on Channel 12 last night."

"They say you planted it," said Frank. "That was on TV this morning."

Dallas jumped into the conversation. "Did anybody check her bank account?"

"Do they have to?" answered Frank. "The allegation will stick a lot longer than the facts."

"What connection am I supposed to have with Willie Robinson?" Ginger asked, her voice hitting high C.

"Several jurors are swearing they saw you talking with Willie . . . 'clandestinely.'"

"Which ones?" she asked.

Looking through his paperwork, Frank came back with names. "Mindy Baker and Joyce Jones."

"Those two didn't come up with the word 'clandestinely' on their own," Ginger said, remembering the two mindless twits who chatted like a couple of magpies.

"They're willing to testify," said Johnnie.

"Do they have pictures?" she said sarcastically. Then she remembered something. "What about the pictures the guard took from that photographer?"

"What photographer?" asked Frank.

"The one outside the courtroom," said Ginger. "The guard took his camera. He's the same guard who was on our floor at the hotel. He gave me copies—Don't you know anything about this?"

Other than for Dallas, they were in the dark.

She continued. "I spotted some slimy little journalist taking pictures of jurors the first day of the trial. The guard reprimanded him once, and then confiscated the bum's camera when he wouldn't stop. He gave me a set of pictures. He even talked to me about them."

"Pictures of the jurors?" questioned Frank, thinking about something. He searched through a stack of newspaper clippings on his desk and came up with two pages filled with pictures. "These pictures?" asked Frank.

Ginger looked at the two pages of photographs gracing the newspaper spread. The pictures were dark and grainy due to the cheap grade of the newsprint rather than the quality of the camera, but they were basically the same pictures.

"Yes." Ginger noticed a small photo of the illustrious journalist who took the pictures next to his byline. "That's the guy I saw at the courthouse."

"Which paper is this?" asked Dallas.

"*The Weekly World*," said Johnnie.

"Oh, that's just perfect," Ginger exclaimed. "Isn't that the rag that said the Beatles are planning a reunion as soon as John Lennon gets back from the moon?"

"I think it was Jupiter," said Matt, knowing that bit of trivia. Nobody laughed.

"Why isn't he in jail?" Ginger asked.

"He said somebody—anonymously—slipped him the photographs," said Frank.

"He took the pictures. I saw him." Ginger's blood pressure was rising.

"It'll be your word against his," said Frank.

"And the guard," she said. "The photographer must have

been on his second roll of film when the guard took his camera."

"Do you still have the pictures?" asked Johnnie.

"No. I left them on Jesus' bed at the hotel."

"I have a couple," said Dallas, reaching into his pocket.

"Well, at least they weren't a figment of your imagination," said Matt rather lightly.

Ginger turned slowly toward him and gave him a cold stare.

Frank intervened before she went for the Ivy-League punk's throat. "Matt, you check out the guard. Ask his supervisor if he turned the photographs over to somebody in authority." Matt didn't know he was being saved from a royal reaming. He left the room. "Unfortunately, Ginger, we have city employees who don't think anything of selling souvenirs as a sideline."

Dallas was turning something over in his head. He spoke up. "Which Willie did he get pictures of?"

"What difference does it make now?" asked Johnnie, thinking it was irrelevant.

"I see where you're going," Ginger said, picking up Dallas's thought. "If it was the *real* Willie, there was nothing clandestine."

Frank shook his head. He held up the paper. "If he was the real one, you were setting him up. If he was the imposter, it was—"

"Yeah, clandestine," Ginger finished the thought for him. "This spin's coming right out of the defense handbook."

Frank was suddenly silent. He had more bad news. Both Dallas and Ginger waited for him to hammer in another nail. "They're saying you and Dallas—and with Dallas's covert military background it's getting some traction. They're saying you two killed off the real Willie Robinson and planted the double, and John Dunbar was an innocent bystander."

"Then why did we blow up our own hotel room?" Ginger asked.

"Nobody's asking," said the D.A. "But I bet Shepherd has an answer, if you're interested."

"Why were we supposed to have done all this?" she asked, getting a little paranoid.

Nobody wanted to say. Johnnie looked at Frank who looked back at Johnnie. Tag, you're it.

"They're saying you're part of a white supremacist fringe group out to get Desmond Williams," explained Johnnie.

"The Aryan Nation," Ginger intoned. "One of those jerk reporters said something about Aryan Nation. I thought he was smoking something. This whole thing is getting out of hand."

"Both of you have backgrounds that—" started Johnnie.

"Wait just a damn minute! There's nothing strange in my background," Ginger said. "Dallas might be an enigma, but my past is an open book. My detective agency was written up in the papers a few times."

"I know you're okay," said Johnnie. "And Dallas, your history is so secret I'm not too sure you even exist. But you put the pieces in the Shepherd spin machine and it comes out pretty murky."

"Then I'll tell my own story," Ginger said.

"You don't have nearly as good a PR team as Malvin Shepherd does," said Johnnie.

"But they tried to kill me. Twice. I think they were after me when they got Janice Rose."

Frank looked again at Johnnie. Ginger knew there was more.

"*What?*" she asked.

The D.A. had this one. "They're saying you killed Janice Rose to shut her up when she found out about the switch. And then you killed Willie's double to keep him quiet."

Dallas asked, "Where are you hearing this shit?"

Frank pulled out a newspaper with large black headlines that read **WHITE SUPREMACISTS TRY TO LYNCH DESMOND WILLIAMS.**

"Who wrote that?" Ginger asked. Gary Johnson's byline was printed under the sensational headline. "I thought Johnson was a TV guy."

"He is. It's the same story he's running on Channel 8," said Johnnie. "But he writes for the *World Globe* when they need a juicy story."

"This isn't a story. It's an outright lie," Ginger said. "Who does he source?"

"Unnamed," said Frank.

"I can name him: Malvin Effing Shepherd," said Ginger.

"We can't force him to come clean. He'd start screaming First Amendment Rights," said the District Attorney.

"I can make him talk," said Dallas matter-of-factly.

"That would really get the media on our butts," said Frank. "This Johnson character is a shining star in their eyes. We go after him and we'll have every major news channel and newspaper coming after us."

"Just because he's a reporter?" asked Dallas.

"That's part of it," said Frank.

"What else?" asked Dallas. "He sleeping with the publisher's daughter?"

"Gary Johnson has a bit of a reputation," said Johnnie.

"That journalistic *Wunderkind* is still being fed false information," Ginger said.

"That's not what I mean," Johnnie said. "He makes things up."

"I don't understand," said Ginger.

"I've gotten to know a few people on other newspapers," explained Johnnie. "They told me Johnson *creates* some of his stories. Did you ever hear him say he covered other high-profile trials? It never happened. He never filed a story about any other trial before this one."

"How did he get his job?" Ginger asked Johnnie.

"He worked for a local paper. Wrote sob-sister stories about the poor being oppressed by society. You probably remember the one he did two years ago about the family who had all their Christmas presents stolen by rogue cops. The paper got hundreds of presents from readers who felt sorry for the—I think they were a Mexican family. It was all a lie."

"The presents weren't really stolen?" questioned Ginger.

"No. There was no family. The entire story was made up."

"Why does he still have a job?" asked Dallas.

Johnnie looked at him and then looked away. This was her worst nightmare. She held the pen in her hand in a death grip. She threw it on the table and stood up. "Have you noticed what color he is?" She stormed out of the room.

After she left, Frank explained. "I didn't know the extent of Johnson's lying before Johnnie told me. I'd heard rumors, but up until now it never affected my office. She did tell me he was fast-tracked at the paper because of his color and not because of the quality of his work.

"It's funny," he continued. "I networked my way up the ladder and never batted an eye. Don't get me wrong. You had to be good to get ahead, but you also had to know somebody to get anywhere in politics. I mean, the good-old-boy network, affirmative action, whatever it takes. But I played by the rules."

Bill James had been sitting quietly at the desk. Finally he spoke. "Frank, if you hadn't been good, and I mean damn good, you'd be in private practice now."

"Thanks, Bill. I needed that."

"Don't get too excited," continued Bill. "Remember, my reputation is on the line, too. I picked somebody I could trust. If you don't screw up too badly, I can cover you. You screw up big time and I'll drop you like a hot rock."

"He's my conscience," Frank said to Dallas and Ginger. "In my position I guess I need one who works full time."

Frank stood up to stretch his legs. Before he could say anything else, the phone rang. He punched the intercom.

"Yeah, Sandy?" he said to his secretary.

"I've got Matt on the line, Mr. Fallen."

"Put him through." A click, click later, and the D.A. said, "Hi, Matt. Whataya got?" into the speakerphone.

"The guard's missing. His name is Samuel Dobson. He didn't call in this morning. They sent somebody to his apartment, but it had been cleaned out in a hurry. He must have left town."

"I'll have them put out an APB. Matt, did anybody say how long Dobson worked for the city?"

"I think he's been around for a while. Everybody knew him. Or maybe I should say, he knew everybody. And it sounds like he asked a lot of questions."

"What kind of questions?" Ginger asked.

Frank repeated her words. "What kind of questions, Matt?"

"About ongoing cases. He was always skulking around in the background. Anyway, that's what a couple guys said. But Dobson seemed to know the right things to ask."

"Matt, check Dobson's phone records and see if he ever made a call to Malvin Shepherd's office."

"While he's at it," said Ginger, "see if he ever called Gary Johnson."

"Why Johnson?" asked Frank.

"Maybe Dobson was Shepherd's intermediary," she said. "Johnson was always coming up with the right story at the right time. Remember his secret witness newsflash? Let's see who's lying to who?"

"Did you hear that, Matt?" asked the D.A. "Go talk to Gary Johnson at Channel 8."

"You want me to ask him if he knows Samuel Dobson?" questioned Matt.

"That, and then ask Johnson who his secret witness is," said Frank.

"The one he said was afraid of us?" asked Matt.

"Yeah. See if his story has changed now that the trial is over. Tell Johnson we aren't going to retry Desmond

Williams."

"We're dropping the case?" asked Matt, stunned.

"No, but Johnson doesn't have to know that. Let's see if it was Shepherd who planted the story about the scared witness."

"Sure, Frank. Talk to you later."

That episode was eye-opening. And it served to bring another question to the surface.

"What kind of shoes do guards wear?" Ginger asked.

"What?" questioned Frank, still thinking about his conversation with Matt.

"Boots. Heavy boots," said Dallas.

"What are you getting at?" asked Frank.

"I heard heavy footsteps running away from the shooting at the hotel. Somebody ran back to the jury side. Jesus said he was going to get something to break through the wall. I bet he went to get the fire ax and Samuel Dobson, our guard, saw him. Jesus either told him what we were doing or Dobson beat it out of him."

"We'll see who else he's been talking to when Matt gets his phone records," said Frank.

Ginger gave a small chuckle. "Now I know why Dobson gave me those pictures. It was after they botched the first job and killed Janice Rose instead of me. He took me aside and said how sorry he was about all the things that were happening. That's when he handed me the pictures."

"I don't understand," said Bill James.

She explained. "If everything went to hell, like it has, they could point to the pictures that they knew I had in my possession—"

"Or on your dead body," Dallas interrupted.

"Right. Then they could say I was involved."

Frank had an awful thought. "But that means they had to get rid of everybody, like Dunbar and the Wille Robinson double."

"It looks like they did," Ginger said.

"Wasn't Dobson trying to kill you two in the hotel?" asked Bill James.

"No," said Dallas, putting the pieces together. "He only took one shot. If he wanted us both, he would have shot Ginger first and then me. Remember, I was standing in the middle of that plank with a flashlight in my hand. No. He got the one he wanted."

"Somebody is orchestrating this show and now they're tying up the loose ends," Ginger said. "Dobson's job was to silence the guy posing as Willie Robinson if his cover was blown. The orchestra leader knew he could finish me off in the media now that the two attempts on my life had failed."

That was a sobering thought. The D.A., Bill James, Dallas, and Ginger waited to hear from Matt.

As for Matt, he was getting nowhere with the obstinate reporter. He went to the Channel 8 studio after getting the phone records for Samuel Dobson. Unfortunately, there were no calls placed from the guard to the television studio, any newspaper, or to Shepherd.

"You didn't know him at all?" Matt asked Gary Johnson when he was granted an audience.

"I don't know anybody named Samuel Dobson. Who is he?"

"One of the guards at the Crawford Hotel watching the jurors on the Desmond Williams case. He disappeared after the fire."

"What's that got to do with me?" asked Johnson, who was fiddling with a few papers on his desk.

"You seem to know a lot of things about the case. The district attorney wants to know if you have any inside info on this guy Dobson."

"Never heard of him. Why's he so important?"

"He had pictures of the jurors taken before they were sequestered. We think some of the jurors were compromised."

"What do you mean, compromised? Bought off?"

"Somebody was doing more than jury tampering," babbled Matt.

"You're kidding." Johnson's curiosity was aroused.

"We think one of the jurors was replaced by a look-alike. He's the one who got shot instead of the woman."

"Who did the replacing? Malvin Shepherd?"

"Probably. It's just the tip of the iceberg. That's why I'm here, to get some answers about the secret witness you uncovered who said they were afraid of the police. Who is it?"

"Huh?" Gary Johnson wasn't listening to the question. He was concentrating on his first Pulitzer.

"What's the name of the witness who told you they were scared of the police?" Matt asked again. "We want to know if Malvin Shepherd paid them to come up with that story."

Johnson came back down to planet earth. "I can't reveal a source. You know that. It would compromise my ethics."

"But if Shepherd is behind this—"

"I'm sorry." Johnson's voice got the ring of righteous indignation. "You or the D.A. can't force me to reveal my sources. You know the rules."

"People have been killed. If your witness—"

"Look, Matt. You got your job. I got mine. And mine isn't to share anything with you. Watch my news report tonight. It'll singe your eyebrows. Now I got work to do."

Matt left Gary Johnson's office. The reporter sat behind his desk and reached for the telephone. He had forgotten he had another guest waiting in his private bathroom.

"Why don't you tell *me* who the witness is?" asked Johnnie Greer when she stepped into his office.

"Oh," said Johnson, startled. "Your boy just dropped the news story of the decade right in my lap." He put down the phone.

"What story is that?"

"Malvin Shepherd bumping off jurors."

Johnnie laughed. "You run with that and we'll see you

in court on a libel charge."

"But Matt said—"

"We need the information about your eyewitness, Gary. I don't know where Matt came up with his story, probably Frank told him what to say, but I can assure you, Malvin Shepherd would never jeopardize his reputation by killing anybody."

"But—

"Come on, Gary. We both know Shepherd isn't above leaking you a phony story. That's in his bag of tricks. Is that where you got the scared witness account?"

Johnson didn't know what his next move should be. "I have the right to protect my sources," he finally said.

"You also have the right to remain silent. If we think you're on Shepherd's payroll, you might just see the inside of a jail cell yourself," said the prosecutor.

"You can't do anything to me."

"If Shepherd is hiding a witness, that's withholding information in a criminal investigation. If he asked a witness to lie for him and you know about it, that's accessory after the fact in a murder case. You want to talk to me, or to your lawyer?"

"There isn't a witness," he mumbled.

"What?"

"I made him up, or her. I haven't figured out who it was supposed to be yet."

"No wonder Shepherd wasn't interested in your story," said Johnnie. "He knew you didn't have anything, because he didn't leak it to you."

"I don't even know Malvin Shepherd. When I asked for an interview, his people told me to get lost."

"So you made up the witness? Cool." She smiled charmingly at him. "That will keep your competition hustling."

Proud of himself, Johnson answered, "Yeah. I can say damn near anything in this town."

"Your editors don't check your sources?"

"They're too busy taking bows for my work."

"Your work?" she questioned. "Not a lot of effort goes into your reporting, Gary."

"Well, let's just say, I make a lot of people *very* happy," he gloated.

"And your network gets a boost in market share. Especially during the Williams trial."

"I've got it made. Channel 8 is creaming the competition."

"What happens when they find out you're making it up?" she asked.

"Like, who's gonna care? Anyway, I write what people want to hear."

"You mean the white supremacist story?"

"I got a tip," said Gary. Johnnie wasn't buying this. "No, really. Somebody called the paper. It was twenty minutes after I tried to get another interview with Shepherd."

"What if Williams goes free?" asked Johnnie.

"That isn't the point. I can run rings around every journalist out there. I'm looking at my own news show in six months. I can hang Williams or save him. It's my call."

"I guess you can," said Johnnie, as she started to leave.

"I read somewhere you and that white guy were an item," said Gary.

"You can't believe everything you read in the papers, Gary," said Johnnie, smiling.

CHAPTER 29

L ess than an hour later Johnnie was back in the D.A.'s office with her news about Gary Johnson.

"You think he was telling you the truth?" asked Frank.

"Yes. And you know why? He thinks we're the same. He thinks I got where I am because nobody would dare fire the black girl, no matter what I did. The smug son of a bitch."

"I'm having dinner with his boss this weekend," said Frank. "His career just ended."

"That's too bad," Ginger said. "Not that the mythomaniac will be unemployed," she hastened to add, "but we can't pin his phony stories directly to Malvin Shepherd. Dallas and I still end up the guilty parties."

"There has to be a link between Shepherd, John Dunbar, and Willie Robinson," said Dallas. "Phone records, bank deposits."

"If Shepherd is as conniving as I think he is," Ginger said, "it was all done by pay phones, cash, and intermediaries, like maybe the missing guard. But no smoking gun."

Dallas stood up, feeling boxed in. "Then we prove Desmond Williams murdered his wife and the fag. Period. That'll end this shit."

"I can't authorize you to do anything," said the D.A. "You'll be on your own. But if you can prove something, I'll run with it."

"Where do you start?" asked Johnnie.

"At the beginning," Ginger said. "What do we know now that we didn't know when the trial started?"

"There's no new eyewitness, either for or against

Williams," said Frank.

Johnnie said, "We don't have any new evidence."

Dallas asked, "Do we have any questions about the evidence already presented?"

"I do," Ginger said, something clicking in her head. "I want to rerun that video of Desmond Williams at the Kirkland Building."

They were watching the video five minutes later. Matt had come into the office and they were staring at the small screen. The tape showed Desmond in the lobby, looking around and then spotting the cops before he went into his crazy act. Ginger was watching the show on the edge of her seat. Not that it was all that riveting, but something bothered her.

"Run that back and show the part when we first see Williams near the elevators."

The video was rewound and played again. A dozen people were coming from the rear of the building. The area wasn't well lit, but as they rounded the corner light flashed across one man's glasses. Just at that point, the cameraman was slightly jostled. When he refocused his camera, Williams had joined their ranks. Desmond walked further into the lobby and glanced up. That was when the police officer called out his name.

"Back it up a little before the cameraman is bumped," said Ginger. The tape was rewound. In slow motion, Matt inched the video forward until the man with the wire-rimmed glasses was featured.

"Stop it right there," said Ginger. "Do you see the light hit that guy's glasses?"

"What is it?" asked Frank.

"The elevator door just opened," she said. "The interior light is reflecting off the lenses."

"Williams got off the elevator," said Johnnie.

Matt stopped the video at the point where Williams was walking toward the exit. Ginger noticed the building's directory over his left shoulder.

"I want to see who has offices in that building," she said.

"Maybe he was looking for another lawyer," kidded Dallas.

"Frank, I'm taking a long lunch," said Johnnie.

Frank covered his ears. "I don't know anything that happened in this room. Remember that," he said.

Johnnie walked out the door first, then Matt. Ginger followed and Dallas brought up the rear. They took Johnnie's car to the Kirkland Building. They entered the lobby and walked to the directory.

Dallas looked at the names. "These are all doctors or shrinks. Maybe Williams was looking for a psychiatrist."

"I don't think he has a conscience," Ginger said.

Matt said, "Maybe he was thinking of using an insanity plea."

"Only after he shoots Malvin Shepherd," she added.

"And he just might," said Johnnie. "Frank told me Desmond and Malvin had words after Judge Cherry ran the movie you told us about."

"Hmm," said Ginger. "Maybe they've had more than a few words." She was reading the long list of doctors on the board and saw something. "What is a 'cometic' doctor?"

Johnnie looked at the directory. "That's probably 'cosmetic,' like that one," she said, pointing to a similar notation in the next column.

"Cosmetic?" Ginger questioned. "Like plastic surgery?"

Johnnie remembered something. "Ginger, the autopsy on Willie Robinson's double found stitches inside his lip."

"Ah. Like maybe a lip reduction by a plastic surgeon?" Ginger suggested.

"Or a 'cometic' surgeon?" said Dallas.

"So Desmond might have been scoping out a plastic surgeon?" said Johnnie.

"Or he already knew of one in the building," Ginger said.

"Should I get another warrant?" asked Matt.

Ginger looked at the young man and cocked her head. "Warrant? I don't need no stinking warrant. I think I'll go ask a few questions. You do it your way and I'll do it my way."

"Mind if I ride shotgun?" asked Dallas.

Dallas had no intention of letting Ginger go it alone. That's a hero for you. They took the elevator to the top floor and were going to work their way down the list. The first two "cometic" doctors were on that floor. The way the office numbers were running, doctor number one would be at the end of the hall.

"Let's see . . . 702. 704. 712 should be down—I bet I know which one it's going to be," said Ginger.

They could see piles of debris and plastic sheeting nailed around what was left of a frosted glass door at the end of the hallway. There were scorch marks around the frame. Dallas pulled the plastic sheeting away from the nails holding it and let her pass through first. The place was totally gutted. He sniffed the air.

"This happened several days ago," he said.

"Was it a fire or a bomb?"

"A fire. There's no evidence of percussion. There wouldn't be any glass left in the door if they bombed it. And look at the cabinets and furniture. They're charred, not scattered. A bomb would have propelled things all over the place."

"So it wasn't blown up like our hotel room?" she said.

"No," said Dallas. "They didn't want to kill anybody, just destroy evidence."

"And something else. Somebody's eliminating all my leads."

"Somebody's trying to eliminate you, too. They think you know something."

"I don't know anything about Desmond Williams. I never even liked his movies."

"Somewhere along the line they think you picked up a

clue. When did all this start?"

"The night Janice Rose was murdered instead of me."

"What was going on in court that day?" he asked.

"I don't remember. Let's find out."

They went back to Frank Fallen's office and looked through the transcripts of the day Janice Rose was murdered. Johnnie was helping them go through the papers. Frank and Bill James were going over their options. Matt wasn't there.

"Here it is," Johnnie said. "Malvin Shepherd was grilling Detective Lawrence Patrick, the officer in charge of the murder investigation. Shepherd was saying it was 'strange' there were no eyewitnesses to the murders and maybe we had gotten rid of some 'mystery witness' who could prove Williams didn't do it. That's playing off Gary Johnson's story."

"I remember that," said Dallas. "The cop was showing aerial pictures of the beach and the neighbors' house."

"I remember now," Ginger said, the image coming into focus. "There was something about one of the pictures. The officer was showing the side yard of the neighbor's house, whichever one was on vacation, and there were newspapers and stuff piled up."

Johnnie had a thought. "If the neighbors were on vacation, they couldn't have seen anything, unless they had a house sitter. But as far as we know, nobody stays at the house and the people are still out of the country. They spend six months in Europe and six months at their place on the beach."

"I think there was a witness," Ginger said. "Do you have the blowup of that picture?"

Frank had the evidence folder brought in and they were flipping through the photographs.

"Here it is," Ginger said, pulling out the enlargement.

"Where's the witness?" asked the district attorney.

"Right there."

Ginger pointed to an oblong box under the eave of the

neighbor's house. It was pointing toward Marcella's house.

Frank studied the picture. "A surveillance camera. I'll have Matt get another warrant."

Before Frank could pick up the phone, Matt rushed into the office.

"Malvin Shepherd is downstairs getting ready for a press conference. He says he has an eyewitness who saw who killed Marcella and Adrian Wells."

"Gary Johnson!" exclaimed Johnnie. "The lying little cockroach."

"What's this all about?" asked Bill James. He hadn't been in the office earlier.

"When I spoke with Johnson today, he said he made up the story about a secret witness. He told me he does it all the time and nobody cares. It sells papers, for chrissake. And Bill, you know the *Globe*. This kind of sensationalism is right up their alley. And if they could run Frank out of office, they'd do it in a heartbeat."

"Who's their witness?" Bill asked. "Another Lolita?"

"No," said Matt. "A guy who was picked up a few blocks from Marcella's house the night of the murders."

"Picked up for what?" asked Frank.

"Armed robbery," said Matt. "But he's saying he's been kept incommunicado because the police want to shut him up."

"Who's his lawyer?" asked Johnnie.

"Take a wild guess," said Matt.

"Where does Shepherd find these people?" asked Johnnie.

"He found this one in jail," said Matt.

"I want to see this for myself," Ginger said.

Dallas stood up. "I'm going with you. I might have to pull you off Shepherd."

"I'll watch it on TV while I get a warrant for that surveillance camera," said Frank.

Reporters and technicians were swarming like ants over

a ham sandwich when Dallas and Ginger got downstairs. Several of Shepherd's minions were making the area ready for their boss as the pair walked out the door.

"Where's the big kahuna?" Ginger asked Dallas, seeing Shepherd's hired muscle making preparations.

"Probably digging up another eyewitness," he said.

"Or burying one," she added.

They watched while cameras, microphones, and lights were set up for another feeding frenzy. As reporters were getting themselves into position, Ginger thought she saw somebody watching Dallas and her from among the camera equipment and TV people. He looked away when she caught him staring, but soon he looked back in their direction and then walked over to them.

"You're Ginger Caulfield, aren't you? The juror who was almost killed during the Desmond Williams case."

Ginger was hesitant to talk with anybody, but he was wearing a Channel 12 *L.A. Comprehensive News* T-shirt and she had her own bodyguard with her. "That depends on which news broadcast you watch."

"I think you might want to listen to this." He handed her a small audiocassette.

"What is it?" she asked.

"Just listen to it. And take a look at this, too." He handed her a videocassette.

"I don't understand."

"You will." He walked away.

Dallas and Ginger exchanged questioning looks. "You want to play it now?" he asked, knowing her answer.

"We'll catch Shepherd's revelations on the five o'clock news," Ginger said, turning away from the press conference. "Anyway, we know there's no witness."

They went back to Fallen's office. Ginger told the D.A. and Johnnie what had happened on the sidewalk and Frank agreed they would run the tape. They were silent the first time they played the audio of Malvin Shepherd telling his boy to find the charm Lolita lost in the police car or burn the evidence. The video followed. It was shot at the remote location in San Pedro where Desmond Williams was filming his movie sequel, though the site had been shut down. Utility lights illuminated a few of the buildings near the cars, but it was still rather dark, but not so dark they couldn't pick out Malvin Shepherd's henchman, Curtis Lee, and another man torching the three studio police vehicles. On the replay Ginger had Johnnie stop the tape.

"Isn't Lolita in the building?" Ginger asked, remembering seeing her earlier.

"Yes," said Johnnie. "We're getting her description of the man who said he was from the D.A.'s office."

"Have her take a look at the second guy on this tape."

Lolita Spring was brought into the office. Johnnie started the video. On the screen, both men finished setting the three vehicles aflame and were standing close to one of the utility lights watching their handiwork. Curtis Lee leaned against a storage shed and pulled out a pack of gum. He unwrapped a piece and offered some to his friend. His accomplice walked toward him and for a moment he stood directly under one of the dangling utility lamps. His face came into view.

"That's him," yelled Lolita, standing up, her tinny bracelet jingling. "That's the man who paid me to say I saw Desmond Williams."

That brightened their day. But Frank had some cold water to throw on it after Lolita left. He had been silent while the rest of the group were congratulating themselves. Finally his silence overcame their exuberance.

"I'll be the first one in line to see Shepherd disbarred, but orchestrating a fire isn't going to put Desmond Williams on death row. And my career is going to rise and fall on a screwed-up murder case, not the disbarment of some shyster lawyer. Present company excepted." He nodded to Johnnie.

They laughed politely, but their mood had been dampened.

Johnnie said, "Maybe Shepherd will admit he master-minded the juror switch if we drop this on him."

"Shepherd isn't suicidal," said Frank.

Ginger said, "So, my reputation is still in the toilet and Williams comes off as an innocent bystander."

"If the witness Shepherd dug up sounds the least bit credible, Malvin will probably have my job after this election and I'll be on the hot seat," said Frank.

"You didn't do anything," Ginger said.

"That's the crime. I went for murder one. If I lose—"

"You mean the media has to hang somebody," said Ginger. "If it isn't Williams or me, it might as well be you."

"Yeah," said the D.A.

Ginger shook her head.

Johnnie was still seeing the silver lining. "Ousting Shepherd will weaken Williams' defense. We'll get him in round two."

"Not if his next lawyer is black," said Frank. "We'd better get Desmond Williams before this round is over."

That was a tall order. The party soon broke up. Dallas and Ginger followed Johnnie out of Frank's office. She was feeling pretty good under the circumstances. She wanted to kick butt and here came her opportunity. Malvin Shepherd was coming down the hall with P. J. Henderson and Curtis Lee, his two bookends. His news conference was obviously over. Shepherd was directing his people as Johnnie, Dallas, and Ginger were coming from the other direction. They spotted each other at the same time. Shepherd had a smug look on his face. Johnnie stopped right in front of him. Shepherd spoke first.

"I take it you saw my news conference."

"Sorry, no. I'll catch the sequel," said Johnnie.

Shepherd was somewhat disappointed, but he went on to say, "We're going for an immediate dismissal due to this new witness."

Johnnie got in his face. "You go for dismissal. We're going for disbarment. Let's see who diss's first."

She held up the videocassette triumphantly and walked away. Dallas and Ginger followed her. That was when Matt came running down the hall after them.

"Johnnie! Johnnie! Wait up. I went to get the warrant on the neighbor's house and checked which home security system they used, and Johnnie—it's been burned down."

"They burned the house?" she asked, stunned.

"Not the house. The security firm, Osborne Security Services. O.S.S. It was a couple of days ago. The same night the doctor's office burned."

"They aren't leaving us much," said Dallas.

"I used to work in the detecting business," Ginger said. "I might know something our little pyromaniacs don't know. Matt, do you have a phone number for the owner of the security firm?"

"I can get it."

Meanwhile, Frank used his cellular phone and dialed a familiar number in private.

"Mark Parsons, *News & Entertainment*."

"Hello, Mark," said the D.A.

Mark hesitated. "Uh, I really don't think I should be talking with you, sir."

"Why? What happened?"

"I got a call . . . Somebody saw us together."

"It's been taken care of. They don't have anything," said the D.A.

"But Shepherd's man won't talk to me. He knows I'm talking to you."

"Shepherd's leaking to somebody else now. They don't need you anymore."

"What?" Mark was stunned.

"The only reason Shepherd's man was giving you stuff is because Shepherd told him to."

"I don't believe . . . He said—"

Frank didn't have time to hold the guy's hand. "I've got a couple things for you, Mark. First, we've got an audio of Malvin Shepherd telling his men to torch those police cars."

"You're kidding."

"Second, Gary Johnson is lying about his mystery witness. You've heard about his reputation? It's true. Shepherd is feeding him."

"I hope he chokes on it. Wait 'til I tell—"

"You do that, Mark."

CHAPTER 30

Dallas, Johnnie, Matt, and Ginger ended up in the base-ment of a West Hollywood bank a little after one o'clock. Just to get there, they had to go through a bulletproof glass tunnel to the vault area of the building, guarded by armed men along the way. From there they went into a cold, col-orless room made of concrete block devoid of any decoration. They were standing beside a long worktable. It felt like a morgue and they were waiting for the body to be wheeled in.

The owner of the security firm, Luke Osborne, was already there, wearing a jacket with his firm's logo, O.S.S., in bright yellow letters on an orange background over the pocket. A bank employee was bringing in boxes from another room.

"That's all for the month of July, Mr. Osborne," she said.

"Thank you," said Osborne. "We'll just be a few min-utes."

The woman left them alone.

"How many houses do you do surveillance for?" asked Matt.

"During the summer, a hundred and ten, a hundred twenty a month. It's our slow season. The beachfront homes are usually occupied during the summer. The people tend to travel to Europe or their places on Nantucket in the spring or fall. The Halburgs are antique dealers. They spend half the year touring the world to stock their shop."

"Do you monitor these cameras twenty-four hours a day?" asked Dallas.

"No. We'd go batty," said Osborne. "We videotape the area round-the-clock; spot monitor day and night, then transfer the data to CDs and store them for two years. We also have the burglar alarm concession. If an alarm goes off, we have a tape running and can provide the police with a picture of the perp."

"What did you do before CDs?" asked Dallas.

"Rented a warehouse to store about a million videocassettes a year. Now we download daily onto these babies. We compress the data from the videos on our computers, then write it to high-density CDs every day."

Matt asked, "How do you know which is which without your records?"

"They're dated and color-coded. You're lucky you had Ginger on this case. She knows the business. You back up everything you do. It's called insurance. All my office files are downloaded onto CDs."

Matt pulled out handfuls of the jewel cases containing the daily CD data, each emblazoned with a bright yellow-and-orange sticker with the company's O.S.S. logo and date. They were all from the month of July, but he couldn't find the ones he wanted.

"I can't find July eleventh," he said. "Here are the ones for July tenth and the twelfth. Are there more boxes?"

The woman from the bank walked into the room.

"Find what you need, Mr. Osborne?" she asked.

"Has anybody been through these CDs in the past few days?" asked Osborne.

"No. Just your business partner."

Osborne looked at Ginger. "I don't have a partner."

That ended their search.

CHAPTER 31

The group went back to the D.A.'s office. Frank wasn't there, but on his desk were piled newspaper clippings— about Johnnie. Now it was her turn to take it hard. The articles were ripping her apart for bungling the Williams' case. They were also starting to delve into her personal affairs— in particular, her affair with Matt. It was turning into the stuff tabloid journalism was made of.

They pretended they didn't see the headlines:

PROSECUTOR: POLITICS OR PARTY GIRL?
DID D.A. USE RACE CARD TO PICK PROSECUTOR?
IN OVER HER HEAD?

They walked to Johnnie's office. It looked like a funeral procession, except for Matt, who grabbed Johnnie's briefcase and was jumping around her like a pet poodle. More newspapers were stacked on her desk. She slid them into the wastebasket. Dallas and Ginger left shortly thereafter. They remained silent in the elevator. It was crowded and they didn't know who was listening. Outside, they found a quiet place to sit and talk.

"That was unpleasant," Ginger finally said.

"Johnnie's a big girl," said Dallas. "This wasn't the first time she's had her sex and her race thrown in her face. She'll handle it."

"You have to develop a thick skin in the public eye. They've got me in their crosshairs. My picture is making the media rounds. I feel like a criminal."

"Are they bothering you at home?" asked Dallas.

"The media is phoning my house, leaving voice mails, e-mails, offering me spots on *Larry King Live, Geraldo,* even *Oprah.* There were messages from the Sunday morning shows asking if I'd sit for an interview. Sam Donaldson called personally and left a plea on the answering machine. I haven't returned any of their calls."

"Good for you."

"I'm not in the P.I. business anymore, so all this free publicity, even the hatchet job I expect, isn't doing anything for me, except tick me off. And what ticks me off most is that they're questioning my credibility. I worked twelve years to earn a first rate reputation. *Nothing* was handed to me. I built up a good name and never screwed anybody. Then the business changed and I didn't much care for the new rules. So I retired. But I left with my name in tact. Now all that's in jeopardy. I'd get my lawyer on their butts...if I had a lawyer."

"Desmond Williams isn't doing too badly," said Dallas.

That really set her off. "He's been the lead story on every television news show since dawn. They've given him celebrity martyr status. You'd think he just graduated from Betty Ford."

"He has a good agent—or should I say mouthpiece?" said Dallas.

"The media tried getting an in-jail interview with Williams," said Ginger, "but Frank Fallen told them where they could put their microphones. Now they're calling me. Have you been contacted?"

"They don't know where I live." He grinned.

"I thought you lived out of that super secret suitcase of yours."

"That's why women make lousy agents. You gals carry too much nonessential stuff. Rollers, makeup. My wife—"

"Didn't you say you weren't married in court?"

"My *ex*-wife hated what I did."

"You told her?"

"Yeah. You can tell the spouse, if you want, unless you're deep cover. I told Angela. She thought it was exciting, at first. I made the supreme mistake of taking her with me on assignment. I put her up in a hotel in Tehran. Told her to stay put. The locals don't cotton to Western women running around their streets. God help us if they're caught driving a car over there. Angie didn't give a damn. She was looking for the nearest mall. They actually have them in Tehran."

"She went shopping?" asked Ginger.

"She borrowed a car and hit the road. Here's a gal who couldn't find her butt with both hands and a flashlight, but she could find the last shopping center left on earth. She was in this one shop and started negotiating with the owner. Somebody told her the only way to deal with Iranians is to bargain with them. Angie was used to plunking down plastic. So she gets into an argument with the proprietor and ends up calling him a pig. She might as well have called him a diaper head. In Arabic countries—"

"Yeah, I know their culture," Ginger said, getting the picture. "What happened?"

"The police were called and she started screaming that her husband was a spy."

"Oh, brother. Is that what ended your career?"

"It ended Thomas Flynn's career."

"Who's Thomas Flynn?"

"It's the name I used when I was married to Angela. We killed him off." He noticed the astonished look on Ginger's face. "The outfit I work for shipped a dead body all the way from Missouri, ran him over in the streets of Tehran one night, and the late Thomas Flynn was shipped back to America as one dead 'State Department' employee who died while in service to his country."

"Does Angela know you aren't dead?"

"She doesn't know anything about any of it. They flew her home twenty-four hours after her scene at the mall.

Thomas Flynn died three days later. His death didn't make the American newspapers. I divorced her four months after I returned to the States."

"You can't go back to Iran, can you?"

"I don't look the same as I did then. I don't think even Angie would recognize me."

"Then Malvin Shepherd's tactics aren't all that strange to you," Ginger said.

"One big difference. I did my stuff for my country. He does his for money."

While Dallas and Ginger were looking for an out-of-the-way place to continue their chat, Johnnie and Matt were getting ready for theirs. Johnnie was standing behind her desk, her fingertips lightly touching the richly polished wood surface, while Matt was toying with a pencil.

"Close the door, Matt."

"We'll get him, you know," he said, as he reached over and pushed the door closed.

"No, I *don't* know, Matt. I don't know anything anymore."

"Shepherd can't spin his way out of this. Both he and Williams will go down."

"What did you do? Read that in the paper? See it on the six o'clock news? Is that where you get your information, Matt? Where do they get *their* information? Like this." She pulled a newspaper out of her briefcase and slammed it down on her desk. "This is my personal business. What is it doing on the front page of the *Los Angeles Times*?"

"They wanted to know about you. What makes you such a good—"

"Like hell they do! Is there anything in there about my working two jobs to put myself through college? Anything about my father dying in Vietnam because he loved this country? Anything about my mother not taking a dime of government welfare because she was raised to take care of her own?"

"They didn't ask."

"They didn't ask!" Johnnie was furious. "Why isn't there anything about all those do-gooders along the way who wanted to mold me into a terrific second-class citizen with all their sanctimonious help? Just don't be too good, nigger."

"I never treated you like that, Johnnie."

"If this story is about me, why didn't you tell them I turned down a scholarship to Harvard when I ranked in the top fifth percentile of high school students?"

"I never understood that," he said.

"No, you didn't. I turned it down and went to George Mason because I knew I would be the *top* student there if I were measured against kids with the same IQ. I wanted to be the *best* against people I thought I could beat. I didn't want to be ground into little pieces at a university where I would be foundering somewhere in the middle even with a straight-A average out of high school."

"I didn't know—"

"You didn't ask, Matt. You didn't ask. But you didn't mind telling the newspaper where we went on dates."

"I thought people would be interested."

Johnnie was circling for the kill. "What types of restaurants did you take me to? What types of clubs?"

"I took you to places I thought you'd like."

"You took me to *black* clubs. This isn't the Fifties, Matt. You don't have to sneak me into back-alley joints."

"I don't mind going to all-black nightclubs with you."

"*You don't mind?* Maybe I mind. Maybe I mind the hell out of it."

"I was just trying to show you that I don't care if you're black."

"Is that all I am? Black. I think I'm a hell of a lot more, Matthew. I've been taking this patronizing shit all my life. See the smart little nigger. See the smart little nigger go to college. See the smart little nigger go to law school. You can all go to hell."

"You take it from Frank."

"I take it from Frank because he pushes me to be better than I am. What do you do?"

"I want you to be better."

"And what do you want out of it? Do you want to show people how liberal you are to take a black woman to a black nightclub? There's nothing brave about that, Matt. You know something else? I've never met your mother."

"She wouldn't understand. She's from the old school." His head was down.

"Ah, yes. The old school. Is she a graduate or did she marry up and get an honorary degree?"

"I wanted to tell her," he said.

"Maybe she'll read it in the paper. Does she get the *L.A. Times* in Boston?"

"She wouldn't understand," said Matt.

"You already said that."

"I slept with you. Doesn't that mean anything?"

"You slept with me? How *white* of you. How fucking white of you, Matt. Someday you might understand how humiliating that is for me to hear. Then again, I don't think you'll ever understand. Good-bye, Matt. Take my number off your speed dial."

CHAPTER 32

Dallas took Ginger to a neighborhood diner for a bite to eat. They grabbed a booth and settled in for a brainstorming session.

"You were in the detecting business," Dallas said. "How do we find out what Malvin Shepherd did?"

"Ask questions."

"Just ask him?" questioned Dallas.

"Shepherd won't tell us, not with all that muscle around him. No, we ask people he's corrupted."

"Like who?"

"First, Gary Johnson," said Ginger.

"Why do you think he'll talk to you?" he asked.

"Because you'll be with me. Didn't you say you had ways to make people talk?"

"Yeah. But he's a professed liar. How can you be sure his 'truth' isn't just another lie?"

"He told Johnnie he made up the story about the secret witness and she believed him. Maybe he was telling the truth, for once in his life. Now Malvin Shepherd is running with it. If we can get Johnson to confess that Shepherd is willfully using a phony story and would put a false witness on the stand, that should be enough for the media and the law to investigate Shepherd's complicity in juror swapping and murder."

"And if he won't talk?"

"The fact we were in Johnson's office will get the defense worried. Shepherd won't know what Johnson told us."

Their first stop was the Channel 8 studios on Sunset

Boulevard. They couldn't just walk in the front door without a pass, but they could take the studio tour. About five minutes into it, they hung a right when everybody else went left. The tour guide was explaining the intricacies of the green room where celebrities cooled their heels before being interviewed. Dallas and Ginger headed toward an elevator.

"Play along," Ginger whispered to Dallas as they approached a few people who actually worked there. "I swear one studio is like any other. Find out their politics and kiss as many butts as you can. I've been here two weeks and feel like I've been here forever. But I still get lost."

Ginger nodded knowingly at the two people riding the elevator with them, expecting commiseration from fellow travelers. The people nodded back.

"Where is Gary Johnson's office?" Ginger asked them.

"He's on three," said one of the young men. "Is he getting the ax?"

"What have you heard?" Ginger asked, concealing her surprise to the man's response.

"Grapevine," he said. "The big cheese wants him o-u-t."

Ginger nodded, again. "I'm giving him his exit interview."

Dallas and Ginger got off on the third floor and headed down the hall.

"He's not in," said a voice behind them. The pencil-thin girl of twenty-something smiled at Dallas and checked him over like a new car. "From what I hear, he won't be coming back."

"Yeah. We're cleaning out his office," Ginger said.

"What did he expect?" the young woman said. "We're a local station. If he wanted to lie, why didn't he do it on one of the big networks where they don't care?" She went into her own office and shut the door.

"What did we miss?" asked Dallas.

Dallas and Ginger went into Johnson's small office. Gary Johnson was a very neat young man. At first Ginger thought the place had been cleaned out before they arrived, but when she went through the Rolodex, it was chock-full of business cards.

"If Malvin Shepherd ever gave him a card, it's gone now. Did you find anything?" Ginger asked.

"Not much in the file drawers. It's like nobody worked in here," said Dallas.

"You don't have to do much research when you make it all up."

The only thing of interest they found was a cardkey to the parking structure at the *World Globe*. That was their next stop.

It was midafternoon and Ginger figured the newspaper's regular staff would be out to lunch, since they put the rag to bed later in the evening. The parking area was almost deserted. She clipped the cardkey onto her lapel and headed for the elevator with Dallas.

They got out on the main floor. It was a virtual maze of low-rise cubicles. Ginger knew what Johnson looked like, but nobody standing up fit the bill.

"Have you seen Gary Johnson today?" she asked a short, balding man sitting in front of a huge computer screen. He was moving news copy around as if playing a computerized jigsaw puzzle.

Without turning around he said, "I don't think he's with us anymore, but his inner sanctum is on five with the rest of the shots."

"Good news travels fast in their business," Dallas said to Ginger as they grabbed the elevator.

The fifth floor seemed virtually deserted. Ginger listened for signs of life. "All the bigwigs must be at a C.Y.A. meeting to see what they can salvage of their reputations now that the news about their errant reporter is out. I wonder who spread the drumbeat?"

Gary Johnson didn't quite have a corner office, but the carpeting was thicker than a newly sodded lawn. The oatmeal color didn't do a very good job hiding dirt and it was positively inadequate in camouflaging the bright red stain oozing into it from Gary Johnson's dead body.

"Uh-oh!" Ginger said, seeing him lying there.

"That's one body they can't blame on us," said Dallas.

"They can if they find us standing over it." Ginger started to leave when she noticed something. "Watch the door."

"This isn't a good time to play detective, Ginger."

"See that purse," she said, indicating the small black bag on the floor beside Gary's desk.

"It doesn't match his suit. So what?"

"You know who that belongs to?"

"It belongs to me," said Johnnie Greer, stepping out of the private bathroom attached to Johnson's office.

"Oh, shit," said Dallas.

"I didn't do this," she offered, helpless. "I came to talk with him. Again. He said he had *very* interesting company coming over and he told me to wait." She pointed to the powder room. "I wasn't in there thirty seconds before I heard voices and then a muffled gunshot."

"I take it you didn't open the door and see who did it?" asked Dallas.

"I was scared out of my mind. I could hear them going through his files. Then nothing. I didn't know if they left or if they were still here. Then I heard your voices. What am I going to do?"

"Get your purse. Anything else yours?" Ginger asked. Johnnie shook her head.

Ginger took a peek out the door to see if they were alone. "Outside. Quick." They hurried into the hallway and Ginger pulled the door shut. "Johnnie, I want you to go out the back way."

Johnnie gave her a look like Ginger had cursed her mother.

"I can't do that. I can't leave the scene of a crime."

Ginger smiled. "That's what I wanted you to say. Come

on. Let's take a stroll."

They got halfway to the elevator before they heard it rumble to a stop. Ginger physically turned Johnnie around and headed her back toward Johnson's office. Dallas made the same 180 and followed the two women. As they got to Johnson's door, Ginger had just enough time to knock, step inside, and let out a loud scream. The people heading to their respective offices came running.

Johnnie, who was already shaking, collapsed in Dallas's arms. Ginger backed out of the room into full view of her handy eyewitnesses.

"What happened?" yelled a man in a nice suit and loosened tie.

"Johnson," Ginger gasped. "Someone killed Gary Johnson."

The police were summoned. The celebrity status of the late Mr. Johnson pushed everything else off the front page, including the three innocent bystanders who had stumbled across the body. Ginger, Dallas, and Johnnie were literally sidelined.

The members of Johnson's estranged press family rose to the occasion. All of a sudden every one of them became a close, personal friend to the troubled, young, dead personality. They would end up being guest stars on the nightly news shows.

As for Dallas, Johnnie, and Ginger, they left by way of the back stairs and made it to the parking structure as more media trucks converged on the stunned and grief-stricken members of the Fourth Estate. Dallas took Johnnie's car while Ginger drove the shaking woman in her own vehicle.

When they were in the thick of midafternoon traffic, Johnnie spoke. "Ginger, I can't believe this is happening. What *is* happening?"

"We're getting close to the truth," said Ginger. "Did Gary tell you Malvin Shepherd knowingly ran with his phony story about the mysterious witness?"

"No. He kept laughing like it was all a big joke."

"Hmm."

"What are you thinking?" Johnnie asked.

"If he was laughing and his visitor hadn't spoken to him yet, Gary was the one with all the aces. The first big story he broke was about a secret witness. He told you he made it up. Malvin Shepherd picks up the same story and runs with it. From what I've been hearing the last hour, Johnson's reputation as a liar has been massively exposed. Not usually fatal for a reporter, but pretty damning for a defense lawyer who tries using the same lie."

"You think Shepherd had him killed?" asked Johnnie. "But Shepherd can say Johnson was killed because he knew too much about the real killer."

"Johnnie, tell me, does any part of you think Desmond Williams didn't kill his wife?"

The prosecutor let herself think deeply about the possibilities. "None at all."

"So, we have to assume Johnson's witness story was a lie."

"What can we do?" she asked.

"Play hardball," Ginger said.

They drove to the Criminal Courts Building and parked at the curb. Ginger saw Dallas pull up half a block away and walk toward them. Johnnie was still shaken by her experience.

"Johnnie, if anybody asks you about going to see Gary Johnson, tell them the truth. Not that you were in the bathroom when Johnson was killed, but that you had an appointment with him, your second in one day. That will explain your fingerprints in his office. If anybody recognized Dallas or me, tell them we were with you. We will alibi each other. Hang together or hang separately. Tell Frank—but only what I just said."

"Shouldn't he know the whole truth?" she asked.

Dallas joined them on the sidewalk.

"We'll tell him later," said Ginger. "Right now, I have an idea. If it works, it'll end this nightmare. If not—I'll need the name of a good lawyer."

"What are you going to do?" Johnnie asked.

"I'm not going to tell you, either. It's better that way. As for Frank, I don't think he would go along with it. I don't know if Dallas will."

"Who do we have to kill?" he said with incredible sincerity.

Johnnie went to her office. She decided the best thing to do was lock herself away until the worst blew over. Dallas and Ginger drove to his place for a war council.

He lived on the top floor over a block of warehouses in downtown L.A. Just to get into the place they went through a door marked **MAINTENANCE**. Ginger doubted if any of the people who rented space below even knew of its existence. The room was cavernous with massive furniture filling the large center section. Huge windows looked out over the city in all directions.

"We know who's behind this, Ginger," said Dallas after they sat down beside the windows that faced west.

"And I'm very sure he thinks he has gotten away with it. He's eliminated or marginalized everybody who could pose a threat."

"What do we do?" asked Dallas.

"We make him an offer he can't refuse."

"I can do that," said Dallas without even blinking. "I've been wanting to get my secret-agent gear out of mothballs."

"Didn't it burn up in the fire?"

"That was my overnight bag. Wait'll you see my world tour gear."

Ginger studied him. "Hmm. What were you?"

"I still am, but I'm . . . between engagements. What's your plan?"

"We'll need a few more people."

"Okay," he said, with no hesitation.

"I need some white guys who look like cops."

"Done."

"And a few others."

"Okay," he said, with some hesitation.

"A specific type," Ginger added.

"Uh-huh," he said with more hesitation.

"With a particular look," she said.

"And that would be . . .?"

"They have to be tall as the ace of spades."

CHAPTER 33

Dallas put Shepherd's rented house in Brentwood under surveillance forty-eight hours later, which was a Sunday night, and his phone lines were tapped. The area was watched round the clock by Dallas's men from that point on. But for the two days before he could get his men in place, Ginger and her husband pulled watch. Fred had been drafted before when Ginger had her private detective firm. She never knew if he enjoyed it for the excitement or he didn't want her to have all the fun in the family. They watched together.

The surveillance team identified the three bodyguards on the premises: Curtis Lee, Malvin's lead goon; Vince, the guy who posed as the man from the D.A.'s office; and another unnamed thug. The ever-present Walter Blue was on hand along with Shepherd's media guy, P. J. Henderson, who came and went as summoned. And in the center of everything was Malvin Shepherd throwing his ample weight around.

Dallas and his crew were planning their sting for Wednesday, but on Tuesday night two more men appeared in the Shepherd compound. The obvious bulge under their jackets led the team first to believe they were more hired muscle. Dallas moved D-Day to Thursday night so they could regroup.

Dallas liked Ginger's idea of making Malvin Shepherd an offer he couldn't refuse, but he wanted to make sure Malvin's minions didn't try to renegotiate the contract. That meant removing a few of the players before H-Hour. First up was P. J. Henderson. Malvin mustn't have liked him much because he didn't live on the premises. He rented an apartment a few miles away and drove home late every evening in his rented car.

On Thursday night, Thanksgiving actually, Dallas had two men tail Henderson from Shepherd's place and stop him within a block of his apartment.

"Was I speeding, Officer?" asked Henderson, seeing the uniform and official vehicle.

"Step out of the car, please."

Henderson complied. "What did I do?" he asked.

"We're picking you up for questioning in the death of William Robinson, a juror on the Desmond Williams murder case."

Even in the dark, P. J. Henderson's face went white. "I need to call my lawyer."

"You'll have a chance to do that, Mr. Henderson, after we get you downtown." Henderson reached for his cell phone. "I'm sorry, sir, but you will not be able to call anyone until you have been processed." The officer removed the phone from his hand.

"I have the right—"

"You have the right to remain silent. If you give up that right and tell us what you know about the death of Willie Robinson, you might get off with a lesser sentence, but I can assure you, sir, you will be prosecuted."

"You aren't cops. I know this trick. Who put you up to this? Do you want money? Is that it? I've got money," said Henderson, reaching into his coat.

The cop spun him around and slapped Henderson's hands on the top of his car. "I'm sure you do, Mr. Henderson. But I am a police officer and you are being taken in for questioning." The cop frisked the man for weapons.

"On what charge?" asked Henderson.

"Accessory before and after the fact in a capital murder. Where is the body of Willie Robinson?"

"You can't do it this way. There has to be a plea agreement. You have to offer me something in exchange for my testimony."

"What's your life worth?" asked the cop.

"I'll tell them you forced me to make a statement."

"You called us, Mr. Henderson."

"What?"

"A 911 call was placed from a pay phone five minutes ago. A person identifying himself as P. J. Henderson said he wanted to give information in the disappearance and subsequent murder of juror William Robinson."

"I'm not stupid enough to make a call like that," said Henderson.

"The voice was yours. A voice match will stand up in any court. Do you think Malvin Shepherd will let you swing alone or will he be joining you?"

P. J. Henderson was weighing his options.

At the same time, Dallas and Ginger were standing in the shadows near the enclosure to Malvin Shepherd's rented estate ready to put the rest of the plan into action. Lights were on inside and occasionally a figure walked past a window.

As per Ginger's specifications, Dallas recruited several black men. One was a mountain of a man named Roger Berry. She had never seen a man anywhere near that size before. He had to be six-foot-four. And muscles. His muscles had muscles. But Roger wasn't a big talker. When he did speak, the ground sort of shook. Very *basso profundo*. The sound came from somewhere deep inside that massive chest and it got your attention. Dallas may have run the operation, but Roger, who must have done similar work before, didn't need much instruction.

The three other men were leaner and scary as hell. Maybe it was the dreadlocks or the black sweat suits or the attitudes, but Ginger wouldn't want to meet them in a dark alley.

They had a few minutes to go before H-Hour. Dallas

touched up the black makeup he had smeared on his face after pulling on a black knit watch cap that covered his long hair. He put on a pair of assault gloves and checked his weapons. Roger was wearing a knit cap, a dark wool pullover sweater, and camouflage all-weather trousers. The other three pulled the hoods of their sweatshirts over their heads, partially cloaking their faces. They resembled three grim reapers.

As for Ginger, she was in a black jumpsuit and black silk jacket with a black cap covering her light hair. She told Fred it was the only outfit she wouldn't mind getting a bullet hole in. He didn't laugh. She was trying to adjust the bulletproof vest Dallas had provided, but was having trouble. Roger saw her struggling.

"Your vest must have slipped."

He unzipped her jacket and reached behind her neck, then yanked up the Kevlar vest. He lifted her several inches off the cobblestones in the process, but she didn't think he realized it. He reattached the Velcro tabs that held it in place, and then looked closely at her blackened face.

"You stay here out of the light. No amount of black paint is going to let you pass for a sister."

Dallas added, "I don't want you any closer than you are right now. You should have stayed at my place until this is over. If things get out of hand, run. If they spot you, run faster."

"I'm wearing a vest," she said.

"The vest is good only if they hit you here." He punched her in the chest. "It won't do any good there." He tapped her head.

Dallas started going over his inventory.

"How did you get plans of Shepherd's house?" Ginger asked, still amazed at what he had accomplished in such a short time.

"She asks a lot of questions, doesn't she?" said Roger.

"Former gumshoe," Dallas said by way of explanation.

"How primitive," said Roger, smiling. He looked at her. "Stay in the shadows." Then to Dallas, "How soon 'til the power goes off?"

Illuminating the dial on his watch, Dallas said, "It blows at nine-fifteen. That's in ten minutes. This entire end of the street will go dark."

"I makes de phone call in five minutes," said Roger, getting into character.

"I'll be outside the library," said Dallas.

"What if he doesn't go in there?" asked Roger.

Ginger had that one. "If the schematics Dallas found on this house are up-to-date, that's where he'll go for security."

Roger gave her a thumbs-up.

"You ready?" asked Dallas.

"Ready," said Rog.

"Rock and roll," said one of the other men.

"Go," said Dallas.

The wall around the impressive home was made of massive stone pillars with iron grillwork in between. Dallas mounted the wall and dropped down on the other side. Roger lumbered over the top and disappeared into the dark. The three others followed at five-second intervals. Dallas headed for the windows outside the library at the rear of the rented baronial estate. Roger planted the explosive devices around the back entrance and then ducked into the shadows. One of the guys with the dreadlocks appeared near the front door. The other two men faded into the trees on the right side of the house. Roger speed-dialed a number on his cell phone and seconds later a ringing was heard inside the house.

Malvin Shepherd was sitting in the living room with Walter Blue and Vince. He picked up the phone.

"Hello?"

"Take dis call away from yo' mens if you knows what's good for you, brother."

"Who is this? What do you want?"

"It's 'bout dose po-lice cars you boined. I have pi'tures."

Malvin thought about it for a second, and then said, "Just a minute."

He punched the hold button and put down the phone. Walter and Vince were watching him.

"I'm taking this call in the library."

Shepherd walked into the library and sauntered to the desk. He hesitated picking up the receiver. Finally he grabbed it.

"Who are you?"

"I'm da guy wit' a bi'ness proposition fo' you, Mistah Shepherd."

"I don't conduct business over the phone. Why don't you come over here?"

"What makes you think I ain't here already?"

Malvin glanced out the window into the darkness. "Look, what's this all about? What pictures?" He dragged the phone across his desk, knocking several books to the floor. He jumped at the noise. He stared into the night, straining to see movement. Dallas had slipped into the shadows and was watching.

"Mr. Williams knows 'bout the videotape wit' yo' people boinin' them po-lice cars. You done fucked up too many times, boy. Mr. Williams done warned you 'bout dat."

"Mr. Williams knows I did everything in my power to protect him from a prosecuting team that's out to lynch him. You tell Williams that."

"Desmond tol' yous not to try yo' half-assed tricks. Now you went an' killed another brother. If you does that to Gary Johnson, you think Desmond trusts you to save him?"

"Johnson?" said Malvin Shepherd very slowly.

"We have yo' boy, Henderson, right now. He be talkin'."

Shepherd hurriedly thought about where P. J. was at that moment. "Wait a minute." He put Roger on hold and speed-dialed his media guy. The phone rang once before it was answered. "P. J., where are you?"

"Hello, Mr. Shepherd," said the police officer. "Mr.

Henderson is unavailable at the moment." The connection ended abruptly.

Malvin hesitated a moment, then returned to Roger. "What do you want?"

"I wanna talk wit' you about a swap."

"A swap? I'm sorry. I don't work that way."

"Then you better loin a new bi'ness."

"Look, you tell Williams I can't help him anymore."

"That ain't what we wants to hear, white boy. You swap what you have for Henderson and the car video, or we be comin' after yo' family."

"Don't you dare threaten me. You tell Williams to get his people to back off, or—"

That's when the explosion went off. Shepherd saw the flash from the library windows. He dropped the phone and froze where he stood.

The detonations blew the kitchen door off its hinges. Roger dashed in, tossing a smoke grenade into the room and another canister down one hallway, and then went in the opposite direction. He smashed a small glass vial behind him that burst upon impact. It was full of sulfur vapor. Rog tightened his gas mask against the fetid stench of carbon disulfide. He looked at his watch, and then pulled his night-vision goggles down just as the lights went off. He continued his journey.

Walter Blue and Vince came running in the direction of the kitchen, but as they saw the smoke cloud they were assaulted by the foul odor.

Walter Blue was the first to yell. "Gas leak. Get out!"

He and Vince tripped over each other as they stumbled toward the foyer and fumbled to unlock the front door. They made it onto the porch only to be confronted by a man sporting dreadlocks and carrying a weapon. Walter was decked before Vince was punched in the stomach and brought to his knees.

One of the new men Shepherd had acquired on Tuesday

stepped out of the ground floor powder room at the far end of the hall only to be knocked out and dragged back into the tiny room. Dallas emerged moments later and raced down the hall toward the stairway. His night vision goggles and gas mask were firmly in place.

Curtis Lee and the other henchman were in the game room on the second floor. They came tearing down the stairs into the cloud of smoke and the pervasive smell of what they thought was natural gas. They saw an eerie light emanate out of the smoky darkness below. They thought it was one of their own men with a flashlight, but were surprised to see a tall, dark figure wearing some weird space alien get-up who motioned them to lie down on the carpet. The voice coming from behind the gas mask was raspy and menacing.

"Gas leak!" gasped Curtis.

"Yeah. I fire a shot and we celebrate the Fourth of July all over again," said Dallas.

Malvin Shepherd was still alone in his library, getting a little jumpy.

"Walter! WALTER! What happened?" Malvin called out.

Shepherd bent down to retrieve his telephone. He felt around in the dark until he found the handset and pulled on it until he located the phone itself. He listened for a dial tone. Silence. He followed the cord to the socket, but the plug was firmly seated. He knew that was a bad sign.

A chorus line of ghostly shadows danced about the room like specters at a masked ball. Flames from a gas log burning in the fireplace were casting wraithlike silhouettes on the walls.

Malvin heard footsteps stomping down the hall outside the library. Nervous, he stumbled toward the door. He managed to push a button near the doorjamb, but a loud thwack and the grinding of gears replaced the clean mechanical sound of the panic door being moved into place.

Malvin tried to push the paneled door shut instead.

Smoke was pressing into the room, but so was something else. He pushed harder. Finally Malvin noticed a tall figure in the doorway wrapped in smoke.

"Vince! Is that you?"

"It ain't Vince, bro."

Malvin couldn't make out the face of the man standing in the doorway. Shadows played across the gas mask and the night-vision goggles jutting out of Roger's head giving him a surreal look of some gigantic insect.

The metal security blinds had rolled into place in front of the library windows, but Malvin Shepherd was far from secure.

At the same time on the sidewalk outside Shepherd's house, Ginger was watching the shadows for signs of movement. The entire street had gone dark and the moonless night offered no help. That's when her cell phone vibrated. Who the hell would be calling at that hour? She answered it.

"What?"

"Ginger," said Johnnie in a panic. "He's out."

"Johnnie? Who's out? Shepherd? He's in his house."

"No. Not—" was all Ginger heard Johnnie say before she heard the voice behind her.

"No. I'm out."

Ginger recognized the voice from all his movies. Her blood ran cold.

Desmond Williams grabbed her wrist and spun her around. He wrenched the cell phone out of her hand and smashed it under his heel.

"You're too late," Ginger managed to say without her voice quivering.

"Too late for what? Killing Malvin Shepherd?" he questioned as he wrapped his gloved hand around her throat.

"No. Getting the video."

"The video of his men torching those phony police cars? Let the D.A. hang the son of a bitch."

Ginger was surprised Williams knew about that video. "When did Shepherd find out about the police car video?"

"He doesn't know about it. You can buy anybody in this town."

Back inside, Dallas was busy hog-tying Curtis Lee and the other thug. He dragged them into the sitting room before heading toward the library. The smoke bomb was still smoldering, the murky air being sucked down the hall to the right wing of the large house. Dallas got turned around and found himself going toward the servant's quarters. He had to backtrack.

Most of the heavy smoke had cleared near the library wing so Roger could pull off his gas mask. The blazing fire in Shepherd's fireplace glared in his goggles so he had to jettison those as well.

That's when Malvin Shepherd saw the huge black man standing in the doorway.

"Who the hell do you think you are?" asked Shepherd.

"I be the man wit' the proposition, Mistah Shepherd. I tolds you I was right chere."

"I no longer represent Williams. You'll have to talk to his new lawyer."

That was news to Roger, but the endgame had nothing to do with who represented Desmond Williams.

"You knows why I's here, Mistah Shepherd. I wants dat CD. Da one of Desmond killin' his wife. You do that, an' he won't be killin' your chil'ren."

Roger removed the metal bar he had used to jamb the lock-down entry, closed the paneled door, and walked toward Malvin Shepherd, who was rapidly retreating behind a large desk.

"I don't know what the hell you're talking about. I don't have any CD," said the lawyer.

Out on the sidewalk, Ginger was still trying to reason

with a madman.

"I'm not talking about the police car video, Desmond."
She said his name as if she knew him.

"What video are you talking about, jury lady?"

He used his other hand, the one not encircling her
throat, to wipe away some of the camouflage paint on her
face.

"The one of you killing your wife," Ginger managed to
say.

He shook her like a rag doll, jangling her teeth. Finally,
he set her down.

"There isn't a tape. You're lying," he screamed.

"I knew Shepherd was smarter than that. He had to keep
something from you."

"He can't hide anything from me. Somebody else told me
about the police car video."

"Somebody in the media?" Ginger questioned, remembering who gave her the tape in the first place.

"They all love me," he said, his capped teeth gleaming
in the dark.

"Not everybody," said Ginger. "Didn't Shepherd's men
talk one of your people into killing the real Willie Robinson
for him?"

"How do you know that?" asked Williams.

"A guy like Shepherd would never do his own wet work.
He'd feed your people just enough information to get the
guy who already has a noose around his neck to do the dirty
work for him. Like getting rid of a juror. That was his insurance policy."

Desmond was getting itchy. "What's in it for you?"

Being a liar is a dangerous thing. Liars always have trouble remembering their own lies. What's harder is remembering somebody else's lies, especially a pathological liar
like Gary Johnson.

"Shepherd's people planted a story about me being part
of the Aryan Nation. I don't know how he found out, but

the son of a bitch threatened to use the information to ruin me."

"Big deal. It's already been in the papers."

"Not the part about me being wanted for murder in Tennessee under my real name. I'm here to get something on Shepherd. If my people can prove he had Gary Johnson killed—"

"Johnson's dead?" questioned Williams.

"The little bastard outlived his usefulness," said Ginger.

"How do you know all this?" asked the inquiring Mr. Williams.

"I have my sources. I used to be a private detective."

"I heard that on TV today," said Williams. "That's why Shepherd wanted to get rid of you."

"Un-uh." She shook her head. "He knew I saw the surveillance camera. The one that took the picture of you killing your wife. Now tell me, how did you get out of jail?"

"I fired Shepherd last night and hired another lawyer. He bought a judge and they released me on bail this afternoon. Now you tell me about that video." He grabbed her arm.

"The people next door to your wife had a security service. Shepherd stole the video. My guys are in there now getting the papers he has on me. Leave me alone and I give you the CD with your face on it. Deal?"

"He can get more information on you," said Williams, but he was still listening to her spiel.

Inside the house a different scenario was playing out. Roger Berry had been leaning on Malvin Shepherd, literally. He had the lawyer pinned on top of the desk. The defense attorney was starting to sweat even though his bravado seemed alive and well.

"You tell Williams he can't threaten me," said Shepherd.

"I don' think you understand what Mistah Williams is gwana do if you don't play ball, Mistah Shepherd. Give me that CD!"

As Roger grabbed Shepherd's shoulders and was lifting him off the desk, three armed SWAT-team members kicked the library door open. They ran into the room, guns drawn, ski masks in place.

"Hands up!" shouted the team leader.

The other SWAT members planted themselves on both sides of the desk, their guns aimed directly at Roger. He backed off Malvin and raised his hands.

Malvin Shepherd got off the desk and straightened his tie.

"Are you okay, Mr. Shepherd?" asked the team leader.

"Yes. I'm fine. Glad you men got here before this maniac did major damage. Did he come alone?"

"We're checking that now, Mr. Shepherd."

In another part of the house, Dallas had found the hall leading to the library, but he was about to find something else. He saw the door kicked open by the SWAT team and was inching toward it. He could hear voices inside. Someone was saying a police vehicle would be arriving shortly. That's when another man approached the library door ahead of him. Dallas ducked into the shadows and waited.

"It took you long enough," said Officer Hastings, stepping into the library.

The three-man SWAT team turned toward the man standing in the doorway. Two of them aimed their weapons at Officer Hastings.

"Hold it. I'm a police officer. Officer Paul Hastings," said the man. He flashed his badge.

"Stand down," said the team leader. Guns were lowered, except the one on Roger.

"I thought the panic alarm wasn't working since the lights went out," said Officer Hastings. "The phones are dead, too. Do they know that downtown?" he continued.

"Yes, sir," said the SWAT leader. "Arnold, you go with Officer Hastings and secure the front. We should have the lights . . ." He looked at his watch and a second later the house lights flashed on. "There you go. Check it out up front."

"Yes, sir," said the SWAT member named Arnold.

Officer Hastings strode confidently to the living room with Arnold close behind him. Dallas had slipped into the powder room with the man he had punched out earlier. The man was rallying so Dallas belted him one more time.

"Looks like Desmond Williams didn't have that good a crew," said Hastings right before Arnold broke a chloroform capsule under his nose and Hastings fell to the floor.

"Put him in here," said Dallas, stepping out of the small bathroom.

"He's a cop," whispered Arnold as he dragged the man into the lavatory.

"Then who the hell's the guy I knocked out?" asked Dallas. "You can't get good intel nowadays," he joked. "The boys in blue are on their way. We go out the back." Dallas gave a sharp whistle and then sprinted for the kitchen with his friend behind him.

Back out on the sidewalk, Ginger was trying to convince Desmond Williams she wasn't a threat, but he still had a grip on her arm.

"When my people are through with Malvin Shepherd, he won't threaten anybody," she said. "You want to see for yourself? Then you can have the CD."

He actually followed her halfway around the large house. When they got to the side yard one of Dallas's men with the dreadlocks stepped out of the shadows and confronted Williams. He cold-cocked him, dropping the B-class actor to the ground. So much for doing his own stunts. The man with the dreadlocks brought his flashlight up to Des's face and got a look at his catch.

"Who let him out?" he asked.

Inside the library, Malvin was ready to make his triumphant entry into the living room. He walked toward the door.

"Wait a minute, Mr. Shepherd," said the SWAT leader. "We need to secure the prisoner and make sure there are no other hostiles in the area. Stay here until I send someone for you. One of my men will stand guard outside."

"Will you have Mr. Blue come in? He was in the living room," asked Shepherd.

"Yes, sir," said the team leader, as he reset the panic room's alarm system next to the door. He picked up the metal bar that had jammed the lock-down entry and took it with him. The metal security blinds over the windows slowly rolled out of sight.

The SWAT leader led Roger away, posting his other man outside the library before closing the door. A few minutes rolled by. Shepherd was wondering why no one was coming to give him the okay signal. He wandered over to a bookcase and fingered several leather bound books. He pulled one out slightly and then slid it back into place. He paced a little more. Finally he opened the library door and was surprised no guard was standing outside. He looked up and down the hall. That's when Shepherd heard police sirens. It surprised him. They sounded far away. First he thought they were going to another incident. Another minute went by. He heard no other sounds in the house. The sirens were getting closer. Shepherd walked down the hall to the living room. He saw a body slumped on the floor near the sofa. Most of the lamps were out so he couldn't recognize the man. He took a few tentative steps forward. Something about this was very wrong. He stopped.

"Walter? Vince? Officer!" he called.

Malvin could hear a rustling noise coming from the adjacent sitting room. He backed away from the body on the carpet and started to turn. A hand grabbed his ankle and dragged him down to the floor. Desmond Williams crawled over to him and wrapped his hands around the man's throat.

"Give me the CD, Shepherd, or I'll break your fucking neck!"

"Let go of me! Vince! Walter!"

"Nobody's gonna help you, you son of a bitch. I want that CD!"

Williams started beating on Shepherd. Shepherd, no slouch himself in the tough-guy department, punched back. They were going at each other on the carpet when the front door flung open.

"Hands up, Williams!" shouted a real cop as he came through the doorway and recognized the actor.

Shepherd backed off and tried to roll out of the way. Williams was way past caring. His hands went around Malvin Shepherd's throat again. It took three officers to pull him off.

Real SWAT members stormed into the house and searched the entire place from top to bottom. Their black ski masks proved very helpful that night. From the rear lawn of the house, Dallas watched the action. Two SWAT members entered the library and checked the area for intruders and then left. A moment later two more guys in identical gear walked into the library. One went to the shelf Malvin Shepherd had been concerned about earlier and removed a few of the leather books. He looked inside them and then looked behind all the other books on that shelf and the one below it. The two men checked the desk and nearby cabinets. The first man turned to face the library windows and shook his head.

The two men from Dallas's team retraced their steps from the library to the kitchen and then joined Dallas in the rear yard. They were over the stone wall and into a neighbor's yard and soon into the rented car Ginger had secured earlier that evening.

"Got it?" she questioned.

"No," said Dallas.

She banged the steering wheel. "Who's got a cell phone?"

she asked. Three were held up to her face. She grabbed the closest phone and dialed a number.

"Hello?" said Johnnie Greer.

"Johnnie, this is Ginger. Get downtown right away. They're bringing in Malvin Shepherd and Desmond Williams. I don't care how you do it, keep Shepherd there."

"But—"

"Make him a material witness in the death of Willie Robinson. Anything. And Johnnie, get him into a room with a view."

"A view?" questioned Johnnie.

"Someplace where he can see and be seen. Do it!" She hung up.

"What are we going to do now?" asked Dallas.

"I need you to make one more call," said Ginger.

Forty-five minutes later Malvin Shepherd was sitting in the police station downtown in an office with glass walls enclosing him like the specimen he was. Visibly shaken, his scheming mind was trying to come up with an option. Johnnie Greer walked into the room and asked the police officer guarding Malvin to leave.

"This will just take a minute," she said. The officer left. "Well, Malvin. What's going on?"

"Why am I here? Am I being arrested?" he asked.

"We're only trying to protect you."

"That bastard was in my house! Your police protection could have gotten me killed."

"You're okay now," calmed Johnnie.

"I want to press charges against Williams and his men."

"That's your right. What was this all about?" she asked.

Shepherd looked at her. "Ask Williams. Now I want to press charges."

Johnnie gazed over his shoulder and saw a few people milling around the outer office. "I'll get somebody in here to take your statement. But we do have some more questions for you."

"Why?"

"Desmond Williams is filing charges against you."

"He doesn't have anything on me. He can't do this."

"He's filed charges. I guess he wants to see you in jail for a change. What do they call it? Poetic justice."

Malvin was getting nervous.

"I'll be right back," said Johnnie as she opened the door. She spoke to the police officer standing outside the glass enclosure and then walked away.

Malvin Shepherd started watching the people in the outer office. It was Thanksgiving night and there weren't many citizens under arrest at that hour except those sleeping off too much Wild Turkey.

He was surprised to see someone he recognized. It was the big black man who had been in his library. The one with the gas mask and the night vision goggles. A police officer was talking with him. Malvin noticed the guy wasn't in handcuffs. He didn't like that. Then he noticed the black man was smiling. Hell, he was laughing. And then the police officer walked away. Roger looked directly at Malvin Shepherd and smiled. Then he aimed his finger at Shepherd as if it were a gun and pulled the trigger.

Malvin ran to the door. He opened it, but the officer posted outside blocked his way.

"That man—" said Malvin, pointing to Roger Berry, who was walking away. "He should be under arrest."

"I'm sorry, sir. I can't do anything about that," said the police officer.

"But he was in my house. He threatened me."

"It looks like they're letting him go. Maybe he got himself a good lawyer," said the officer in all innocence. "Do you have a lawyer?"

"I *am* a fucking lawyer!"

The next morning there was a knock on Ginger's front door. Through the window she saw an A-1 Courier truck at the curb. She opened the door.

"Special delivery for Ginger Caulfield."

"That's me."

She signed the logbook and he handed her the small parcel. Shutting the door, she took the padded envelope to the entryway table and felt it. She could tell without opening it what it was, but she pulled the tab and let the plastic jewel case fall into her hand. The orange and yellow label from Luke Osborne's security firm, O.S.S., confirmed her deduction.

CHAPTER 34

The grainy, colorless video taken from the surveillance camera hanging under the neighbor's eave flickered on the screen. The images were brought closer by computer enhancing. Lights were on at Marcella Williams' beachfront house. Two figures could be seen through the sheer curtains in the living room. A dark form appeared at the side of the house and stopped near the window. A gloved hand went up to the glass and smashed it. The two figures on the couch sat up as the hulking shape stepped through the broken glass. Marcella leaned back on the couch while Adrian raised his hands to pooh-pa this obvious show of machismo.

The intruder raised the shotgun and fired several times, then stepped forward to make sure the deed was done. The figure slowly backed toward the window. He turned to dodge a piece of hanging glass and stepped directly under a recessed spotlight in the whitewashed ceiling. Desmond Williams' face was caught on camera. Freeze-frame.

The dulcet tones of John Roberts with Channel 11 *View on L.A.* could be heard on television sets across the city. "And that was the video run today by Assistant District Attorney Johnnie Greer, lead prosecutor during the second trial of Desmond Williams, former television and motion picture actor, who has been accused of the brutal murder of his former wife Marcella Williams and the celebrated restaurateur Adrian Wells. Mr. Williams' new lawyer, Randolph Calhoun, stopped the proceedings today and had his client plead not guilty by reason of insanity—"

Frank hit the mute button on the remote control. Their little club was meeting in Frank's office. Johnnie was there with Dallas Long, Bill James, and Ginger Caulfield.

"They must be insane," said Johnnie. "They're reviewing it like a damn movie."

The news program was still running in silence on the TV set behind them. Channel 11 was doing a montage of the Williams case. There was picture after picture of the murdering pig. Then in slow motion they showed the end of the video where Desmond Williams was skulking away from the murder scene. The news producer began with a long shot, grainy and dark, and then zoomed in for that up-close and personal shot of Williams' cold, hard face.

Ginger said, "He should have known better, especially in the business he was in. You're only as good as your last picture."

"I wonder what the next big case will be?" Frank yawned.

"Do you ever get tired of it?" Ginger asked.

"I get tired, but not of this," he answered. "Because with every one we win, we get that much closer to providing justice." He held his fingers a gnat's whisker apart.

"Do you ever want to pull what Malvin Shepherd did?" asked Dallas.

Frank thought about it. "I come about that close." He measured the same distance with his fingers. "But I can't quite pull the trigger."

Bill James looked over at his longtime friend. "Shepherd didn't mind pulling the trigger, or getting somebody else to do it for him. He didn't even mind if he lost a case. He just wanted that big, fat, stinking reputation. The stinkier the better." He added, "Somebody once told me, a friend of his, to tell the truth; he said Malvin hated the scum he represented, but he loved the fight. He loved working everybody into a frenzy until nobody could see the truth."

"He got a lot of scum off death row," said Frank.

"And he put a lot of scum back on the street," Ginger said.

"I don't think he thought about it that way," said Bill. "That wasn't his game."

"What makes a guy like that do it?" asked Dallas.

"He was a street punk back East when he was a kid," explained Bill. "Had a bad reputation himself. He fought his way out of the slums and into college and into the head-lines. But he just couldn't do anything the legit way. He liked being a wiseguy."

"But he valued something more than the fight," said Ginger.

"His reputation?" suggested Johnnie.

"No. He sold that to the media."

"Power?" guessed Frank.

"No. If he wanted real power, he would have gone into politics."

"His life," said Dallas.

She shook her head. "No. His family."

"What do you mean?" asked Johnnie.

"The video wasn't the only thing in the envelope." That surprised everyone. "Shepherd sent me a note written on a yellow legal pad along with a child's hair ribbon. He knew giving up that CD would put him in jail, but he had to stop Williams because he feared for his family."

They all gave her questioning looks.

"He had to ask himself: What do I value most?"

*Less than a month later in an average house
somewhere in Los Angeles . . .*

The TV was on with Warren King sitting behind the Channel 12 *L.A. Comprehensive News* anchor desk with a piece of paper in his hand, looking grave.

"This just into the Channel 12 news desk. The mutilated bodies of two—"

The channel was switched.

Myrna Blankenship, the young newshound from

Channel 11 *View on L.A.*, sat at the news desk with a paper in her hand, looking grave. She started to speak, "...the wife of former..."

The channel was switched again.

Mark Parsons was sitting at the Channel 10 *News & Entertainment* desk with a sheet of paper in his hand, looking grave.

The channel was switched again and again and again.

Channels 8, 6, and 3 were also flashing news bulletins across the screen along with their accompanying musical fanfare.

In that house somewhere in L.A., the average man switched his TV back to the football playoff game. From the kitchen his average wife called to him.

"What was it, honey? A car chase?"

"No. Just another murder."

About the Author

Gayle Bartos-Pool was born in Omaha, Nebraska. Her father was a pilot in the U.S. Air Force and the family lived in various countries from Okinawa to France, as well as on military bases in the States. The family settled in Memphis where she attended college. G.B. took a year off from college and worked on a small-town paper as a reporter and then as a private detective with a local Memphis firm, taking assignments in Atlanta, Chicago, and Little Rock. Upon graduation from Rhodes College in Memphis, she worked a short time as a draftsman and then moved to California, where she started her writing career and then launched her own publishing company. Married to a Texan similar to the "Fred" character in the Ginger Caulfield Mysteries, G.B. writes mystery novels, spy novels and Christmas stories.

Just a day at the races, then they find the body . . .

HEDGE BET

Coming 2005

Is it a reckless bet on the ponies or a high-stakes gamble in the stock market that leads to five deaths and the return of Ginger Caulfield to her former profession as a private investigator?

Deirdre Delvecchio, the all-business wife of self-made millionaire Donald Delvecchio, turns up dead at the racetrack. Hot-tempered Phil Lester told her to bet heavy on a long shot. Suave Paul Bradshaw said he'd loan her the money. Deirdre didn't take either man's advice. Ginger Caulfield overheard both conversations.

Donald, the grieving husband, asks Ginger to get back into the detective business and find out who killed Deirdre. His alibi: He was with another woman when his wife was murdered. The next day, Donald Delvecchio drops another bombshell. Ginger's husband, Fred, says, "Here we go again."

From HEDGE BET: Chapter 6

That's when the perfect day took a decidedly dark turn. A few minutes later a voice came over the P.A. system: *"Ladies and gentlemen, may I have your attention, please. There has been an incident at the track, and we would ask all patrons to keep their seats for a few minutes until we can get the situation under control. We have been advised by the Pasadena Police Department to keep all guests where they are and this situation will be cleared up as soon as possible."*

I looked at Fred. "Deirdre," was all I said as a chill ran through my body.

There were plenty of blue uniforms in the area in a matter of seconds. I guess with all that money floating around, the police expect trouble, even if they seldom get *big* trouble. This looked like *BIG* trouble. Racetrack security was on the scene right away and soon an ambulance drove onto the patio. They had an ambulance or two in the wings just in case a jockey lost more than the race. Minutes later a police car pulled up.

The crowd was now strangely quiet. They were all seated, talking among themselves. Most eyes were focused on the tunnel and the activity below. I could imagine a few side bets were being made as to whether it was a dead body or not. I was actually wondering about that myself, but I had that horrible sinking feeling that I knew the answer.

"Mrs. Ginger Caulfield, please come to the Directors' Room in the Turf Club, fourth floor. Mrs. Ginger Caulfield."

I slowly looked over at Fred and might as well have been looking in a mirror. We both had the same stunned look on our face. I mumbled a slight profanity and stood up. I swear every eye in the stands turned in my direction. I could have been going to the powder room for all they knew. But they knew, because I was the only person in the whole damned grandstand who stood up.

And this time I knew it would happen. It would be head-over-heels down the steps, flat on my butt in front of thirty thousand people. How I got to the Directors' Room without mishap, I'll never know. Doors were opened for me and I passed into the restricted chamber.

Donald Delvecchio was seated. He was the only one in the room not on his feet. Most of the people doing the talking were police types. I guessed the expensive suits with the worried looks were racing officials, and this was going to be a huge headache. At this point I didn't know if Deirdre was among the living, but all signs pointed to the negative.

Somebody suggested that I speak to one particular gentleman standing near Donald. I quietly moved closer as Donald looked up. I expected his eyes to be red and his demeanor shaken, not stirred. Nope. Donald was pissed.

"Why in hell are you asking *me* anything? I don't know what happened," Donald was yelling at the man.

"Mr. Delvecchio, sir, I have to ask you a few questions. It's just routine."

"That's what you say right before you guys slap on the handcuffs," Donald roared.

"Mr. Delvecchio, I need to ask you where you were."

"I was in the can taking a leak. I told you that before. I'm sorry I didn't bring a witness. I didn't know I needed one."

"How long were you gone?"

"About two Scotches worth."

"Please, Mr. Delvecchio, I'm only trying—"

"Wait a minute. Ask her."

Donald pointed toward me. Oh, God.

"Who are you? Were you with Mr. Delvecchio?" asked the man.

"Who are *you*?" I said in reply.

Why I asked the question and why I wasn't handcuffed on the spot as an accessory, I don't know.

"I'm Detective Randolph Pierce. I'm the officer in charge of this investigation."

"What's happened?" I asked.

"Mrs. Delvecchio was murdered. Now, let me ask a few questions. Who are you?"

"My name is Ginger Caulfield."

"And your connection to this case?"

"She's a private detective," spurted Donald.

"Donald, I'm retired. Detective Pierce, I'm just a friend of the Delvecchio's, but I—"

"Would you please wait *outside*?" said the officer.

He indicated with a jerk of his head for one of his men to remove me from the premises. Donald must have been the one who had me paged over the loudspeakers. This was really turning into a bad day. I started to slink away.

"I knew you couldn't get away with it," said someone behind me.

I was being tossed from the room in front of all these people and somebody was going to rub my nose in it. But the voice . . . Where had I heard that voice, that tone . . .?

"Is she in custody or can I talk to her?" the person asked, as pressure was being applied to my elbow as I was escorted out of the room.

The man pushing me stopped. So did I. Now I had a chance to see the face that went with the voice.

She smiled first and then shook her head. "They always come back to the scene of the crime."

That caught the attention of Detective Pierce. He wrinkled his eyebrows, very handsome eyebrows actually, and stopped writing in his notebook.

"Do you know this woman, Trin—Lieutenant Lopez?"

"Yeah. We go way back. She started her private detective firm before we got out of the academy. She was pretty good, until she decided to hang up her .38s."

Pierce studied me a little closer, but still had his brow furrowed. He went back to his notepad.

"Do I get to stay?" I asked Trinidad Lopez, a police officer I had met during my former occupation.

"Yeah." Trinidad winked.

Trinidad Lopez's father had served two tours of duty in the U.S. Marines. Sergeant Lopez met Trin's mother, a native of Shanghai, while in the service. He got out of the service and joined the San Diego Police Force. He flew Trin's mother to the States and married her after his first year on the force. Trinidad came along a year later. Both her parents looked like movie stars, and Trin turned out to be a beautiful mix of the two.

I lowered my voice to ask her my next question. "Do you outrank him?"

"No, I sleep with him," she said in less than hushed tones. Everybody heard. Since nobody batted an eye, I gathered anybody who mattered already knew. "Do you know this guy, Delvecchio?"

"Sort of. I knew his wife a little better, but I—"

"Come over here," insisted Detective Pierce, interrupting.

I obeyed.

"Do you know this man?" He indicated Donald Delvecchio.

"We're acquaintances."

"Did you know his wife?"

"Yes, and I'd—"

"Can you vouch for his whereabouts at about four-forty-five this afternoon?"

"No, but—"

"Did you speak to him anytime after your brief stay in the Turf Club lounge?"

For a good-looking man, this guy was becoming a real pain. "No."

"Mr. Delvecchio seems to think you might be able to help him."

"If you'd stuff a sock in it for a minute, I'd like to say something."

That quieted the room.

I explained. "I saw Deirdre enter the tunnel right before she was killed. And I saw a man follow her down the steps—"

Watch for the second in the Ginger Caulfield Mystery,

HEDGE BET, Coming Soon . . .